Chatham
June 1984

DISC

Also by Henry Carlisle

Voyage to the First of December (1972)
The Land Where the Sun Dies (1975)

The
JONAH
MAN

Illustrated with etchings by Joe Lee

The
JONAH
MAN

HENRY
CARLISLE

ALFRED A. KNOPF
NEW YORK   1984

THIS IS A BORZOI BOOK
PUBLISHED BY ALFRED A. KNOPF, INC.

Library of Congress Cataloging in Publication Data
Carlisle, Henry.   The Jonah man.
1. Pollard, George—Fiction. 2. Essex (Whale-ship)—
Fiction. 3. Chase, Owen—Fiction. 4. Nantucket (Mass.)—
History—Fiction. I. Title.
PS3553.A72J6 1984   813'.54   83-48869
ISBN 0-394-52942-1

Manufactured in the United States of America
First Edition

A Jonah is he?—And men bruit
The story. None will give him place
In the third venture. Came the day
Dire need constrained the man to pace
A night patrolman on the quay
Watching the bales till morning hour
Through fair and foul. Never he smiled;
Call him, and he would come; not sour
In spirit, but meek and reconciled;
Patient he was, he none withstood:
Oft on some secret thing he would brood.

From *Clarel*, Herman Melville

Part One

FIRST SOUNDINGS

1

I first saw the vessel when I was seventeen. I was on board the *Eliza Slade,* returning to the Island on a blue, windy September afternoon in 1808; we had rounded Brant Point and the town came into view, the wharves, the gray-shingled houses, the four windmills on Popsquatchet Hills, the steepled churches on Orange Street and Academy Hill, a glimpse up Main Street as we rounded into the wind, the ropewalk, the Cliff beyond; we let go our anchor astern of her.

ESSEX
NANTUCKET

She was a bluff, broad-beamed, black-hulled whaler of medium tonnage for those days (small for today), a stout, businesslike ship with no frills. Though not newly built, she was new to Nantucket (at the time I prided myself on being able to name most of the forty-odd vessels that sailed from the Island), and I looked her over with a seamanly eye, musing on my bright prospects in the whale fishery.

That day was a proud one for me. Not two hours before, with Great Point lighthouse off our port bow, Mr. Bench, the mate of the *Slade,* standing with Captain Clasby on the afterdeck, had called me over to them and the captain had growled, "Well, Pollard, I guess it's back to the potato patch for you now. Eh?"

"No, sir," I said.

"No, sir?" he said in mock surprise.

"I intend to ship on another whaling cruise."

"Ship again! God's Britches, did you hear what this young man just said, Mr. Bench?"

"Truly amazing."

The captain shook his head in wonderment. "You mean to tell me, Pollard, that with all the trouble the whales have given you, not to mention Mr. Bench, that you actually want to go whaling again?"

"Yes, sir. I mean to spend my life at it."

"Worse than I thought," said Clasby. "Much worse."

"Hopeless, I'd say," said Mr. Bench.

Then the captain eyed me narrowly and said, "Well, then, in that case I guess I got no choice but to recommend you for boatsteerer your next voyage out. 'Course the say-so'll be your next skipper's and the owner's, but the Starbucks'll have my view of the matter, and you can use it as you like."

"Thank you, sir," I told him. "Thank you very much."

Captain Clasby studied me for a moment, then, still looking at me, said to the mate, "Reckon he'll always think I've done him such a favor, Mr. Bench?"

At the time the captain's question made no sense to me. As we neared our anchorage my gaze swept the town. I felt elated on this first homecoming, assured that I had acquitted myself creditably, and all that I could see ahead on that bright September afternoon was clear sailing.

My Uncle Hezekiah met me at the wharf, the news of the arrival of the *Eliza Slade* having not yet reached my family in Polpis, six miles upharbor from the town. Hezekiah Coffin, the husband of my mother's younger sister Nancy, was about thirty then, a rugged rock of a man, a seasoned whaleman with a Nantucketer's reverence for hard facts.

"How many barrels?" he asked me. First things first.

"Sixteen hundred," I told him proudly.

He nodded noncommittally and said, "Goin' out Sconset way. Drop you home if you like."

"Be most obliged."

"No trouble. Goin' out Sconset way."

I slung my bag over my shoulder and we started down the wharf toward his box wagon. My legs still felt the roll and pitch of the ship, my head was teeming with tales of scrapes with whales and wild seas, but my uncle made no further inquiries about my voyage.

"How's Aunt Nancy?" I asked him.

" 'Bout same."

"Owen and Edward?"

"Same." Then reluctantly he added, "Grown some, I guess, since you seen 'em."

"How's everyone in Polpis?"

"Same. 'Bout same. Heard Betsy had a boy, ain't you?"

"Hadn't heard she was married." My elder sister was eighteen.

"You been to sea longer'n I thought."

"She *is* married?"

"Yup. Tom Hussey. Livin' in town now. How long you been out?"

"Nineteen months."

"Be shipping again?"

"Yes, sir."

"Your old man could use you handily on the farm."

"Can't help that."

After a moment he said, "Sixteen hundred barrels in nineteen months?" He let himself smile at me. "Not too bad for a first voyage."

My uncle was right about the farm at Polpis. Everything was about the same there. Flights of terns screamed over the house, the barn, the sandy fields, the green salt marshes against the still blue of the harbor. Sheep bells tinkled. Chickens squawked. My mother greeted me as a ghost returned from the dead. My father was pleased to see me. My safe return had settled an argument in his favor.

"See, Tamar," he said that evening, poking at the fire in the kitchen hearth. "He's home in one piece. What about all them gloomy predictions?"

As if she hadn't heard him, my mother looked at me and said, "Glad you're home, son, and hope you'll stay awhile. We need you here."

My younger sister, Susan, was looking at me expectantly. I reached into my pocket and handed her a package. With delight she opened it and took out the amber necklace I had bought her in Valparaiso.

"It's pretty," she said and kissed me on the cheek.

"Pearls next time," I told her.

My mother looked at my father. "Next time," she said.

In the days that followed I helped with the last of the harvest, feeling that everyone was blind to the changes that had happened in me. They were still treating me as the Polpis farmboy I had been before I put to sea. Couldn't they understand that I was now George Pollard, Jr., whaleman? A boatsteerer, by God's Britches!

Everything was the same except me.

I felt like a stranger on the farm and determined to go to sea again before I became trapped in its sandy furrows. I was by then certain that I was put on earth to kill whales.

2

On the night of my birth, July 18, 1791, no comets were seen in the sky. As soon as I got my bearings I found myself six miles upharbor on Nantucket Island, thirty miles from the continent. My father, George, Sr., was, according to the season, farmer, carpenter, sheepshearer. From him I would inherit my tall stature, physical strength, unruly brown hair, large plain features, blue eyes, and little else, for my father was a placid, unseeking man, at peace with himself and our Island, while I had been born on it with a squall in my gizzard that would not let me rest. My mother, Tamar, was a slender dark-haired woman with green eyes that from morning to night were filled with care and warning. From her I would inherit a sense of the mystery of life, a tolerance for books, an abiding suspicion of priests. She took laudanum now and then, saying that it was for lumbago, though I suspected that it was more to tranquilize a sensibility unsuited to the needs of a Polpis farmer's wife. In contrast with my father, my mother, I believe, did not feel at home on this Island a day in her life. I had two sisters, Betsy, who had the airs of a princess, and Susan, who collected seashells and thought the best of everyone.

In most respects my childhood on Nantucket was quite an ordinary one. I was not, of course, the only Island boy to be born uneasy and self-searching, though I expect that, to my disadvantage, I remained enthralled by my singularity rather longer than most. I assumed until rather late in my youth that God was taking a personal and benevolent interest in me. Indeed, for a long time I could not get it out of my head that He had singled me out to accomplish some high mission. Only as I grew older and no angels descended and no blueberry bushes burst into flame did I begin to see the trap I had fallen into, and by then it was too late. God had set it for me—more exactly, the Old Wizard had tempted me to set it for myself: He had let me believe that he had set me down on the farm at Polpis for some favored destiny, only to reveal in time that pride alone had lured me into such a belief, and that in the very realization of what had happened I had gained a knowledge that would forever exclude me from community with my fellow Islanders. I had believed that I was set apart, and so I had become—not as God's favorite but as an outsider on his own—flawed beyond understanding.

Of course, as a boy I did not yet grasp my situation in such terms. I did not wake up one morning and say to myself, "Ah, Pollard, you have done it this time! You have set yourself apart, you have killed your faith, you have forfeited your birthright, and now where are you?" It did not happen that way. But though it would be years before I would realize it, it happened.

As I grew up I ventured to question my mother about our origins and our place in Nantucket. Her replies were disappointing. I learned that though, like most Islanders, we were grafted to that gnarled family tree of Gardners, Coffins, Folgers, Starbucks, Swains, Husseys, Macys, and other descendants of the first white settlers, we were, in a manner of speaking, but its outermost twigs. We lived out of town, we were not members of the Society of Friends (in a community where a large part of its citizenry, including most of the propertied class, were Quakers). On my first excursions to town on my father's vegetable wagon I had discovered that the better sort of Quakers wore broadcloth and beaver hats. My father and I wore homespun and sennit hats. The Quakers addressed each other as "thee" and "thou" and "Friend," but hardly addressed us at all. My father's friends were other farmers, grocers, cod fishermen, carpenters, and members of the night watch. It soon became painfully obvious to me that almost everyone of any account on Nantucket was somehow engaged in the whale fishery: in the oil houses, cooperages, chandleries, refineries, ropewalks, sail lofts, or on the ships themselves, unloading or outfitting at the wharves, riding at anchor in the harbor, or at sea. The heroes of the Island were its successful captains, its lords the owners of the ships and wharves, its emperors the owners who were their own captains. I could not for the life of me understand why my father, who as a young man had shipped on a whaler, had abandoned the calling that was the pride and livelihood of our island. He seemed indifferent not only to the challenge and adventure of whaling but also to the rewards which accrued from its successful pursuit.

I swore great oaths to myself that I would not miss my own chances.

One summer evening I was sitting with my mother on the harbor beach. That year she was reading to me from a book of stories of ancient Greece. How earth and heaven had been made. How Prometheus had shaped men and women out of clay, giving them life from the good and evil of many animals, and how Athena had breathed the divine spirit into them and how they didn't know what to do with it until Prometheus showed them. She had read me about the abduction of Helen, Achilles and Ajax, Hector, the Trojan Horse, the fall of Icarus, the voyage of Odysseus, which was my favorite tale. In my mind Odysseus and all the gods and heroes were of the same earth and Olympus inhabited by Nantucket's first settlers, old Tristram Coffin, Thomas Macy, Peter Folger, Chris-

topher Hussey, Stephen Greenleaf, and the others, and by
Mary Starbuck, a leading spirit of the Society of Friends on
the Island, known as the Great Mary. It was all one world to
me. I must have been eight or nine. Betsy, barefoot with her
skirts hiked up, was splashing at the water's edge. Susan was
scampering for shells and stones. Overhead, terns dove and
wheeled, screeching. To the west a whaleship was clearing the
harbor, her sails turning crimson as she changed course to the
northeast. Half hearing my mother's voice, I watched until
only her royals and skysails were visible beyond the Coatue
sandspit. Then I lay back and gazed up at the birds. My
mother was reading about Atreus's banquet. The screeching
birds became menacing. The stories were fine, except that
they left me confused about what was real and what was not
and what was necessary to do to become a man. That uncertainty, more than the image of the grisly feast, was the source
of the fear that seized me then. And the birds. I felt anger
then, at my own fear. I wanted her to stop and to talk about
something that was real beyond any doubt. I sat up, inter-
rupted her.

"How long will that ship be gone?" I asked her.

She looked out where I was looking. "Two years, maybe."

"How long was Father's voyage?"

"Two years. That was during the war. He was lucky to get
back at all."

"Why did he never go whaling again?"

"Too much sense."

Braving her vehemence, I said, "But most of the men in your
family were whalemen. Some Pollards too. Some of them captains. Whaling's what Nantucket men do."

"What some do," she said. "It's a sad, cruel business. It's not
for you."

"It is for me!" I told her hotly.

She looked at me sorrowfully, then said, "Anyway, it's too
soon to be thinking about that."

"It's not too soon!" Then, looking out at the departing ship, with great determination, I repeated, "It *is* for me!"

"Then may God help you," said my mother.

After that my mother read me stories from the Old Testament.

That same summer, one Sunday—the Quakers' "First Day"— I was walking with my father past the Meeting House on Main Street just as the Friends were filing inside. They were dressed alike, the men in broadcloth breeches, reefer coats, great black hats that shaded their cheerless faces, the women in tent-like dresses and coal-scuttle bonnets. They didn't appear to see us. To them we Pollards were of "the world's people," by which they meant heathens who walked in darkness at high noon. Yet on that day I wished with all my heart that I was one of them. I envied them for that Inner Light which seemed to guide them unerringly toward whales at sea and prosperity ashore.

When we had passed I asked my father, "Why aren't we Quakers?"

He said at once, "Because we wear buttons and don't pry into other people's business."

"Could we be—if we didn't wear buttons?"

"Don't doubt it—if you're willing to let a committee of toothless old men examine your secret thoughts."

"I'm not," I said, wondering whether my father's harsh view of the Friends was true.

"Nor am I," he replied. "Nor was your grandfather or his father or most of your mother's people. That's why we're not Quakers."

"What are we, then?"

He thought a moment, then said, "Nonsectarians."

"Where's our church?"

"Right here."

I looked around. "On Main Street?"

"Main Street. The town. Polpis. The whole Island."

I glanced at him doubtfully. "Uncle Hezekiah and Aunt Nancy are Congregationalists. They have a real church with pews and a minister."

"And one day you can join it if it suits you. Your Aunt Nancy saw to that."

My father and mother had never forgiven my aunt for conniving with my Grandmother Bunker and having me secretly baptized as insurance against Hell Fire.

I glanced back as the doors of the Meeting House closed behind the last of the Friends. Then, fighting back anger, I asked, "How is it that Quakers who don't kill people even in wars are so good at killing whales?"

My father smiled sadly. "That one always stumped me too. Kind of a puzzle, ain't it?"

With my heart in my throat I said, "You never did take much to whaling, did you?"

"Never did. Never felt easy about it somehow."

Though I half expected it, his reply distressed me. "You fish cod."

"Not the same," he said. "Whales are special creatures, more like us than they're like codfish. Hard to explain till you've been up alongside one and looked in his eye and heard him breathing just like you. Whales aren't fish, you know."

I was so unsettled then that I said something that I instantly regretted. "Main difference I see is that a whale can kill you and a codfish can't!"

"True enough," he said evenly. "Only I wasn't afraid of going whaling. I was afraid of not going whaling." Then he smiled at me and added, "You get over that."

So it was that my parents' refusal to view the fishery as the noblest of callings set the hook of my ambition. At the farm I spent hours harpooning shoals of haystacks with a wooden pitchfork. In town I haunted the wharves and ran errands for the mates and the owners' clerks in exchange for being allowed on board whaleships. On Main Street I imitated the rolling gait of the sailors. I peered into the windows of the owners' houses as if I were peering into my own future. I resolved that if my mother was right that I was not born to be a whaleman, I would then make myself over and so become one—and the best at that. Another member of our family understood that ambition and encouraged it.

3

Aunt Nancy. To think of her *now* as she was when I was a boy!

Twelve years younger than my mother, she was then a lithe brunette with darting brown eyes, a mischievous smile, a contrary nature, and an air of propriety that was somehow extremely seductive. A complicity had always existed between us, which only strengthened after her marriage to Hezekiah Coffin in 1801, when I was ten.

One morning in that year, when she was visiting the farm, we strolled to the barn on the pretext of seeing a newborn calf. In fact I wanted to sound her out on the troubling questions my parents had raised in my mind.

"Can you keep a secret?" I asked her.

"You know I can, George. What are friends for?"

So I told her about my mother's warning, adding, "How can she say whaling's not for me? How can she know?"

She looked at me steadily, then said, "Do you know that your mother believes she has a Gift?"

"Of knowing what will happen before it does?"

"Especially terrible things."

"And does she?"

"Of course not," said my aunt firmly, with a toss of her head. "No one can see into the future, but Tamar thinks she can. She was always predicting horrors, and of course in whaling horrors sometimes happen, so she could think she had a gift of prophecy. When your great-uncle Ben Pinkham's command, the *Juno,* was lost with all hands in a storm, she said she had seen it—before the news reached the Island. That was when some people got the idea that it might never have happened if she hadn't seen it, and they whispered about her."

"Is that why my father never went back to sea?"

She shook her head. "They hardly knew each other then. That was his own idea. He could have shipped as a boatsteerer and been a captain by now." She glanced back at the little gray-shingled house just as my mother came out the back door to feed the chickens. She threw the feed to the ground as if she wanted to kill them. "Of course," continued my aunt, "there's nothing *wrong* with being a farmer. People must eat." Then she took me by the shoulders and said, "But you're meant for better things, George. If you want to go to sea you must go. Don't listen to anyone who would hold you back. You must live your life to suit you and no one else. You can, you know. Not everyone can, but you can." She stroked my shoulder lightly. Then she bent close to me and whispered into my ear, "I know because you're so like me."

Of course I came to believe that Nancy Coffin was the best and wisest human being on God's earth—as well as the prettiest and best-smelling, and I was by then hopelessly infatuated with her.

That year, in September, I began attending classes conducted by the Reverend Zebediah Matthews, for in those days there was no public education on Nantucket. Zenas Coffin, the richest man on the Island, did not believe that public funds should be squandered on educating the young, any more than he believed that whale oil should be wasted on lighting the streets of the town. Finding one's way, whether through the mazes of universal knowledge or down Federal Street at midnight, should be a private undertaking. Zenas was not alone in this conviction. Education bred gentility, and gentility was not to be debased by promoting it with public revenues. So, under our patriarchal government, dominated by the Friends and rooted in the customs and prerogatives of the first settlers, it was Quaker schools for Quakers and come-what-may for everyone else.

There were twelve of us pupils, including Bill Riddell and Jed Hamblin, who were to become my companions, and Owen Chase, who was two years younger than I. We had no schoolhouse but convened every weekday morning in the parlor of the Riddell house on Pleasant Street. I was the only boy from out of town, and it was up to me to transport myself from Polpis as best I could, on foot or by hitching a ride in a wagon. In foul weather I sometimes spent the night at Aunt Nancy's house on Broad Street.

The Reverend Matthews was a cadaverous, hollow-eyed off-Islander, with a shiny bald head and tufts of white hair floating over his ears. Stern and humorless, he taught us by ferreting out our ignorance and exposing it to ridicule. Since I was farm-bred and large of frame, Reverend Matthews decided that I must therefore be slow-witted. He took to treating me as the dunce of the class, only to find that I was quicker than he at arithmetic and possessed of wit enough to stand toe to toe with him in theological debate.

As a Calvinist of the harshest stripe, Reverend Matthews taught Scripture both as the literal history of the world from Creation to Crucifixion and as revelation. His object was not to save our souls, since according to his belief our salvation was entirely out of our hands. His purpose was to teach us that all our lives we might squirm toward a state of Grace and still sizzle for Eternity. We were born in sin, and all the prayers and good works in the world would not save us from damnation if God had not, for reasons of His own, chosen in advance to pluck us out of the Fire. He had already made his choices! Each of us was trapped in his fate like a netted fish with no power to escape it.

For some reason this state of affairs seemed to afford Reverend Matthews considerable pleasure. I, on the other hand, liked nothing about it, all the more because he had apparently formed an opinion of who in our class showed signs of Grace and who did not. Contrary to the Bible's teaching on the subject of rich men getting into Heaven, Bill Riddell, whose father was a dry-goods merchant and auctioneer, had an excellent chance; and Jeff Folger, Caleb Mitchell, and Jason Starbuck, inseparable friends whose families owned ships and wharves, had little to worry about; and Owen Chase, of a whaling clan settled all over Cape Cod, and to whom it had never occurred not to be devout, or not to prepare his lessons, or to be anything other than what he was expected to be, was a sure winner, while Jed Hamblin, whose father was a carpenter, and Tim Jenkins, the son of the town crier, were in serious doubt. And as for me, a dirt-poor farmboy with infernal notions of self-importance, there was no hope at all.

Reverend Matthews made this clear one day when, in the course of one of his tirades on Original Sin, Grace, and Damnation, I raised my hand.

"Question, Pollard?" he said, vexed to be thrown off stride.

"Yes, sir," I said. "If we can't do anything about what happens to us, if doing good doesn't save us, why should we try to please God if it's all to no purpose?"

Reverend Matthews closed his eyes, put his bony hands to

his temples, and said, "Oh, Pollard, Pollard, if you've ever prayed in your life, pray to God that He didn't hear you say that. Sweep that thought from your mind. Throw it in the Devil's face. To please God and walk in His light is the reason you are on earth, my poor boy—no matter what awaits you."

"Doesn't much sound as if He even wanted us to please Him."

"It is not for you, young man, to guess His mind! It is for you to submit to His will. Remember that wherever you are, you are in the Lord's sight. You cannot escape Him. Remember what befell Jonah when he tried to flee from the Lord."

There was a respectful silence. Of all the stories in the Bible the tale of the reluctant prophet who was swallowed by a great fish—presumably a whale—had captured the imaginations of us Nantucket boys. We had all heard lurid accounts of misfortunes in the fishery, but for a man to be swallowed whole and live for three days sloshing around in seaweed and cuttlefish and then be vomited onto dry land, that was a yarn that had won our respect if not our credence.

"What does the story of Jonah teach us? Riddell?"

"That you can't run away from God."

"Hamblin?"

"That it pays to obey Him."

"Chase?"

"That He is merciful."

The look of gratification on Matthews's face told me that once again Chase had hit the nail on the head and could count himself among the Elect. Again I raised my hand.

"Another question, Pollard?"

"Yes, sir. If God was so merciful, why did He make Jonah tell the people of Nineveh that they would be destroyed?"

"Because He wanted to warn the Ninevehans to make them mend their ways. But foolishly Jonah became angry because

God relented and was merciful. What are we to think of such
a man, Pollard?"

I pondered a moment, then said, "Strikes me Jonah was
lucky God didn't need to prove He was any more merciful than
He did."

"Pollard!"

"No wonder Jonah got angry. He'd been put through a lot
of trouble to make God look good."

"*Enough,* Pollard!"

By then Bill and Jed and some of the others were having some
trouble not smiling. Reverend Matthews was glaring at me as
if flames were already licking at my pants legs.

I remember Chase in those days as a boy who, as I say, took
the world pretty much as it came, without question or complaint. He seemed as content with his existence as I was determined to change mine. Most males in Chase's family had been
whalemen; his father was a captain. Chases and their kin were
a prolific, God-fearing clan with a sprinkling of deacons, well
rooted ashore, at home on the sea. Owen Chase was strong
and broad-shouldered, with a handsome, steady countenance
that seemed to reflect a nature neither so shallow as to be
unfeeling nor so deep as to allow his feelings to bother him
much. His vision of me as a person of dubious character
would inspire me to pull surprises on him so as not to let him
down.

Those years before the second war with England were prosperous ones for the Island. Buildings were going up everywhere,
and all day long, one-horse drays trundled up newly cobbled
Main Street hauling bulging black casks to the Starbucks' refi-
nery on New Dollar Lane, returning with smaller casks of

finished oil, the best in the world. Jed's father was never out of work in those days. The Riddells were thriving. It was at the Pleasant Street house that I first met Mary.

Her sight is failing now. She can no longer read or sew. As I write she is entertaining female friends in the parlor below this room. When they leave she will prepare our supper. After our meal I will read aloud the news of the Island from the *Inquirer*. Then I begin my nightly rounds. I would long ago have been lost without her.

I had never thought much about Bill's younger sister except, as Bill himself did, as an intruder into our masculine world. Then, one afternoon of a warm spring Saturday, I went to the Riddell house in the hope of finding Bill. Mary opened the door. It was the first time we had ever been alone together. I must have been about thirteen then, Mary about nine, though she seemed older in worldly understanding.

"Hello, George Pollard," she said with a smile, as if she had been expecting me.

"Bill home?" I asked, making clear the reason for my visit.

"No, George Pollard," she said. "I'm home."

This reply threw me into confusion. With my sister Betsy I was used to female mannerisms and with Susan to female sweetness, but here was something else altogether: a girl with steady, unflusterable blue eyes who very plainly and directly was challenging me to pay attention to her—and successfully. At first, I suspected that as a Riddell with friends in all the better families in town she was making fun of her brother's rustic acquaintance. I felt that earth and dung clung to my homespun clothes, that my body and hands were too big and ungainly, my peat-colored hair too unruly, falling from under my cap, which

I had neglected to remove. Having always assumed that a compact existed between us that we have nothing to do with each other, I was now surprised that she would not cooperate.

"Will you tell Bill I was looking for him?"

"Of course I will, George Pollard."

"Why do you call me by my two names?"

"Because I like your two names. Why not try calling me by mine?"

I hesitated, then answered her smile. "All right, Mary Riddell."

"See how easy it is?"

I left the house with my cap still planted firmly on my head, marveling at the power of females to scramble a person's thinking. From that day on, instead of avoiding Bill's sister, I took to walking out of my way past her house, on the chance of seeing her.

That encounter left me all the more determined to go on a whaling voyage at the earliest opportunity. I very much wanted to show Mary Riddell who I was, and at the same time find out for myself. As I passed the open doorway of the Starbuck countinghouse that day, looking for Bill, I saw two boys only a couple of years older than I signing their first shipping papers, and I longed for the day when I could do the same. At Straight Wharf a whaleship returning from a long voyage was being warped into the dock, and I gazed up at the officers and crewmen on deck, their faces browned by the Pacific sun, and I heard one of the mates call down to the wharfmaster, "Twenty-one hundred and all sperm."

On the bench outside the blacksmith's on North Wharf I found Bill and Jed Hamblin and Owen Chase sitting with the former whalemen who gathered there to swap well-seasoned tales, and banter as unhurried as the creaking of the wharf's piles. Gaunt old "Captain" Jeremiah Swain was holding forth to three cronies and the boys when I upended a candle box for a seat in their midst.

". . . so there we was, in with a shoal of sperm whales, when no sooner'd Cap'n Coleman got fast to one when another of 'em bore straight down on us with his great jaws gapin' like the caverns of Hell. Well, all of us 'cept the cap'n went overboard just as those jaws closed on our bow, catchin' the cap'n so's all we could see was his arm stickin' out of that whale's mouth as it sounded. Well, sir, that, we figured, was the end of the cap'n, but in about a minute damned if the whale didn't broach and fling him 'bout five fathoms 'cross the sea. Well, we thought he was done for, but when the mate's boat got to him we saw that he was still alive but his arm was mauled up something awful. On board ship the cap'n sized the situation up, called for the medicine chest, got out a doctorin' book and a saw and some knives. Then, looking at what was left of his arm, he said to the mate, 'Mr. Swift, the plain fact is I ain't going to make it ashore if me and this wreck don't part company. I've seen it done once and I'm going to tell you what to do and you're going to do it. And, by God, if you faint even once I'm going to have you thrown overboard. So let's get on with it.' And the mate done it and Cap'n Coleman lived to ship out again. You see, he was bound and determined not to die as long as there was anything to be done about it."

He fell silent and Elisha Jenkens said, "Swain, you know damned well you never shipped with Cap'n Coleman."

Not the least perturbed, Swain replied, "Jenkens, if I never shipped with Cap'n Coleman, then you sure as hell never shipped with Cap'n Levi Hussey."

"Ah, now Cap'n Hussey, there was a real whalin' man," announced Jenkens, not troubling to deny Swain's suggestion. " 'Member the time we was on a real old-fashioned Nantucket sleighride, towed four-five miles from the ship. When our whale tired we hauled up to him and Hussey lanced him but the whale turned and the last act of his life was to catch us from underneath with his flukes, smashing the boat to splinters and flinging us all into the sea. Well, there we was in the water, ship nowheres in

sight and night comin' on and sharks beginnin' to take an
interest; so, usin' his lance to get a purchase, Cap'n Hussey
helped us climb aboard the dead whale, where we spent the night
hanging on and singing but mostly hanging on. Next morning
the ship found us. Cap'n Hussey never let a whale get away from
him if he could help it, and he never lost a man to one."

At that, after a respectful pause, I spoke up, asking Swain a
question that had been troubling me since my disagreement
with Reverend Matthews.

"Cap'n Swain," I asked, "could a whale really have swallowed Jonah whole and three days later spit him out alive?"

Swain puffed on his pipe, considering the matter scientifi-
cally, then said, " 'Pends what kind o' whale you're talkin'
about. Couldn't be a sulphur-bottom or a bowhead or a right
whale. They got gullets no bigger'n a hawse hole. Blackfish's
too small. That pretty much leaves Old Cachalot. Ain't sayin'
it's likely, but if he set his mind to it a sperm whale could
swallow a man, and it stands to reason that if he could swallow
him he could spit him out again."

"Not after three days," objected Jenkens. "No sir, a sperm
whale's got mighty powerful innards. 'Fact he's got seven or
eight stomachs, so a man wouldn't stand much of a chance
being digested for three days, 'specially without no air. No, sir,
only way I figure it is, Jonah didn't get swallowed at all, he got
inhaled. See, if he got breathed into the whale's lungs he'd have
air and wouldn't be gettin' digested neither, so you figure that
way he would have lived three days, maybe five or six. Then
he'd be *coughed* up. That way it wouldn't be no miracle at all,
just a mite unusual."

In those gams Bill and Jed and Chase and I heard a lot of lies
and just plain nonsense, but we also formed an idea of what
whaling was and what was expected of a man at sea. The

Nantucket captains and mates those old sailors admired were admirable men, give or take a tyrant or two; the best of them were as brave, skillful, and resourceful seamen as ever walked a quarterdeck. All of us felt the powerful call of the Pacific, of adventure, of the kill, of testing ourselves. The dangers of the business only whetted our desire to go to sea; for a young Nantucket boy will not really, down deep, believe that anything calamitous will happen to him, while allowing that the very worst may happen to others. The only questions in his mind are: How brave am I? How good a whaleman will I be? What name and fortune will I make for myself on the Island?

I recall the evening when, going on fourteen, I announced to my parents my decision to go to sea that very year, 1805. It was February, bitter cold and blustery outside, a fire of peat and timbers from beached wrecks blazing in the kitchen hearth. We were at supper, my father, mother, sisters, and, as our guests, my Aunt Nancy and her husband of four years, Hezekiah. I had chosen the moment deliberately, expecting that the presence of my aunt and Coffin uncle would moderate whatever objections might be raised over my plans, while at the same time hoping to enhance my importance in the eyes of my aunt, of whom I was fonder than ever. My calculation that both Nancy and Hezekiah would lend me support proved correct; my error was in thinking that my father would side with my mother, who remained unalterably opposed to my going whaling.

When I made my announcement she said in a soft but intense voice, "You must not."

"Why?" demanded Nancy. "It's not so strange an ambition for a boy."

My mother looked darkly at her sister, saying only, "Whaling's not for everyone."

Then to my surprise my father said, "True, Tamar, but

George must decide for himself what he'll do with his life. I could use him here, but farming's not for everyone either. If he's a mind to go to sea, then I guess he'll go to sea."

"Of course he will," said Betsy, emboldened by my father and adding to me, "I'll be so proud when you strike your first whale."

Hezekiah said, "Won't be strikin' whales first voyage out. Second maybe, dependin'."

And Susan said, "Will you bring me a trinket, George? Maybe a pearl?"

"Pearl ain't no trinket," Hezekiah said.

"I'll bring you a whole necklace of pearls," I told her.

My mother turned to Nancy. "And will you be sending your Owen off whaling?"

Owen Coffin, my first cousin, was then not quite three years old.

Nancy replied, "I won't be sending Owen off anywhere, but when the time comes and he should decide to ship on a whaler, I wouldn't stand in his way. I'd be proud to have him follow in his father's steps."

I glanced at my father. If he found any offense in Nancy's words, his calm, weathered face showed no sign of it. My mother glared at my pretty raven-haired aunt—who smiled at me to vex her. The sisters had never been close.

There were two berths for green hands on the *Eliza Slade,* one on the *Ellen Mitchell.* Since Owen Chase was still too young to go whaling, Bill and Jed and I had to determine who would sail together, who alone. We decided it as we always decided such matters, by drawing lots. That way, whatever happened, no one could say it wasn't fair. The choice was left to chance.

I held the straws. Bill was my closest friend that year and I wanted desperately to sail with him, so I prayed to God and, for good measure, the Devil that Jed would take the short one. He did.

But four days before we were to sail, Bill took sick with fever. I prayed some more that he would recover in time, but this time it didn't work. He got worse and had to be replaced. When I went to say goodbye to him, he was burning with fever and downcast about not going on the cruise, though maybe, as I think back, a little relieved too.

Mary met me at the foot of the stairs. She looked at me with a twist to her mouth, half worried, half vexed, and said, "You come back safe now, George Pollard."

"I will, Mary Riddell."

She took my hand in both of hers and squeezed it so hard it hurt. "You be sure you do."

"I think I'll even miss you," I said.

"You'd just better."

4

Manhood is reached by many small steps, and the fourteen-year-old green hand stepping off the gangway to the deck of the *Eliza Slade* still had leagues to go. Even now I can feel a twinge of what I felt then: the gut-gnawing disparity between the bundle of raw forces I was and the man I was yet to be.

In those early years of the century, Nantucket ships were sailed by young men of the Island for the most part, in contrast with the polyglot crews of today. Boys of all classes and conditions were represented. The other young apprentices on the *Eliza Slade* were a nephew of one of the Starbuck owners, a Gardner, a Folger, three blacks from the New Guinea section of town, and the son of the town crier. Owing to the parsimony of the owners, there was a high proportion of green hands, and the burden of offsetting this disadvantage through intensive training and discipline fell upon the first mate, Silas Bench.

I was standing on deck by the gangway gazing up at the lofty maze of standing rigging, wondering how I would ever sort it all out, when the mate came up the aft companionway and approached me.

"Everything shipshape, Pollard?" he asked—and I found myself in the presence of the strangest-looking individual I had ever seen. He was tall and lean with long arms and huge hands, a small round face twisted by burns, an irregular stub where his nose should have been, small, cunning eyes. When, amazed by his appearance, I didn't reply at once he said, "It is Mr. George Pollard, isn't it? From Polpis?"

"Yes, sir."

"Mr. Bench. I'm the first mate on this ship."

"Pleased to make your acquaintance."

"That what you think you've done?"

I must have turned beet-red, to judge from the mate's look of satisfaction. "No, sir," I said lamely, my wits crippled by frustration and embarrassment.

"Private sort of person?"

"At times, sir."

"Ah," he said. "Who'd have guessed? Well, George, looks like you and me are going out after whales together."

"Yes, sir."

"Any special thoughts about that?"

I could feel myself flushing. Finding no defense against the mate's intimidating humor, I was doing my best to weather it —and failing. When he had thoroughly wrung me out he said,

"Now, George, go forward and claim a nice snug bunk for yourself, and be sure to let me and Captain Clasby know the minute anything ain't suited to your liking."

I was to learn that Silas Bench was a native of Rhode Island. During the Revolutionary War, as a boy of ten, he had shipped as cabin boy on a whaler out of New Bedford. His vessel had been captured, and he survived two years on a British prison ship, losing his nose to rats. Ever since his release he had sailed on whaleships. He was to be my tormentor, taskmaster, and first teacher of the glorious, greasy art of whaling.

I went forward and descended into the fo'c'sle and as my eyes adjusted to the darkness threw my seabag on the nearest vacant bunk.

"Taken, Pollard."

I identified the owner of the voice as Caleb Mitchell. He and Jason Starbuck were seated on a lower bunk adjacent to the one in dispute.

"Nothing to claim it," I told them.

"There's us to claim it," said Starbuck.

"For Jeff Folger," said Mitchell.

Already discountenanced by my run-in with Mr. Bench, I was in no mood to submit to an affront by my fo'c'sle mates. The full truth is that, having entertained the hope that I now might be accepted as an equal by these sons of prosperous Quaker whaling families, I was now infuriated by their hostile reception, and even more by my foolishness in expecting anything else. I knew that I could successfully take on either Starbuck or Mitchell and possibly both together, but I was not about to jeopardize my career in its first five minutes by starting a shipboard fight; so I swore that at the earliest opportunity I would show these proud, privileged young men whom they were dealing with. I would make use of their disdain to harden my will to excel. I had no need of them. Looking for an honorable way out of the confrontation, I then made out three blacks lounging in their shelves on the port side, watching me with amusement, and on an upper bunk, little Tim Jenkins, the town crier's son.

"Come over here, Pollard," he called. "You're welcome here."

Fixing Starbuck and Mitchell with my grandest look of defiance, I took up my seabag and tossed it on the bunk under Jenkins's.

"I thank you, Tim," I said. "Air seems fresher over here anyway."

So began my sea career—inauspiciously, but with my determination stirred to fever pitch. I would lie low and learn the business at hand until I had a chance to prove myself. All I wished was to serve my apprenticeship as inconspicuously as possible.

Silas Bench, however, was not to cooperate.

By the third week at sea, it was clear to everyone that the mate had singled me out as the prime target of his stinging wit. Aloft, I would pause in my work a moment, scanning the horizon in the wild hope of being first to raise a whale, and his high-pitched voice would float up from the afterdeck. "Look alive, George! Ain't no strayed sheep out thar." On our first boat drill when, in my overeagerness, I pulled at my oar a split second too soon: "What's wrong, Polpis? That's an oar you got thar, not a hoe. Get it in the water when I tell you, not before."

After the first week of harassment by Mr. Bench and ostracism by Starbuck, Mitchell, and Folger, I began to learn the tricks of the sea trade very rapidly. By the third week everyone on board had noticed my progress. Among the novices I was the best steersman, and was the first up the rigging in any weather, and never again did I snag an oar. Of course, Mr.

Bench took sole credit for my improvement, but he also eased up on me and my confidence soared. By the fourth week I was not only admitted into the company of the Quaker aristocracy but had become a leading spirit in the fo'c'sle on my own account.

Still, as we had not yet raised a whale, the greatest test lay ahead of me, and the more time that passed the more concerned I was about just how I would meet it.

It came on our thirty-first day at sea.

We had been ghosting along under a clear blue sky with fluffy clouds at the horizon, in light airs, leaning gently into long, sun-flecked swells, scattering flying fish from our bows, as peaceful as could be, indeed far too peaceful, with not a drop of oil in our holds, and Captain Clasby pacing the quarterdeck, now and then casting stormy glances at the masthead watch. Forward, one of the blacks was scratching a mournful tune from his fiddle, accompanied by the languid creaking of timbers and the occasional snap of canvas catching the halfhearted breeze. From the cookhouse the inviting smell of boiling salt beef wafted over the vessel.

But the midday meal was to be delayed that day.

Suddenly from the crow's nest the second mate sang out what we had all been waiting to hear.

"There she blo-o-ows!"

Instantly the captain shouted aloft, "Where away? How far?"

"Four points off the starboard bow. Six miles. Lone sperm whale."

By then Mr. Bench had dashed up on deck and was ordering all hands to prepare for lowering the boats. Captain Clasby dove below, returning with his glass, leaped into the shrouds, and climbed nimbly to the masthead. From there he conned the helmsman on a new course, while we readied the boats to be swung outboard: the captain's, the mate's, and the second mate's.

Owing to the light winds it was three-quarters of an hour before the captain judged us to be at the proper lowering distance from our quarry (which sounded but always surfaced again on the same course), and during this time I, and no doubt other of my shipmates, took the opportunity for meditation on the hazards of our occupation.

My place was at the stroke, or sternmost, oar of the mate's boat, one of four oarsmen who with the harpooner, Jason Morse, in the bow and the mate at the steering oar made up the crew of our twenty-six-foot cockleshell, about to accost a robust member of the largest class of living creatures ever to inhabit land or sea. A dozen times on the voyage we had practiced for this moment, shipping the mast and raising the sail, maneuvering both offensively and defensively, but now that our huge prey was in sight, a sheeny black island in the blue water, and the ship steadily closing the distance between us, my thoughts were agitated. Watching the whale I saw the glint of his mammoth flukes that could bat us into Eternity; and I reflected on his jaws, like those of a barracuda the size of a church, able to chop us in two with no trouble at all. And I asked myself, "Pollard, what are you doing out here in the middle of the Atlantic, venturing your one precious life in order to fill the Starbuck coffers? Are you really so set on supplying the world with clean-burning oil?"

And at that moment I saw that the mate was looking squarely at me, and I guessed in his ravaged face what was on his mind just as he was guessing what was on mine. The mate had sensed my trepidation and was wondering whether or not at the crucial moment my hands would grow numb with fright, causing me to foul a life-saving maneuver, or, worse, whether I might become so addled in my terror as to require the clout of a lance pole to settle me down.

At once, under his gaze, my thoughts steadied and the fearsome questions crawling in my guts were resolved.

I would do well. I would face what was to be faced and master my fear. I would do well not for the Starbucks or for Captain Clasby or for Mr. Bench and my boatmates but for myself. I felt an intense urge to experience the unknown that lay ahead. At that moment I would not have changed places with any man in the world.

Without a word passing between us the mate seemed to understand from my answering look that I was not about to get gallied on him.

"Stand by to lower boats!" called down the captain, who then descended, took his place in his own boat, and gave the order to lower, leaving the cook, the cooper, and the cabin boy as shipkeepers.

All three boats struck the water at the same time, but it was ours, the mate's, that by tradition had the honor of striking the lone whale first, the other two being close by to strike again should we fail to get fast, to bend on more line if the whale sounded deep, or to retrieve whatever was left of us and our gear if we got fluked. Since there was so little wind, we didn't ship the mast but prepared to row, urged on by the mate's exhortations.

"Line your oars, boys. Now pull ahead, long and strong. Spring, I tell ye! Lay back and spring!"

We raced the other boats, gaining the lead, fairly flying through the swells. I glanced over my shoulder. The whale was less than a quarter-mile of sapphire sea ahead of us. He looked immense, indestructible.

"Eyes astern, Pollard. You do the rowin' and leave me 'n' Jason do the lookin'. All you beauties just feast your eyes on me. Now all, lay back and spring. Spring!"

Ten minutes passed like an eternity. My shoulders ached. Then at last, with his free hand, the mate slowed the rhythm

of our rowing and in a lowered voice said, "Easy does it now,
boys. No noise. Oh, what a whale! Ninety barrels if he's a gill!
We're in his wake. Now—*now*—pull hard and pull silent. Stand
up, Jason."

As I bent to my oar I saw the whale's flukes rising and
falling in the clear water not ten feet abeam of us. Then we
were alongside his glistening black flank, and with a sweep of
the oar the mate headed us directly toward him, calling, "Let
him have it, Jason! Give it to him!" We heard the harpooner
grunt as he heaved his iron, then the mate, no longer mode-
rating his voice, shouted, "Now, stern all, boys! Stern all, if
you want to see your sweethearts again! Stern all, if you want
to see Nantucket!"

The strength we found then, despite our exertions, fairly shot
our double-ended craft away from what by then was seventy-
odd tons of writhing fury, slapping his flukes on the water with
an awful noise that seemed to echo down from the sky, then
diving, going deep, as turn after turn of line unwound from the
tub, burned around the loggerhead in the stern, and bored into
the water off our bow.

We were fast.

The fight had begun.

As if it were his intention, the whale was towing us rapidly
away from the other boats, with their spare tubs of line, and we
put some strain on the fast-escaping tether—to put more would
have pulled us under.

Then, without warning, the line went slack, and I experienced a thrill of terror, imagining that deep below us the
whale had turned and, locating his puny tormentor, was at this
instant boiling up from the depths directly under us. The mate's
grim look then was not reassuring.

"Stern all," he said, quietly this time, adding as if to himself,
"No sense running over him."

We obeyed with a will.

After an endless time we witnessed a sight that, even after many another eventful encounter with cetaceans, I shall never forget. Suddenly, about fifty yards abeam of us, the enormous black stub of the whale's head broke the surface and the creature rose straight up, as if reaching for the sun, for life, the harpoon in his side, the line wound once around his body, until he almost stood on his flukes, then very slowly toppled to one side, with a great splash, and lay in the water, still.

"All right, Jason," said the mate then, "come astern and steer us straight to his life. Give me a crack at him now, will ye?" And the mate and the harpooner changed places, Mr. Bench taking up the long, razor-sharp iron lance and standing braced in the bow for the kill, as Jason Morse took over the steering oar.

"Now, boys," said the mate, "line your oars and pull, and look alive, I tell ye. That whale ain't finished yet, and he may have a nasty trick or two in him."

So, again, we pulled directly toward the whale's flank, to the spot called the "life," which when struck brings speedy death.

As we approached the great creature we could hear his labored breathing. Then we heard the mate's strangled cry as he buried the lance deep in the whale's vital organs.

"Stern all!" he shouted then. "Stern all, for your lives!"

Instantly, as we pulled, the water around us was churning white-streaked carmine as the whale flurried; then slowly, as in a nightmare, he turned away and raised his flukes over us until they shadowed our terrified faces.

"Stern all!" cried the mate, now with panic in his voice, and we pulled clear of the descending tail that smashed down not six feet from us, drenching us with gory brine.

We worked to a safer distance, then stood off, watching the whale's death throes. He spouted a red geyser, swam in a tight circle, raising first his head, then his flukes, blood now stream-

ing from his blowhole, strangling his desperate breathing, until
at last he slowed, rolled to one side, his fin up, limp and useless,
his small eye fixed sightless on the sun.

For a day, a night, and another day, watch on, watch off, the
officers and harpooners, now in their role of seagoing butchers,
severed the great head from the carcass secured alongside, directed the draining of the "case" of its precious spermaceti,
stripped the thick blubber from the body, using seven-foot scal-
pels, for us to hack into pieces and feed to the boiling try-pots,
working in a reddish cloud of stinking vapor. In a continuous
process we fed the copper cooking vats, then drained the oil into
casks, and when they had cooled wrestled them across the
slippery, rolling deck and below, eighty-seven barrels all told.
The mate had been close to the mark.

When this was done we released the head and carcass to the
sharks and fell to scrubbing down the vessel until, as we
resumed our southeasterly course, there was not a trace of the
cutting-in. Then, exhausted, we fell into our bunks.

Just before sinking into sleep, I thought of the expiring whale
as he had risen from the sea like a black tower, and I felt, as
my father must have, a sense of awe at the death of so wondrous
a creature, no doubt, as my father believed, more kindred to
ourselves than we know.

So, what sort of man, feeling this, would at his very first taste
of whaling be confirmed in his ambition to make it his life's
occupation?

The young man I was then.

For the truth is that I had also felt a savage joy in the chase
and the kill. It seemed as if there was a part of my being, beyond
reach of reason or fear, that drew its strength from the hunt and
the death of the whale. For days afterward I felt whole and
confident.

I was more certain than ever then that I was born to the peculiar enterprise of the Island and could only prosper in it.

5

In the same year I returned from my first cruise on board the *Eliza Slade,* I shipped as boatsteerer on the *Edward Cary,* Captain Peleg Barrett, an able master more at home in the stern sheets of a whaleboat than most men are in their parlors. On that voyage, on the Brazilian grounds, the third mate and two seamen were killed when a cow sperm whale, blinded by a lance, splintered their boat with her flukes. I then became third mate. We returned in the summer of 1810 with thirteen hundred barrels and seven thousand pounds of bone. After four months ashore I shipped again on the *Cary.* We now faced a new danger, for by then the British and the American War Hawks were at each other's throats, and impressment of sailors was a threat to every Yankee ship, so that our masthead watch had to scan the horizon for English men-of-war as well as spouts. We rounded the Cape and took sperm whales in the Pacific, returning in June of 1812 to learn that a state of war existed between America and England. Captain Barrett had commended me for a promotion, but it did me no good, since no ships were sailing and those at sea were at peril. As had happened during the Revolutionary War, Nantucket's lifeline to the oceans was cut and we faced heavy losses of men, ships, and revenue, all because of a squabble between mainlanders and Englishmen that meant only destitution for the Island.

I was impressed—not on board a British ship but on the Polpis farm, navigating a plow in the lee of a flatulent mare, cursing both Yankees and English for beaching me at the outset of my whaling career.

I stuck it out at Polpis for nearly a year. Then, in the spring of 1813, I signed on Amos Kendall's blockade-running sloop, the *Southern Cross.* It was tricky work. British warships plied the Sound, and we sailed for the mainland ports only on moonless nights, often in bad weather, Captain Kendall navigating by ranging on lighthouses, dead reckoning, a sixth sense of the set of the sea and the landfalls, and also, as I look back, a lot of luck.

Those were bleak times for all who had stayed on Nantucket. The few returning whaleships that managed to elude the blockade brought news of many other vessels captured and some burned. There was little food or fuel. The poor were reduced to begging, while our leading citizens, having requested assistance from President Madison and received none, petitioned the British for permission to provision the Island and save its six thousand inhabitants from starvation. For a time that permission was granted, but then it was withdrawn and we were worse off than before, now mistrusted by both British and Americans alike. Except for the South Tower bell that tolled each wasted hour and the town crier's announcements thrice daily, the town was as still as the cemeteries that bordered it. Most of the Main Street shops were closed. At night the houses were dark, parlors closed, with only the glimmer from meager fires showing in kitchen windows. The old men who had gammed on the bench on North Wharf were gone, in the Poor Asylum, or dead. The whaleships in the harbor—among them the *Essex*—had become roosts for gulls, wind harps.

Yet, bleak as those years were for the Island, they were not the worst times for a young blockade runner. To be near the sloop, I was lodging at my Aunt Nancy's house on Broad Street, paying my rent in wood and food and helping her with the education of Owen and Edward, and looking after her third-born, an affectionate girl of four, Ann. Hezekiah was still at sea. Of the two young boys, it was with Owen Coffin that I formed a special friendship. I enjoyed his cheerful company.

As I write these words my brain is burning. To tell what was without revealing *what was to be* seems like a lie. "A special friendship." "I enjoyed his cheerful company." Yet it was true. It is true! Nothing—save madness—can alter the past; while our future is constantly created by our own choices, in collusion with chance. Through a window of fire I remember my life before that appalling *what was to be*—yet I do remember it. It has not been taken from me.

I remember Nancy Coffin as she was in the winter of 1813. I remember her well. She was thirty-one and prettier than ever. I was twenty-two. Her mind was quick and, being barren of serious preoccupations, receptive. She refused to let the hard times or the uncertainty of her husband's fate dampen her high spirits. Sitting near me by the fire one freezing night, knitting, her dark hair loosened and falling to her shoulders, she taunted me about what she took to be my state of melancholy and prescribed a remedy for it.

"You *are* stubborn," she said.

"Stubborn?"

"Mary Riddell is not going to wait forever."

"She's just eighteen."

"Yes, but a very pretty eighteen. Less attractive girls marry younger."

"Then I'll have to take my chances. I haven't a penny in the bank. How could I support a wife now, with this damned—this accursed war?"

She stopped knitting, looked at me, and in a strange voice said, "George, you can say 'damned' with me. I'm not the prude you think I am."

"I never thought you were a prude," I said. Then in confusion I glanced up the stairs to the closed door of Edward and Owen's room. "I wouldn't want to set an example to the children."

For some moments she was silent, the brass clock on the mantel ticking in counterrhythm to the click of her needles, then she said, "The children aren't home."

"Where are they?" I asked sharply, as if my cousins were in some danger.

"Polpis," said Nancy, smiling at me. There was a luminous cast to her face, animated by the firelight. The little oval oil portrait of Hezekiah next to the clock gazed down at me impassively. Naturally ardent, I had no mistresses then but the Pacific island maidens that my imagination presented to me at night. As for Nancy, there was every reason for me not to think lustfully of her; she was my mother's sister, my godmother, nearly a decade older than I, a married woman. Moreover, the special understanding that had always existed between us had implied—I had always assumed—a chaste intimacy in which attraction between us was nothing but a harmless amusement. And yet, increasingly, I did occasionally think lustfully of her, at first without concern, chiding myself halfheartedly for my forbidden thoughts; until in time it occurred to me, from certain looks and blushes, silences, that Nancy herself might be experiencing similar feelings. I could not be sure. I was still woefully inexperienced. Having been fearful of contracting disease from women of easy virtue and entanglements with the other sort, I had never lain with a woman; and my virginity had become a burden and an addiction, for which there appeared to be no ready cure but marriage. Yet in that instant, from the way Nancy told me that we were alone in the house, I let myself believe that she had arranged this country visit for her children with but one purpose in mind, and my confidence that our relationship must remain an innocent one vanished in an instant. The clock ticked loudly. Her needles flew. I glanced at the portrait of Hezekiah. I looked at Nancy, my thoughts in turmoil, my desire for her mounting with each tick of the clock, each click of the steel needles. She looked up from her work, and for the first time in my life I was gazing into the eyes of a woman who was giving herself to me. There could be no doubt of it. I said nothing. I did nothing. The communication between us was perfect. What had seemed impossible only moments before was now inescapable—unless I were to—God help me— refuse this greatest of gifts on the pretext of some scruple that no longer meant anything to me. *That* would be the unforgivable offense. And yet what if I was wrong? What if it was only in my heated imagination that Nancy was at this moment offering herself to me? Then, abruptly, she thrust aside her work. She smiled at me without affection. She arose and said, "Goodnight, George. I'm going to bed. Don't forget what I said about Mary." And she took the lamp beside her and went upstairs. The last two steps creaked accusingly.

After several minutes, hearing no sound from upstairs, I took the other lamp, went up the stairs, and started down the hall toward my room at the back of the house. Nancy's door was ajar. It had never stood open at night before. I stopped outside her darkened room. That was my decision. After a moment she said, "Come in, George." That was hers.

I recall the giddy young man at Nancy's breakfast table the next morning with disbelief. As if it were now his right, he took Hezekiah's place at its head. Still hearing her cries of pleasure, he let Nancy serve him porridge and warm milk. He believed that he had accomplished something extraordinary. A fire of driftwood sawn and split by the absent master crackled in the hearth. He smiled at Nancy to assure her that everything was all right. It was a splendid morning. She smiled back faintly, then not at all.

"What's the matter?" he asked.

"Nothing."

"Regrets?"

"You're a funny boy."

"What is it, then?" He reached across and took her hand.

She was silent, then said in an even voice, "The children. I dreamed that they were dead."

"They're surely safe."

"I dreamed that Tamar killed them."

I stared at her in amazement.

"You know that's ridiculous."

"It was a dream. A dream is never ridiculous."

"But then you wake up."

"Do you?"

"What are you afraid of?" I demanded, and hearing the sharp edge in my voice I added, "I'm very fond of you."

She smiled at the young man from a great distance, then said, "And will you protect me and my children, George?"

He replied, "I can't protect you from your nightmares."

He felt her hand tremble. Then she drew it away. And for all his blindness, he understood then that Hezekiah was still master in this house.

6

It would be edifying to relate that I was soon swept by remorse and fears of Hell following my night with Nancy, but it was not so. If anything, the giddiness that I had experienced settled into a feeling of satisfaction. I had cast off the albatross of virginity. I could now meet whatever life had in store for me without that at least dogging my steps. If there were a dexterous God overseeing the matter personally, He could not have played His cards better.

As for Nancy, lacking my own splendid independence from the bonds of moral law, she made it plain that what had happened should never happen again. This also suited me.

I saw Mary more often after that. What my aunt had said about her was true enough. She was by then a very pretty woman with many friends and a mind of her own. One of her male admirers was Caleb Mitchell, the heir apparent of the Mitchells' whale-oil business. There were others. Nantucketers do, as a rule, marry young. I was convinced that Mary would soon make a "good" marriage and not wait for a penniless blockade runner from Polpis to make his mark.

One afternoon we were walking on the beach at Brant Point, I in a dark mood, when Mary said, "George, what on earth is the matter?"

"Nothing," I told her.

"What is it?"

"This—accursed war," I lied.

"It'll be over someday."

"Then what?"

"Times will be better. Ships will sail. And you'll not be so gloomy."

"Mitchell ships will sail."

"George Pollard, you are the most foolish person I've ever met in my life."

"Then you must be even more foolish to keep company with me."

"I do only as a charitable act. Lord knows what would happen to you if you were left on your own."

She turned from me and walked briskly down the beach, then turned again and called back, "You'd probably fall off Straight Wharf and drown."

"Then you'd be rid of me," I yelled, adding for good measure, "Isn't that what you really want?"

"Yes!"

We stood there glaring at each other—then both began laughing. I went to her and took her in my arms and kissed her. Her eyes searched mine, then she said, "You are very silly, you know. You can be anything you want on this Island. Everyone knows what a fine whaleman you are. You can have ships of your own one day, if only . . ."

"If only what?"

"If only you'd believe it."

"What makes you think I don't?"

"Do you?"

When I didn't answer she said, "Sometimes, George Pollard, I think your Polpisy ways are all play-acting and you really think you're better than anyone on this Island."

"You know all my deepest secrets," I said teasingly.

"I'm not in the least interested in your deepest secrets," she said. I kissed her again.

"In fact," she said, "I doubt very much whether you have any deepest secrets."

"You'd be surprised."

She frowned. "I don't wish to be surprised."

Then, remembering my mother's premonitions, I said, "How good are you at guessing the future?"

Her mouth twisted in annoyance. "You don't guess the future. You make it happen."

"Don't the stars have anything to do with it?"

"Not unless you let them."

7

New Bedford has replaced us as the Western Hemisphere's first whaling port. Zenas's sons, Henry and Charles, inheritors of the moors and beaches, are already envisioning Brightons rising out of the sand. Our Island community is now united only in uncertainty. The Quakers are split into factions, Hicksites against Gurneyites and both against Wilberites. In the small hours, as I walk up Main Street, the stately homes of the whale-oil merchants loom on either side of the cobbled street, monuments to the memory of a dying trade. ⬥

Catty-corner from this house where I write is, today, an imposing mansion with a commanding facade and soaring chimneys, the only three-storied brick on the Island, built a decade ago by a wealthy cousin of Zenas's named Jared Coffin. Made with whale-oil profits, the dwelling was only briefly occupied by its builder, who sold the property to the steamship company, which reopened it as a hotel for the better class of visitor. Ocean House.

There lies our future: innkeepers at the graveyard of American whaling.

. . .

Owen Chase, they say, is failing. After his long and successful career at sea, his reason is slipping. They say that he markets for more food than he needs and hoards the surplus in the eaves of his house on Orange Street, deranged only now by the ordeals we suffered thirty years ago.

I survive, still with all my faculties.

On my desk as I write lies a copy of Chase's *Narrative of the Most Extraordinary and Distressing Shipwreck of the Whaleship* Essex *of Nantucket.* Its foxed, brittle pages remind me of the time that has passed since it was published late in 1821, the year of our rescue. In his introduction he wrote, "It was my misfortune to be a considerable, if not a principal sufferer in the dreadful catastrophe that befell us; and in it, I not only lost all the little I had ventured, but my situation and the prospects of bettering it, that at one time seemed to smile on me, were all in one short moment destroyed with it." Apart from the grammatical curiosity of that sentence, something else about it galled me for years: the words "if not a principal sufferer." I asked myself how many principal sufferers he was accounting himself with, assuming the omission of those who at sea had ceased to suffer, however horribly. The five survivors from the boats? Four of them? Three? Two? Or none but himself? Could he be saying, I used to wonder, that he was *the* principal sufferer?

Then what of Ramsdell?

And what of me?

Our first cruise together was on the *Essex* in 1815, the year the war ended. Under Captain David Russell, I shipped as second mate, Chase as boatsteerer. On that voyage many a whale was taken that might have escaped were it not for the rivalry that sprang up between Chase and me, to the enrichment of ourselves, Captain Russell and the crew, and, to be sure, Gideon Folger & Co. In 1817 we shipped again on the *Essex* under Russell, I as mate, Chase as second; and toward the end of that voyage our mounting respect for each other as whalemen had somewhat eased our relationship. Homeward bound, we spoke of our girls at home, and once on a night watch under a star-filled sky exchanged views on the magnitude and antiquity of the universe. But we remained rivals for advancement, and, what was more, I could not help feeling that whenever Chase's steady gaze settled on me he was discerning some calamitous flaw.

8

Each year on the 20th of June the greater part of the population of Nantucket vacates the town for the grassy shores of Miacomet Pond to partake in the festival of Sheepshearing. Its name describes its utilitarian purpose, serving, as it does, a need of our Island's second industry, which is the raising of sheep; or, more accurately, the encouragement of sheep to raise themselves. There are at any given time on Nantucket upward of ten thousand woolly quadrupeds, and nowhere will you find any folds or fences or a single shepherd with a crook. Nantucket sheep, once ear-nicked or otherwise mutilated for the purpose of identifying their owners, are sent forth into the wilderness of moors, bogs, and hummocks to forage as best they may, unsheltered from the elements. The lambs that survive their first winter will multiply, perpetuating a hardy breed. For the annual washing and shearing the animals are rounded up and herded into the only confinement they will ever know, the ramshackle pens at Miacomet Pond. As long as I can remember, and a century or so before that, Sheepshearing Day has been a principal Island holiday, our Maypole Day, our Bartholomew Fair, the occasion of much social merriment, revelry, flirtation, feasting, dancing, and competitions, indeed the most our Quaker-ridden Island can offer in the way of public license.

Sheepshearing, 1818, was a memorable moment in the life of the not-quite-twenty-seven-year-old first mate, fresh from a successful Pacific voyage on which he had, by everyone's account, acquitted himself well, Captain Russell's praise ringing in his head, the ground still rolling and pitching under his feet, a little money in the bank, and feeling for the first time that summer whole and confident, the equal of any man on Nantucket.

It was a blue-sky day with a mischievous north wind catching skirts and bonnet strings and flapping the sailcloth rigged over the shearing pens. By ten o'clock several hundred people had gathered along the western shore of the pond, families with hampers of food, children darting everywhere, needy women selling cakes, preserves, homespun, and crochet work. Near the pens a fiddler struck up, and couples were soon dancing in a circle of trampled grass. There was an off-Island magician, a blind one-legged ex-sailor with a talking parrot, an acrobat. There were people of all conditions, from the beaver-hatted whale-oil merchants and shipowners and their bonneted women and proud-faced children to the paupers who, by custom, gathered the wisps of shearings that the breeze lofted to the bayberry bushes and wild roses. As I passed through the crowd, greeting acquaintances, I felt admiring eyes on me as if the whole Island could at last see me for what I had striven so hard to become: a promising young whaleman to whom the owners if not the gods had taken a fancy.

I took a turn beside my father in the shearing pens.
"Will you win the iron throw?" he asked me.
"Will you win the shearing?"
"Let's show 'em what two Polpis men can do!"

I sat with my mother and Susan. Then in her middle twenties, my sister had remained the gentle soul she had always been, the collector of shells and stones, with the mind and feelings of a child of ten.

My mother said, "You'll want to be with your friends." And she glanced over at the Riddell family encampment on a rise near a stand of wind-twisted pines.

"We're his friends," said Susan. "Aren't we, George?"

"You surely are," I said, "and what's more you're dancing with me."

Delighted, she sprang to her feet, and we joined the circle of couples dancing to the fiddle. In those years Quakers did not dance, nor did those who sought to emulate the Quakers. In giving pleasure to my sister I had the further satisfaction of observing glances which seemed to say, "Young Pollard is making a name for himself but he hasn't forgotten who he is."

Among the onlookers was Nancy Coffin. Susan saw her too.

"Look out for her," she said in my ear.

"Why?"

"Mother says she's taken too much medicine again."

"Dr. Damon's Elixir?"

"Do you think it does everything it says on the bottle?"

"More," I told her.

. . .

After the dance I escorted Susan back to Tamar and started
through the crowd to join the Riddells. Nancy intercepted me.
She was puffy-faced and unsteady.

"You're very good to poor Susan," she said.

"I like dancing."

"So do I." When I did not reply she added, "What a shame
we can't have a dance together."

"We can," I told her.

She shook her head. "Not on this talkative island."

She was looking at me with a strange smile. I said, "Who
would talk about us?"

"Who indeed?" she said, adding quickly, "You must visit
us now that you're back. The boys and Ann are very fond
of you."

"I will."

"Now go to your Mary. She's looking for you."

I left her and made my way to the Riddells.

That afternoon my father won the shearing contest. Mary and
I had watched him, cheering him on. By custom the victor was
seized hand and foot and tossed into the pond, and he submitted
to this treatment with good grace. He emerged from the water
stripping off his shirt and swinging it in a circle, scattering his
assailants, laughing and having a high time of it. He was in his
element, and I was as proud of him as I had always been as a
child on Sheepshearing Day. Just then, close behind us, I heard
an aloof male voice say, "Come, Martha, we've seen enough of
Polpis at play." I swung around, instantly possessed by fury, to
confront Caleb Mitchell. He was with a pale, frightened-look-
ing girl, but I had no doubt that the remark was intended for
my ears and Mary's.

Mary said, "Caleb, don't be any more foolish than you have to be."

"I meant no offense," he said in a thoroughly offensive manner. I squared off, prepared to strike him. Mary restrained my arm.

"George Pollard, don't you be silly either."

Enraged, I was conscious that people were forming a circle around us—when I saw that Owen Coffin was approaching, leading his young sister by the hand. Owen was sixteen then, tall and strong for his age, with a lean angular face; Ann was nine, a shy, serious creature with wide, wondering eyes and no trace of her mother's coquetry. On both young faces was such dismay at finding their kinsman prepared to do battle that my anger quickly cooled.

"Accept his apology," said Mary.

I said menacingly to Mitchell, "I'm very glad that you meant no offense."

With that his frightened friend hurried him out of danger and Mary said, "George Pollard, you must watch that temper of yours. You've no reason to be so angry."

Then Owen Coffin said, "Cousin, they're clearing the field for the iron throw."

And Ann said, "I know you'll win, because last night I said a very special prayer that you would."

I did win, my harpoon striking the farthest target dead center. Owen Chase was second. My shipmates from the *Eliza Slade,* Jason Starbuck and Charlie Gardner, took fourth and fifth respectively, while James Hussey was sixth in a field of twenty. Little Ann rushed up to me and kissed me on the cheek. I said, "Annie, that was a very fine prayer and I thank you for it."

"You're most welcome," she said. "But you'd have won anyway."

"Not a chance. You brought me luck."
"God brought you luck. I just reminded Him."

Two gentlemen approached me: Gideon Folger, the principal
owner of the *Essex,* and Zenas Coffin, patriarch of the Coffin
tribe.

Folger said, "Pollard, you and Chase have done me and the
Essex proud."

I thanked him, and Zenas said, "What's wrong with Coffin
ships, young man?"

"Nothing in the world," I told him.

"Keep it in mind."

Folger protested, "Now look here, Zenas. Don't try to recruit
my best men right under my nose. George Pollard sails under
our flag."

Zenas frowned. "Gideon, from what I hear you'd just better
make it worth his while." And to me that flinty old man repeated, "Keep it in mind."

9

1819. I was twenty-seven, Mary twenty-three, by Nantucket
standards an old maid. I would like to believe that she had
refused all other proposals only because she was waiting for
mine, but that was probably not the way it was. Rather I think
that more than the security and joys of marriage she valued her
independence and was in no hurry to lose it. As for me, I had
held off proposing until I felt confident that I was on my way

to a successful career in the fishery. The fact that that—most illusory!—moment coincided with Mary's readiness to surrender her spinster's freedom in favor of marriage was my good fortune. Or so I interpret the matter. It is not impossible that she was waiting for me.

In any event, though I had only a little capital, I had excellent prospects of supporting a family in some comfort. Upon the retirement of Captain Russell, Gideon Folger had offered me the captaincy of the *Essex*. The former farmboy from Polpis, not yet twenty-eight, was to be the youngest whaleship master in Nantucket. The Island was prospering and I was prospering with it. I felt then that I had gained everything a man my age could reasonably want—including, most precious of all, a good name.

At a prearranged hour on a squally April afternoon, I came calling on Mary at the Pleasant Street house. Entering, I heard female giggling upstairs. Mary met me in the hallway, greeting me with more ceremony than usual. We went into the west parlor. She sat on a small settee, I perched on a wing chair nearby. On the mantel, oil lamps were burning to brighten the dark afternoon. On the walls the portraits of Mary's Riddell and Starbuck ancestors gazed down sternly at the stranger in their midst, waiting, it seemed, for him to speak. Suddenly I found that my confidence had fled and with it all memory of the words I had carefully rehearsed.

"Mary," I said at last.

"Yes, George?"

Rain beat against the windowpanes.

"I cannot offer you very much. Not at first."

With a slight smile she said, "Why should you offer me anything at all?"

I took a breath. "Because I want you to marry me." And

when she didn't answer at once I added impatiently, "Well, will you?"

"Yes, George," she said softly, but my head was pounding so that her reply did not reach my brain. I recalled my prepared speech.

"Of course, you know that my profession is a hazardous one and that I'll be absent at sea for long periods of time."

"I do know about your profession, Captain Pollard. I said yes, I will marry you."

Understanding at last, I said brusquely, to cover my confusion, "Well, then, it's agreed?"

"George Pollard," she replied with severity, "you're not bargaining for a load of potatoes. You're taking a wife. You have proposed to me and I have accepted. Isn't there something you're forgetting?"

Only then did I go to her, draw her to me, and kiss her.

She studied me in silence, then said sharply, "Of course, you must ask Father's permission."

"Of course."

"Oh, he'll give it, if I have anything to say about it. Besides, he thinks you're a man of promise. He said so."

"He's right," I said happily. "It's all I have in the world."

She frowned. "It's nothing to joke about. You have a fine future, and I'm not going to let you forget it. So you can just forget your Polpisy fears about being Polpisy."

"I am thinking only of successful voyages, ships of my own, a fine house on Main Street full of children and grandchildren."

She tried not to smile. "If that's what you want."

"I want nothing more than that. But it will take years."

"We have years."

"You could have a fine house now if you married Caleb Mitchell."

She shook her head in exasperation. "George Pollard, must you begin our life together by showing how little you know about women? If I wanted to marry a house I would marry a house. I am marrying you, and if you know what's good for you you'll not make me sorry I did."

And marry we did, that June, at the Congregational Church on Academy Hill the Sunday after Sheepshearing Day.

That summer of 1819, so propitious for me, was a tragic time for Nancy Coffin. The day after our wedding, the whaleship *Martha,* Captain Amos Parnell, returned with the news that Hezekiah was dead. While leading a boat party ashore on the coast of Timor to collect water and wood, he was set upon by natives and clubbed to death. Two seamen met the same fate. Three more escaped in the boat, the survivors reporting that they owed their lives to Hezekiah, who took the brunt of the attack and fought back furiously, while shouting to his men to flee while they could. He was to the end a good and brave man, dying before his time.

So Nancy was left alone with Owen and Ann. Edward was by then at sea, sailing on board the merchant brig *Tom o' Shanter* between New York and Barbados. Owen Coffin, then seventeen, consoled his mother as well as he could, but though he was gentle and mild-mannered, his will was strong, and, just as I had at his age, he had made up his mind to ship on a whaler himself. I think his determination was only strengthened by the loss of his father. He must have felt that fate was testing his resolve and that he must stand firm in the face of his mother's appeals.

"I need you here, Owen," Nancy told him one evening when Mary and I were at supper at her house. "I can't manage alone."

In the weeks since she had received the news of her husband's violent death my aunt had visibly aged. Grief had lodged in her face and her hair was streaked with gray. Owen lowered his eyes a moment, then met hers and said, "My father would want me to go."

He looked at me in appeal.

I said to Nancy gently, "You once said you wouldn't stand in his way."

In a dead voice she answered, "I remember."

Mary then said, "Maybe you could wait a little, Owen. Just a while. You're still very young."

"Not so young as Cousin George was," said Owen, then he turned to me and in a firm, manly voice said, "I want to sail with him on the *Essex.*"

Nancy looked from him to me, her eyes filled with dread, and to herself she uttered words that I shall never forget.

"And if Tamar is right about you?"

I was soon fully occupied with preparations for my first voyage as master, consultations with Gideon Folger, and before I knew it farewells to my family and bride.

On the 12th of August, 1819, a warm, sultry day, as the South Tower bell was striking twelve, I stood proud and tall on the quarterdeck of the *Essex* with my first mate Chase and, favored by a light southeasterly breeze, gave the order to weigh anchor.

Part Two

THE CRUISE

1

As Great Point lighthouse vanished into the summer haze astern I set our course for the Western Islands. I remember Thomas Nickerson, a dreamy giant of a boy, standing at the windward rail gazing aft for a last glimpse of home—and Chase coming up from behind and clapping his hands over the lad's ears, as if to expel from his head any wistful thoughts and remind him of his new situation. I saw Owen Coffin in the maintop, his first time aloft, working under the boatswain's eye with a fierce eagerness to learn that put me in mind of myself on my own first voyage. That afternoon I had Chase give the order to sweep down ship, then for all hands to assemble amidship to hear my address to them.

With Chase at my left, second mate Matthew Joy and third mate Thomas Chappel, an Englishman, at my right, I watched the men gather. For the first time I had an opportunity to look over my full crew, who until then—except for Chase, Joy, and Chappel, with whom I had sailed, and my young cousin—had been merely names on the shipping papers.

I was not pleased with what I saw. As was so often the case, there was a dangerously high proportion of apprentices. Almost a third of the crew were blacks, a fact which promised trouble, not so much from them in particular as from the enforced mingling in close quarters for months on end of young men of different races who were not used to associating with each other ashore. Nor did I like the frozen looks of some of

the more experienced hands, whose appearance of abject obedience struck me as counterfeit. Owen Coffin, however, was
looking at me with intent concentration, as were the other
novices. Then, just as I was about to speak, I saw Isaac Cole,
an able seaman, grinning past my shoulder, and I turned in
time to see Thomas Chappel winking at him. I experienced a
sudden wave of fury at what I took to be defiance of my authority—with Chase looking on!—but I mastered my feelings
so as not to begin the cruise with a dressing-down of one of
my officers. I ordered Chase to read out the watch lists and
the complements of the three boats. Then I addressed my
crew, telling them that whatever the reasons they signed on,
we were now together on a whaling voyage to the Pacific, and
that our lives as well as the success of the cruise depended on
one another, each doing his best, that there was no room on
board for shirkers or cowards, that the green hands were expected to learn quickly from the experienced ones and the
officers, that there would be frequent boat drills, and that by
the time we cleared the Western Islands I didn't want to see
a single lubber on board.

I don't remember what else I told them, but I do recall—and
shall forever—Owen Coffin's trusting eyes on me then. I had
already decided not to show him any favors, out of fairness and
also so as not to turn his shipmates against him. I did, however,
instruct Chase to assign him to my own boat so that I could
oversee his training and keep an eye on him.

My object was to be personally responsible for his safety.

It was not long before the *Essex* and her crew were to be
subjected to a sudden and violent trial.

The first day out was clear with blue skies, fresh wind from
the southwest, blue sea, mild swells. We conducted boat drills
in the morning. All that afternoon a school of bright-hued

dolphins played alongside as if to welcome us to the open sea. On August 14 the waves increased, the wind became gusty, the sky overcast. I gave the order to shorten the sail. On the morning of the 15th the sky was an eerie ocher color. By noon, approaching from the southwest, a black squall loomed over us, spitting lightning to the oily slate sea. I was on the afterdeck with Chase. Before we knew it, strong gusts were battering our quarter and then blackness, thunder, and lightning were all around us.

"We'll run before it!" I shouted to Chase, then yelled to the helmsman, "Put her down!"

It was too late. As the helmsman spun the wheel a gust of hurricane force hit the weather quarter, lifting the stern of the vessel and easing her over on her beam ends until the yardarms touched the lashing waves.

From below, over the howl of the wind and the crack and rumble of thunder, we heard terrified shouts. A blaze of lightning revealed the forward watch in the scuppers, clinging desperately to the rail. Then we saw that the helmsman too had lost his footing and was at the taffrail holding on for his life. Both Chase and I managed to seize the wheel and were struggling to bring the vessel up into the wind, but we had lost all way and were at the mercy of the elements.

Then, as suddenly as it had arisen, the squall passed to the northwest and the wind itself, working against the careened ship, brought her up into it, and the *Essex* slowly righted until she rode on an even keel, saved by the same force that had nearly sent her to the bottom.

I immediately ordered all hands on deck to determine if any were lost or injured. Though badly shaken, all were accounted for and none had sustained serious injury. I and my officers then inspected the ship for damage, finding none that would impair her seaworthiness, though the cookhouse had been swept overboard and, far more serious, the two port whaleboats had been smashed beyond repair, leaving us with only the two starboard ones.

Ordering the ship set on her former course, I then met with Chase, Joy, and Chappel in the cabin. I was dismayed by the loss of the boats, and my first thought was to return to the Island to replace them. Chase disagreed.

"With the wind shifting to the northeast we'd be a week beating back, and we'd be sure to lose hands in Nantucket."

"Are they so gallied as that?"

"Almost capsizing hasn't lifted their spirits any, but it's more than that. Some of them signed on more to impress their friends and sweethearts than anything else. Now they're homesick and plain scared. My guess is that as soon as we made Nantucket we'd have seen the last of quite a few."

"Do you agree with the mate, Mr. Joy?"

"Yes, sir, I do."

"Mr. Chappel?"

"Yes, sir. Word's going around the fo'c'sle that the *Essex* is an unlucky ship."

"Who started that damned lie?" I demanded. "This vessel has an excellent record of safe voyages."

Silence. Under the harsh light of the gimbaled lamp I stared at the Englishman until he replied.

"Mamula."

"Get him."

John Mamula was our steward. A native of the island of Haiti, nineteen years of age, he was already a very unstable young man, I am sure, at the time he signed on the *Essex*. His sullen, brooding disposition had undoubtedly been exacerbated by his physical ugliness: his eyes protruded, his ears extended, his woolly hair was an unpleasant dark-rusty shade, and his shiny anthracite skin was cratered with pox. Keeping always to himself, he was given to muttering with the pagan gods in his head. Until the squall struck us, the raffish element of the crew, egged on by Chappel, had treated him as a humorous curiosity, the butt of their cruel wit and mean pranks. When cornered by tormentors he would alternately cringe and then lunge like an animal at bay, repeating over and over the words "Tee Dombella too puissant," apparently as a charm to protect his spirit.

Up to then he had served me and my officers well enough, and I had had no cause to complain of him. Indeed, looking back, I suppose that we were not displeased to have such a comically freakish fellow on board as a sop to the aggressive instincts of the crew and an entertainment for ourselves. Undoubtedly, by not prohibiting the baiting of him, under the pretext that a Negro boy so ugly and outlandish could not possess ordinary feelings, I had been an accomplice to the persecution he suffered on board the *Essex*. I must have felt some guilt on that account, but the truth is that I don't remember feeling any—only the anger that seized me when I understood that the miscreant was at work disaffecting my crew.

Chappel brought him down the companionway and stood him at the table facing me. He was trembling, his eyes bulging, his lips forming the pagan incantation.

"Mamula, is this an unlucky ship?" I demanded.

At first he could not reply, then in a convulsive croak he said, "De light!"

"What light are you jabbering about?"

He pointed upward.

"Very bad," he said. "De light in de rigging."

Then Matt Joy said, "St. Elmo's fire. I saw it too, during the squall. Hazy blue light at the ends of the yards and masts."

Chase said, "It's nothing to worry about. St. Elmo's fire is a good sign. Means the storm's passing."

"No!" shouted the steward, looking directly at me. "Not good for this ship!"

Even today I cannot account for what overcame me then. No doubt the near-loss of the vessel had strained my nerves. I remember the moment vividly. With the roll and pitch the overhead light slowly roamed our tense faces. I felt certain at that moment that the black possessed a power against which we were helpless. I lunged across the table for him. Chase and Chappel restrained me. Joy hustled the steward up the companionway. Then there was silence in the cabin but for the slow working of the ship's timbers. Chase, the man of reason, was studying me as if trying to solve a riddle.

Chappel, appraising me warily, said, "Bloody nonsense."

Matthew Joy returned. He was ill at the time, more than we knew, and he had more reason than anyone aboard to return to home port; yet he said, "I don't think we have an unlucky ship. I agree with the mate that we would lose men if we returned. I believe we should thank God for saving us all from death—and continue the voyage."

I looked to Chappel and Chase. Both nodded.

"We continue the voyage," I said, as if nothing had happened.

We enjoyed fair weather and favorable winds for the rest of the leg to the Azores. The spirits of the crew revived, the carpenter built a new cookhouse out of the wreckage of the whaleboats, our hour of peril was all but forgotten. Chase and Chappel now gave me a somewhat wider berth. Only Matthew Joy was forthcoming with me. The crew must have sensed that something was awry between me and Chase and Chappel. On a ship like the *Essex,* with only inches separating the officers' cabin and minuscule staterooms from the boatsteerers' and boatswains' quarters in the steerage, such things are impossible to keep secret. I longed for a sighting of whales, but as we sailed under clear skies with fair winds, the masthead watch was silent. I offered a prize of two pounds of tobacco to the first man to see a spout.

On the morning of the 30th we raised the pale-blue island of Flores in the western Azores, and that afternoon stood in to the roadstead at Santa Cruz for the purpose of taking on fresh water and provisions. We lowered out two boats, mine and Chase's, and no sooner had we cast off than Chase's harpooner, Ben Lawrence, called out, "Shall we show 'em our wake, Mr. Chase?" Chase threw me a challenging grin, and I yelled to him, "Go ahead and try it, Mr. Chase." Then as one we gave the order to pull, and our boats were soon flying through the waves toward the white beach under the now azure-green mountain.

On our two other cruises on the *Essex,* Chase and I had often raced our boats, but never had we competed with such determination, as if I was defending my worthiness to command and Chase was challenging it; and I think that our respective boat crews understood what was at issue and responded with all their forces.

In my boat Owen Coffin pulled the stroke, or aftmost, oar; Sam Reed, a black, behind him, the tub oar; Charles Ramsdell the midship oar; Seth Weeks, an able seaman, the bow oar; while my Portuguese harpooner Brazilla Ray pulled the forward-most harpoon oar, when not occupied in the more urgent business of striking a whale.

"Spring, boys! Spring!" I shouted as I steered us toward shore. "Let's put 'em astern of us. Spring, now!"

To my satisfaction I saw that with each stroke we were gaining on Chase's boat, so that by the time we were in the breakers we were two lengths ahead. Suddenly I heard Chase shout and at the same time saw a large rock jutting out of the water dead ahead of me. I swung the steering oar to clear it, but in so doing lost my footing and tumbled headlong into the surf. I came up spouting salt water in time to see my boat broached to and Chase's running on the beach, its crew raising a great cheer and then laughing heartily at the sight of their captain emerging drenched from the waves. I put a good face on the mishap, pretending to laugh it away, while inwardly I was hot with anger, all the more because my ungraceful dunking could be no one's fault but my own. I was, it will be recalled, not yet thirty.

In the village of Santa Cruz we bought vegetables and a few pigs. Then, on the 1st of September, we cleared the island of Flores and set a course south by southeast for the Isle of May in the Cape Verdes for more pigs.

In that sixteen-day passage we raised no whales, but as we coasted the south shore of the Isle of May we came upon an even more welcome sight. Heeled over on the beach was a whaleship, her standing rigging still intact. Chase was with me on deck. I handed him my glass.

"Where there's a whaler there must be whaleboats, Mr. Chase," I said.

And so it proved.

The beached wreck was the *Archimedes,* out of New York. In a storm she had struck rocks, and the captain had managed to save the lives of all hands by running her on the beach. The captain and his crew had returned to New York leaving the wreck in the custody of Portuguese chandlers in the town of Englishport. Uncertain of their responsibilities, they agreed at last to sell us two of the four whaleboats salvaged from the ship, one of the two being in poor condition but serviceable as a spare. When the boats were aboard I said to Chase, "*Now,* by God, let anyone say that the *Essex* is an unlucky vessel!"

The acquisition of the whaleboats raised my spirits. Like the bright-hued dolphins, it seemed a good omen. For the first time on the voyage I felt entirely master of myself and of the *Essex*. Everyone aboard noticed the change in me; and as we set sail from Englishport bound for Cape Horn, we were united in high hopes.

On the second day, on the blue-gray horizon under a mackerel sky, the masthead watch raised a shoal of whales. It was Owen Coffin, who had never seen a spout before, who won the prize of tobacco. We altered our course, and a half-mile from them lowered our three boats. Soon mine, Chase's, and Joy's were among the whales, and we each struck one. My whale and Chase's made off to the south at a furious rate abreast of each other. As we hammered over the water I called out to Chase, "We'll show you our wake, mate!" Chase called back, "Just try it, Captain!" And this exchange assured the green hands that if they were about to die it would be in the company of lunatics immune to fear. All during our Nantucket sleighride I kept an eye on my cousin and saw that though he was normally apprehensive his bearing was manly and brave. Even as I was half-blinded by spray, I saw him looking at me with a confidence that drew upon mine.

Throughout the leg we took whales. By day, steam and smoke from the try-pots enveloped us as we cut blubber from the swinging stage, grappled casks, and worked the heavy tackle. By night, the fires shone on our oily bodies and cast our shadows on the slimy deck. The appalling smell was everywhere— sweeter to me than the scents of our Island moors. This was my element. There was an awful beauty about it.

As we neared Cape Horn, the weather grew worse and there was no more whaling. We shortened sail, and I ordered the ship cleaned down until there was not a drop of oil to be seen anywhere—and 350 barrels in the hold. The crew were exhausted. Where before, idleness and the specter of a profitless voyage had dampened their spirits, now the constant labor, lack of sleep, and exposure to danger had disheartened them more than I realized. As I grew more confident, thriving on the work and its perils, I was unaware of the trouble that was brewing in the fo'c'sle.

The problem was pigs.

In our preoccupation with securing the whaleboat on the Isle of May, we had overlooked the original object of our going there. We had taken on board a few more pigs, but hardly enough to supply fresh meat for the long voyage south, much less the treacherous passage around Cape Horn and north to the coast of Chile; so now the crew were receiving increasingly smaller portions of our dwindling supply of salt beef and salt pork.

One gray, squally day in late October, with high seas and westerly gusts wearing the vessel and our nerves, Mr. Chappel, who had taken Joy's deck watch, summoned me from my stateroom. Without a word he led me just forward of the companionway, where I saw a bucket of pudding and potatoes laced with stringy scraps of meat. The midday rations for the fo'c'sle —refused.

I became enraged. That they should dare defy me! Would any crew have so provoked Clasby? Zenas Coffin? Russell? Never! Who did they take me for? Was it my youth that let them think they could get away with it? I glared at Chappel. His clowning with the crew had surely weakened the authority of the quarterdeck. And how could he have failed to see who had brought the rations aft? The limejuicer, I decided, must be part of the conspiracy.

"Who put that there, Mr. Chappel?"

"I don't know, Captain. I was at the taffrail. I didn't see."

"You must have seen."

"I didn't. Whoever done it must have kept the binnacle 'tween me and him."

I turned to the helmsman. Seth Weeks. His meek, feral face was white as a sheet.

"Weeks, who put that bucket there?"

"Didn't see neither, sir. I was watching the sails not to let her fall off. When I looked down again, there it was."

Lying, I decided. "Mr. Chase!" I shouted down the companionway. "Come on deck."

I told the mate to call all hands amidship. As they assembled on either side of the tryworks I watched them narrowly, searching their faces for signs of guilt. The blacks gathered in a knot on the port side, most of the others starboard, Owen Coffin and Charles Ramsdell foremost among them. As I studied that pair, it struck me that, from his look, Owen was no longer the compliant young man who had wished for nothing so much as to sail with me, but had grown withdrawn and contrary—and that the cause of the change was his ill-chosen companion.

When it was still I said quietly, "Who put those rations aft?"

No one answered. I fixed my gaze on my cousin's friend. "Ramsdell?"

"Wasn't me, sir."

"Who was it, then?"

He pressed his lips together.

I looked from one blank, apprehensive face to another, deliberating my next move.

Then Owen Coffin said, "May I speak, sir?"

I looked at him in surprise. If I had seen defiance in his face before, it was gone now. "You may," I told him.

"No harm was meant, sir. But it's not easy to do the ship's work on such rations."

Murmurs of assent echoed his words.

It was a delicate moment for young Captain Pollard as he

stood facing his first disciplinary crisis. Here was the crew siding
with his young cousin, whose earnest manner seemed to exclude
the possibility of sedition. Here was the bucket of slop. Undenia-
bly, I as captain was ultimately responsible for the lack of proper
rations, and there was, moreover, nothing to be done about it
until the ship reached the Pacific ports. That was the state of
affairs. Another man might have answered Owen Coffin's complaint with a reasonable explanation and assurances that better
fare would be provided as soon as possible. Not young Pollard.
Observe that at the time he was still finding his way as a whaling
master and there is nothing that exasperates an emerging authority so much as to be cornered into adopting a sensible course
of action. Glaring at Ramsdell, convinced that he had turned my
cousin against me, half out of my head, I resolved to show the
crew once and for all that their puny demonstration would not
be dignified by a reasonable response. I threw down my hat,
ripped off my jacket and stamped on them. Then I shouted,
"You throw your rations in my face, do you? Haven't I given you
all the ship can afford? Haven't I treated you like men? Do you
want me to coax you to eat, chew your food for you? By God, I'll
take the luff out of you!"

To my great satisfaction the crew now appeared very
alarmed, my officers amazed. It was all I could do not to laugh
at them. They actually appeared to believe that they were in the
presence of a raving maniac. Mollified, I said in a milder tone,
"If I hear any more about provisions I'll tie you up together and
whip the devil out of you."

Then I nodded to the mate to dismiss them, thinking, "Now,
Chase, which neat compartment in that orderly mind of yours
will you put me in?"

On the 18th of December we reached the latitude of the Cape
and beat west—as the winds rose and shifted to that quarter.

We had expected a fairly easy passage, since mid-December was considered to be the most favorable time of year, but it was not to be. The wind reached gale force, and under shortened sails we climbed and plunged through the appalling seas. The helmsmen struggled every instant of every watch to hold the vessel's bow on one tack after the other against the green mountains rising toward us, and sometimes, in the worst of it, we hove to, losing distance, time, patience, everything but the determination to prevail.

For five weeks.

On the 10th of January, 1820, we altered our course to north by northwest and entered the Pacific.

2

I remember our first clear dawn in the South Pacific, the sun that we had not seen in more than a month breaking out of the blue ice-crowned peaks of the Grafton Islands off our starboard beam, steaming the drenched decks and canvas, warming our bones and spirits; wind steady from the west, horizon razor-sharp, the vessel creaking languidly as she leaned into the swells, masthead watch set; Sunday.

Forward the crew were hanging out clothes and bedding to dry. Now, with the prospect of reprovisioning soon, I had ordered extra rations for the morning meal. We officers had breakfasted, the boatsteerers were at our places in the cabin, Chase and I were at the taffrail taking separate sightings of the sun, Owen Coffin was at the wheel, Chappel at the masthead, when Matt Joy approached me with something on his mind.

"Sir?"

"Mr. Joy?"

He studied me a moment as if already doubting the success of his petition, then said, "Captain, there's some forward saying it wouldn't hurt if you were to assemble the ship's company and say a few words to thank the Lord for seeing us 'round the Horn safely."

At once I was on my guard. Though I sensed that Joy had not a conniving bone in his body, his request did not set well with me. I felt that Chappel, aloft, somehow knew what was going on, might even have put Joy up to it, and was even then looking down in amusement. Owen Coffin, seeming to share Joy's sentiment, awaited my response. Chase, who knew me as the Doubting Thomas of Reverend Matthews's class, said, "That's if you felt the same way about it, sir."

I thought: You know damned well I don't feel the same way about it, and I said to Joy, "Let every man offer his silent thanks and his prayers in his own way."

"Not the same, sir," he persisted.

The picture in Joy's honest mind was of me standing reverently on the quarterdeck, head bared and bowed, leading the ship's company in thanksgiving to the Almighty, uniting the men of the *Essex* in communion with Him. No more than that. As captain I was mariner, navigator, whale hunter, surgeon, judge, the absolute temporal power on board; why should I not also be pastor? In my cabin were a prayerbook and a Bible belonging to the ship. I had only to send below for them, have Chase assemble the crew, and the thing could be done in a minute. So why was I unwilling? Though few whaleship masters observed the Sabbath, it was not unheard of. A common feeling was that no great harm could come of it. Someone else in my circumstances would have shrugged, mumbled a few pious-sounding words to comfort his flock, and called it a day, but not young Pollard.

No, I decided, I would be damned if I would stand up before my officers and crew as a hypocrite. I would not hang my head to the Lord without faith in Him.

Still, as a practical matter, out of concern for the crew's tranquillity, I did not dismiss Joy's request out of hand and was seeking an alternative way of complying with it, when John Mamula came on deck, heaved a bucket of slops to the lee, and with a fierce glance at me went down again to the cabin.

As he disappeared below I hit upon a solution to the dilemma posed by Joy. Not wishing to empower any officer to intercede with the Deity in my place (such confidence was not yet mine), I decided to delegate Owen Coffin. I called over to him, "Coffin, will you give us a prayer and a verse or two?" And, pleased, he said, "Yes, sir, I will gladly."

So I had Chase assemble the crew, except the masthead watch (I was not about to lose whales on any account), I called down to Mamula to fetch up the prayerbook and Bible, and, ordering that Coffin be relieved at the wheel, I directed that the steward, when he appeared on deck, give the holy books to him. To my annoyance he persisted in holding them out to me. Three times I had to order him to give them to Coffin before he complied. At that moment an unsettling incident occurred. I was suddenly aware of a whirring at my right shoulder and felt the rapid flutter of wings against my neck. I was terrified. I dodged away and struck out with my hand, knocking a black-and-yellow finch to the deck, where it lay gasping, its legs crumpled under it. To most of the crew and to Chappel, the scene was comical. That their captain, fearless in engagements with fifty-ton cachalots, should be frightened by a little land bird no bigger than a canary was hilarious. John Mamula, however, saw the thing differently. He looked from the wounded bird to me with an expression of dread, and I sensed that in his primitive imagination the alighting of the creature on my shoulder must be an omen, and not a favorable one. I then realized that many of the crew were reading the steward's response the same way and were no longer amused but, as the bird struggled for life, apprehensive. At that moment I determined that Mamula would be put ashore at the first opportunity. I then nodded to my cousin that he might speak for the ship's company before the Throne.

The boy bowed his head and said in a strong, clear voice, "Lord, we give thanks for our safe passage 'round the Horn and we humbly pray that you will continue to watch over this vessel. Amen."

The crew responded with a ragged "Amen" and Coffin then read the Twenty-third Psalm and led us in reciting the Lord's Prayer.

"Our Father Who art in Heaven . . ."

By then it was plain to all of us on the quarterdeck that the steward was behaving more and more strangely. As we prayed, Mamula muttered his heathen chant, under his breath at first, then louder and louder, his enormous eyes rolling wildly, until the entire crew saw that the misshapen pagan, from the deeps of his dark nature, was countering our sorcery with his. His conduct, which I took for criminal insubordination, disturbed me, but I was hardly prepared for what was to come. At the close of the prayer I dismissed the crew, but they, fascinated by the steward, showed no inclination to disperse. Owen Coffin, who almost alone had always shown kindness to Mamula, came up to him and put his hand to his shoulder, intending to guide him away from trouble. Violently the Haitian drew away from him, as if the touch had burned him, and, glaring at Coffin with the most demonic look I have ever seen on a human face, said, "You will die."

That was too much for me. I shouted, "Steward, hold your tongue and get below!"

Instead, Mamula, whose whole body was now convulsed with jerks and twitches, turned his hellish gaze on me and said, "You—Jonah man!"

I lunged for him and seized him by the throat, falling with him to the deck. I was vaguely aware of Chase, Joy, and Coffin all trying to pull me off, Coffin pleading, "Captain, stop!" I was aware of my victim's eyes starting from his head and of the convulsions of his body; and I remember feeling that I was as helpless as my victim.

Suddenly the muscles in his neck went limp and I eased him to the deck. As Chase and Joy pulled me away from him, Mamula lay twitching feebly, his skin the color of blue steel, as if he was in the throes of death.

I felt my officers and crew looking at me in awe.

Soon, to my relief, the steward showed signs of recovering. The twitching abated, he opened his eyes and gazed up at me, no longer with ferocity but fearfully and, as it soon appeared, with no recollection of anything that had happened since he had come on deck with the prayerbook and Bible. When he could speak he said to me, "Please, Captain, put Mamula ashore."

I replied, "We will oblige you, steward." And to the amazed crew I said, "Lay forward—the holy offices are over."

Little by little as they dispersed, the men appeared to find humor in my remark and began to side with me against my recent victim. There seemed to be no more question in their minds as to whose magic was stronger, or any more illusion that we were embarked on a reasonable enterprise.

By then the little bird was dead. Joy threw it overboard.

A few winters ago the late Dr. Frederick Gorham, then an octogenarian physician of this Island who in his declining years had befriended me, was visiting downstairs. I had given him an account of that half-forgotten Sunday in the South Pacific, as truthfully as I could remember it, not glossing over my own conduct, and he said in response that from my description of the steward's behavior he had little doubt but that the man was an epileptic. Indeed, he thought it very likely that Mamula was suffering a seizure at the very moment I was strangling him. He further told me that according to some medical authorities, at the onset of such an attack the subject is visited by a sensation that curtains of the mind are suddenly drawn open upon what is ordinarily concealed. That, he said, would set in an interesting light his prediction that Owen Coffin would die, as well as his desperate desire to quit the *Essex*.

As for my conduct toward Mamula, the doctor could offer no explanation. Or perhaps chose to offer none.

3

Our first Pacific port of call was St. Mary's Island, a rendez-vous of whalers ten miles off the coast of Chile. On the 17th of January, 1820, a clear, blustery morning, we dropped anchor in the roads, astern of the *Lydia* of New Bedford. Within an hour we officers and the starboard watch were aboard that vessel for a gam. We learned from Captain Stevens that she was home-ward bound with seventeen hundred barrels, and none too soon, he told us, since the entire Chilean coast was a war zone, with the naval forces of Bernardo O'Higgins's new independent government sweeping the seas of Spanish shipping and bom-barding royalist strongholds. The civil war had spawned priva-teering on both sides, and no unarmed vessel under any flag was safe in the area. It was evident that Stevens, a bluff bulldog of a man in his early fifties, was impatient for his boat crew to return to the ship with casks of water so that he could weigh anchor for the Horn and home. We spoke of the subject always first in the thoughts of whalemen: where the whales were. He said that some were being taken in the cruising grounds off northern Chile and that the previous year, later in the season, many more were taken in the Peruvian grounds. Touching again on the political turmoil in Chile, he said, "Above all, steer clear of Valparaiso. 'Fact, I'd steer clear of all the mainland ports north to Peru."

"We're shy on fresh provisions," I told him.

"Masfuera, then."

"The Juan Fernándezes are safe?"

"Hell of a lot safer'n Valparaiso, by my reckoning."

I resolved to take the captain's advice. Even more than privateers I had feared that in Valparaiso, dissipation, illness, and desertion would decimate my crew; and now I had another reason not to touch there. I would sail northwest and provision at the island of Masfuera.

Before leaving the *Lydia* I entrusted two letters to Captain Stevens: one to Gideon Folger, describing our situation and prospects, including a brief account of the defection of the steward and my decision to put him ashore at the first suitable port; the other to Mary.

My first letter to my bride said little about the voyage as we were experiencing it, still less about my own fragile state of mind at the time. What is clear now is that the writer's omissions concerning himself say more about the fledgling captain from Polpis than would have any "honest" attempt to see himself whole. Preserved by Mary all these years, the letter reads:

My very dear wife,

In a day's sail we shall put in at the island of Santa María, off the southern coast of Chile, for wood, water, and news from any whalers that we may meet there. Thus far, though we have not been spared the usual vicissitudes of our calling, the voyage has already yielded 350 bbls of oil, with the imminent promise of much more from the bounteous Pacific cruising grounds. We are for the most part strong in health and spirit and prepared for whatever lies ahead. Chase and I, after some initial adjustments owing to our different natures, now work together exceedingly well, as if each of us inspired the other to put his best foot forward at all times. An exception in point of health is my second, Matthew Joy, who is ailing I think more than he will admit, though from what disease I do not know; however, he is as strong in *spirit* as any man aboard, and I am confident that with the return of fair weather he will mend. Alas, my third mate, Thomas Chappel, exhibits the opposite symptoms. Though in rude good health his spirit is, if not corrupted, in constant peril of becoming so owing to the chronic impishness which inhabits it. "Life is a lark" is his motto, and his familiar ways with the crew have set a bad example.

When you next see Nancy, tell her that her Owen is well and is proving to be an exemplary apprentice. He learns quickly, is brave and willing, and despite his young age and slender physique shows every sign of becoming a fine whaleman like his father. That said, he also possesses a mind of his own, as would be expected of a son of Nancy and Hezekiah, and is not afraid to speak up for what he believes is right, though always within the bounds of what is permissible. He is a fine lad and I only wish that I had more like him on board.

I think of you often, dearest Mary, and look forward to the happy day when we will be reunited. On my return we shall look for a house of our own in town, and one with enough rooms for any little visitors who might join us. You will have your rose garden. There will be a brass knocker on the door, a weather-vane on the roof peak.

Convey my respects to your parents and tell your father that I appreciate his offer of financial assistance. After this voyage his help will probably not be needed, but I do appreciate his generous offer. I shall write again at the next opportunity. With affection and esteem, your husband

Geo. Pollard, Jr.

From St. Mary's Island we reached northwest to Masfuera in the Juan Fernández group, taking on yams, fish, and six pigs. From there we sailed north to the cruising grounds off northern Chile, where we took eight whales without suffering any mishap. The log of the *Essex* showed a series of pleasant days with light westerly trade winds, its pages ornamented by ink-stamped whales each signifying a cachalot saved. Through February and March our try-pots boiled and the decks were aslither with oil. By early April we had stowed away more than eight hundred barrels. Our spirits were high. We were confident. How Chappel laughed when Matt Joy, standing in the bow of his boat after planting a lance deep in a whale's life, was turned into a red Indian by the animal's bloody spouting! This was a sight too commonplace to be construed by anyone as a prophetic sign.

With the coming of a murderously hot summer, we cruised north to the Peruvian grounds, where between June and September we took sperm whales. Then on the 1st of October we steered for the small harbor of Tecamus for water and provisions. At daybreak on the 2nd an awesome view stirred our water-weary spirits. Ahead of us, higher than we could believe, the broken ridge of the Cordilleras eclipsed the sun. We stood in for the indigo shadow where the town was. When the sun cleared the ridge, blazing on the ice fields and rock cliffs in the sky, we sailed on the edge of the receding sha-dow, under that immense mass which rose ever higher, under the sun. All of the crew were on deck or aloft, frisky at the prospect of their first real liberty ashore. Now the town had appeared in the remnant of night beyond the water. The sunlight outdistanced us, and for a time the western slopes of the Cordilleras towered above us like an engulfing wave. Then, even as we watched, feeling the heat of the day settle on us, Tecamus appeared in the sun, and when we looked up again the sierra had vanished into haze.

To any but land-starved seamen the town would have ap-peared a miserable place. The beach was black sand and kelp-strewn rock, with a spindly wreck of a pier staggering into the waves; beached double-ended, lateen-rigged fishing boats that could have been Phoenician; nets spread to dry. Beyond the beach, there were one- and two-story stone dwellings and shops, flanking an arcaded plaza. Overlooking the town from a rock promontory at its southern extremity was an ocher church built in mission style, puny against the scale of the invisible mountains. Not a tree or a shrub anywhere. The light offshore breeze we were beating against carried the voices of women in the plaza and the crow of a rooster fooled by the false dawn.

It was at this place that I had decided to put the steward ashore, providing that he still wished to take his chances on finding an Atlantic-bound vessel that would sign him on. When we were at anchor I spoke to him in the cabin, warning him of reports of press gangs in the town and of the reputation of the local people for inhospitality to indigent strangers. Nothing would dissuade him.

"You still wish to leave this vessel?"

"Yes, sir."

"Even if you escape the press gangs you could be beached here for weeks or months."

"I know, sir."

"You've not a penny coming to you. You signed for the cruise."

"I know, sir."

Feeling compassion for the man then, I reached in my pocket and found five Spanish dollars, which I held out to him. When he didn't move I said, "Here, take them. You'll need them. What's the matter with you?"

"You owe Mamula nothing!" he told me, his eyes wide with fear.

"I'm giving them to you, you idiot!"

Stubbornly he refused the coins, as if to accept them would be to bring evil upon himself.

"Go to the Devil, then!" I said.

So that morning the Haitian went ashore with the provisioning parties, and I never saw him again, nor did I ever learn what befell him.

That afternoon I gave the crew their liberty in the town. Little Joe West and Doc Thomas got into a fight with some *paisanos* and were locked up in the calaboose until Chase secured their release with a small bribe. Chips got so drunk he was brought back to the ship unconscious. Chappel had managed to get into a scrape over an unmarried young woman. I considered myself lucky when by sunset the crew were on board again with no permanent damage to any.

. . .

Early the next morning we put Tecamus astern of us, sailing
west by northwest for the Galápagos; and by the time the sun
broke over the sierra we were out of sight of the last human
settlement that most on board would ever see.

$$4$$

As I read over this account of my experiences up to the morning we cleared Tecamus bound for the Galápagos, I see that,
as yet, no very clear portrait of that young captain has emerged.
The diarist seems incapable of capturing his youthful self in a
constant light. His feelings about him swing wildly, from indulgence to impatience, from protectiveness to an urge to display,
indeed to flaunt, his worst side. We see him on the quarterdeck,
dancing a jig on his clothes, acting the madman over a trifle.
We see him flying into a rage that nearly leads him to commit
murder, when a heathen black, possessed himself, calls him a
Jonah. Then there is the thorny matter of his reluctance to bow
his head or pray to an Almighty he fears may not exist. There,
of course, is the key: his pride, the source of all his shortcomings
—proneness to anger, sense of homelessness, overweening ambition, fear of love—all the flaws of that intricate young man
who survives in me, even as I have changed so much as to feel
toward him like a despairing father.

In all these years I have not revisited my memories of that leg
between the Peruvian coast and the bleak archipelago of dead
volcanoes five hundred miles to the west. With fair winds it
would have been a passage of four or five days; but we were not

to have fair winds, but for much of the time a torrid calm that would work insidiously on our spirits. It is said that cockroaches and spiders act strangely before an earthquake; though, if the insects' behavior gives advance warning of a cataclysm, it cannot be presumed that the creatures themselves know the significance of their squirming and scampering. No more did we.

Our objective in touching at the Galápagos was to take on board a quantity of the large land tortoises which abounded there in those years. These great stump-footed beasts, many of which attain a weight of a hundred pounds or more, a few as much as four hundred, were to provide us with a supply of fresh, delectable meat throughout the season of sperm-whale fishing on the equator to the west, between the Galápagos and the Sandwich Islands. I still could not put out of mind the incident of the crew's rejection of their rations, and was determined to see that they would have no further cause for complaint; and here was an opportunity—of which, be it said, American whalers in those years routinely availed themselves —to stock the ship with several tons of an epicurean delicacy at no cost to the owners.

The first day out, carrying full sail, we ran before a warm easterly breeze under a blue sky, while on the southwest horizon great anvils of white towered and to the north another line of clouds billowed higher throughout the afternoon. That evening electrical storms flashed and thundered on either beam like warring armies.

In my snug stateroom that night, I took the ship's Bible from the shelf over the headboard and, for perhaps the hundredth time in my life, read the story of the temptation of Abraham, and for the hundredth time was astonished by it. It is a simple story, a mysterious story, so simple and mysterious that it seems already inscribed deep in one's brain. The Lord asks Abraham to offer his only son Isaac, whom he loves, as a burnt offering. Without a moment's thought Abraham saddles his ass and takes his son to the mountain where God has directed that he sacrifice the boy. He lays firewood around a stone altar, binds his son to it, and raises a knife over his heart. At that moment an angel of the Lord tells him to spare Isaac: Abraham has proved his faith to the Lord's satisfaction. A ram is sacrificed in the boy's place. Abraham is blessed and so, through his seed, are all nations of the earth.

I remember thinking, that night in my cabin, what different men were Abraham and Jonah. Jonah had taken to the sea to try to evade God's service, to escape a task he didn't believe in, and when God sent the storm and the whale, Jonah gave himself up to the whale's jaws rather than doom the sailors. Abraham did not hesitate *one instant* to doom the son he loved. He is the consummate man of faith. Jonah is the man on the run. Before extinguishing my lamp, I remember thinking: Mamula was right after all—I *am* a Jonah man.

Upon awakening the next morning, I knew at once that we had lost our favorable wind. Instead of the crisp breeze and clear skies that would follow thunderstorms in the temperate zones, the equatorial disturbances had left us floating on an undulant green glass sea reaching into haze, with limp sails half filling fitfully only to collapse again, as little Billy Wright, the helmsman, wrestled the wheel to hold our heading.

I glanced aloft—to find the crow's nests unoccupied. Chappel, the watch officer, was nowhere to be seen. I asked Billy where he might be.

"Went forward, sir," said he with an anxious look.

Since the tryworks obstructed my view of that region of the vessel, I advanced to the waist, starboard, and saw that Owen Coffin was standing watch in the bows. He was shirtless, gazing out to the still sea in a curious pose, his right elbow cocked upward with his fingers resting at the nape of his neck. His lean, graceful torso was now as nut-brown as a Pacific native's.

Just then, from the other side of the tryworks, Chappel appeared and, not observing me, advanced stealthily toward Coffin and, coming up to him from behind, placed his fingers over the boy's eyes. Coffin made no move. When Chappel released him, my cousin turned and, showing no surprise at all, smiled most warmly at him, as if this tender game had been played a hundred times before. So intent were they on each other that though I was in plain sight of them, not concealed in any way, neither saw me, and, as I watched, the mate and Coffin proceeded to spar with each other, and then, when they had tired of this, to wrestle playfully, until the two of them were rolling about on the foredeck like a pair of puppies.

Then, stout Tom Nickerson, Little Joe West, and Charles Shorter came on deck and took in the situation. There was the third mate frolicking with an apprentice, who was moreover the captain's kinsman; and there was the captain looking on without ordering a stop to what he must consider, at the very least, unbecoming conduct. Nickerson and the two blacks—soon joined by others from the fo'c'sle—formed a circle around the wrestlers, cheering them on, as if to ratify the captain's indulgence of this innocent diversion.

Soon Chase and Joy came up from the cabin and joined me at the starboard side. When they had taken in what was going on, I asked, "What do you make of that, Mr. Chase?"

"Nothing new. Except they're at it when you're on deck."

"They're as thick as that?"

Joy said, "For some time now, Captain."

"And so leery of me?"

Chase said, "No longer, apparently."

"Seems to be no harm in it," said Joy, adding then: "Except to him."

As Joy spoke, Charles Ramsdell had come on deck and was taking in the scene, just as Chappel, who was the stronger of the two, pinned my cousin to the deck, where the vanquished accepted his defeat with a melting smile at the victor. As a cheer went up from the onlookers, Ramsdell turned his broad back on the proceedings and went to the starboard bow, where he stood gazing fiercely at the silken sea. Ramsdell, I well knew, had been Owen Coffin's inseparable companion on Nantucket and, for a time, on board the *Essex,* until (as I was to piece together from reports) Chappel had befriended them both, then gradually concentrated his attentions on Coffin, who soon submitted to the third mate's charm and began to find Ramsdell cheerless, sulky, and less interesting than he formerly had been.

Especially when I could see it as Ramsdell must have done, I could not put my cousin's smile at the radiant Englishman out of my mind.

As the gladiators got to their feet and observed that we officers had been watching them, Chappel, without betraying a hint of embarrassment, came over to us and addressed me cheerfully, " 'Morning, sir. Seems the night took our wind with it."

"I can see that, Mr. Chappel," I replied, with more severity than I intended. "What I do not see is the masthead watch."

He looked taken aback and said, "Captain, we've no way to speak of, so I figured the forward watch would raise any whales we could lower for."

"With you skylarking with him? How could he do that?"

Chappel looked sheepish. "Sorry. It was only for a minute. It was my fault, not his."

"What were the standing orders?"

"To set a masthead watch at the first light. But under the circumstances I thought—"

"I'll do the thinking on this vessel, Mr. Chappel. Now kindly set a lookout aloft, then come to breakfast."

"Yes, sir."

So that, thereabouts, was what happened. The young captain had taken it into his head to rebuke publicly his most popular officer for what amounted to exactly nothing. (A three-man watch went aloft to stare out into haze for two hours, then came down, and none was sent up again.) After leaning over backwards to tolerate the Englishman for more than a year, I had suddenly come down hard on him for no visible reason. I had acted like a martinet, unnecessarily, whereas the custom on board an American whaler is that discipline springs spontaneously from the captain's guts or he lets the matter be. As for Chappel, though sensitive to other people's feelings and purposes, he seemed immune to humiliation and bore no resentment of my treatment of him, but rather adopted a charitable interest in what might be wrong with me that morning. The crew, with little enough to think about, reflected on this novel incident and were inclined to imagine the worst. But what was the worst? Had Chappel given the captain reason to suspect him of some far more serious offense? Sedition? Or something beyond the imagination—unspeakable? If so, what were the grounds for his suspicions? Or was the captain himself under some bizarre influence? No, the thing could not be explained; therefore there must be something momentous behind it. By the upside-down logic that prevails on long voyages, it was the very absence of clear meaning to the incident that made it seem important.

My cousin was greatly affected. As Chappel chose three men from the watch to go aloft, Coffin stared at the deck, then, with an anguished jerk of his head, looked squarely at me; he was near tears, his chin quivering despite his efforts to present a manly appearance. In his look I read defiance and shame, pride and guilt: everything that a young man will feel when he is trying to squirm away from judgment, and the sternest judge is himself.

For three days we drifted on the sea's southwesterly set, nearly dead in the water, sometimes gaining steerageway from a feeble shift of air only to lose it again. I directed my officers to keep all hands occupied with scraping, painting, tarring, and various makework tasks. We held boat drills. In the evenings the crew gathered at the forward hatch for musical entertainment provided by Peterson, who played the fiddle; Shorter, who kept time with a tambourine; Isaiah Shepherd, who sang and danced "Jim Crow" with great comic effect; and Chappel, who possessed a fine tenor voice and a repertory of old English ballads, tunes of love and loss that, to give the devil his due, seemed to charm everyone on board, even our one remaining pig, in its pen by the cookhouse.

So we passed the time, but by the third day adrift in the equatorial heat our nerves had worn thin. A fight broke out in the fo'c'sle when Ben Lawrence accused Billy Wright of stealing a biscuit. In the cabin feelings emerged that had been hidden before, and nothing was quite the same.

By then we four officers had sat together at that round, scarred walnut table, under the skylight and the gimbaled lamp, three times a day for 420 days, making 1,260 times in all. So we knew one another pretty well, as far as we let ourselves be known; for I can only guess (from realizing now how much I concealed from them, even the watchful Chase) how much they concealed from me, their private selves being, I have not the shadow of a doubt, no less complex, troubled, and unfathomable than mine. The truth is that the occupation of whaling does not, as a rule, stimulate the sharing of deep feelings among those engaged in it. Nor are most whalemen much given to reflection or speculation. Ours is not a work that calls upon the highest part of the brain. The style of conversation at an officer's mess is, as a rule, closer to "Pass the duff" than the sort of high palaver you might hear at a meeting of the Nantucket Philosophical Institute. The three Nantucketers among us were of a breed not known for small talk; only the Englishman had an off-Islander's taste for it. This streak—together with his Anglo-Saxon good looks (tall and slender with wavy amber

hair, long narrow face, quick brown eyes) and the impression
he gave of being on the cruise for the sport of it, as if we were
engaged not in our life's work but in an entertainment to work
off youthful energy, a sort of nautical fox hunt—set Chappel
apart from us, though it often seemed that we were the foreign-
ers and he the native. In the plainest terms, I was convinced
that he did not take the voyage seriously, and I perceived
danger in his attitude, which could prove to be contagious.

And yet, in the very act of calling the Englishman to account—seeing Coffin's look of pain, sensing Chase's and Joy's
and the crew's bewilderment—I became aware that I was
behaving impoliticly if not irrationally. Chappel's physical
grace, his free spirit, wit, and high good humor—together
with his skill and bravery as a whaleman—had won him an
admiring following among the crew, and he had lifted their
spirits during the weeks of boredom between lowerings and
landfalls. I admitted to myself that disciplining him publicly
for no reason was a mistake. I therefore resolved to change
my behavior toward Chappel in accordance with my new understanding of him: he was not seditious, he was very simply,
for all his cleverness and fancy English ways, a child. The
ardent core of this boy-man was not malice but glee. Disin-
herited, he claimed only laughter as his birthright. Instead of
coming down on him, I determined to let him play the mad-
cap.

Chappel, of course, could not appreciate my altered attitude
toward him at once. At first he was on pins and needles with
me, eyeing me warily; but then, finding me more than usually
cordial to him, he soon regained confidence and was himself
again, indeed in higher spirits than before.

I remember the conversation in the cabin at the evening meal
that third day becalmed, the 7th of October. I remember it

because it was not in the least typical. Between me and Chappel in particular, the usual restraints were set aside.

We had just been served a steaming mess of Tecamus vegetables, flavored with strings of salt beef. By then our provision of meat was critically low and the loss of wind had delayed our recruitment of tortoises at the Galápagos for an indefinite time. Our one pig survived, which would provide two or three meals for the ship's company at the most. These were the circumstances under which Chappel suddenly speared an onion with his fork, held it up, and announced, "Man is a carnivorous animal."

Chase and Joy looked my way to see if I would take the remark badly. To their surprise I replied in good humor, "Gentlemen, I believe that Mr. Chappel is suggesting that we kill the pig."

Chappel popped the onion into his mouth and while chewing it said, "No, Captain. Not kill. Sacrifice. We sacrifice the pig to the gods of the wind."

"We are not pagans," I said.

"Pity," said the Englishman. "Great pity."

"I only meant that pagan gods would not receive an offering from us."

Chappel was fascinated by the notion. "But how do we *know?*" he demanded, then turned to Joy, whom he loved to bait on the subject of the latter's Christian piety. "Maybe there's more savage in us than we imagine, eh, Matt? How do we know?"

Joy smiled and said, "And maybe there's more God-fearing Christian in you than you know, Tom—or more than you admit."

Chappel now lanced a carrot, inspected it with displeasure, ate it. "Won't deny it," he said. "Had it all drummed into me when I was a lad." Then with a grin at Joy he said, "All right, Matt, we'll have it your way. We'll sacrifice the bloody pig to God."

Chase with a grimace said, "Too hot for such talk."

With a glance at the uncomfortable first mate I said, "Maybe He'd expect more than a pig."

Chappel examined this idea in his mind while studying me, apparently, in a new and more favorable light.

"A definite possibility."

Joy said, "Perhaps all He wants is our prayers and He isn't hearing them."

Chappel, his brown eyes bright with deviltry, said, "No, Matt. Prayers may be all very fine in Nantucket, but this is the Pacific. A prayer don't carry a ship's length out here. Even a good one. Many a poor bloke in a cannibal's stewpot's found that out."

"Stow that," said Chase.

"Facts are facts," said Chappel. "Am I right, Captain?"

I looked at him steadily and saw that he knew that he had gone too far. I said, "I'm sure that the Lord is fully as attentive to our needs here as He is in Nantucket, Mr. Chappel."

Half encouraged, half leery of me, the Englishman said, "Captain, just what did you mean by 'more than a pig'?"

After a moment I said, "The fact is, I was thinking of Father Abraham."

To this Chappel replied almost gleefully, "*There* was a man of faith!" And with a sidelong glance at Joy added, "Isn't only heathen gods who expect human sacrifice. And his own son, at that."

Hotly Joy said, "God didn't want Abraham to sacrifice Isaac. He just wanted to see if he was ready to."

"Scurvy trick," declared Chappel. "Wouldn't you say it was a scurvy trick, Captain?"

"It was a test of his faith," I said solemnly, reflecting that the Englishman was not such a bad fellow after all.

"Yes, a trick to test his faith. To see where Abraham would draw the line. And he didn't draw the line, did he? He was dead set to carve his son's heart out if God had so much as whispered, 'Do it.' That's the kind of faith God *relishes*. Men who'll do anything He asks and suffer anything He inflicts. Look at Job and Jo—" He broke off, looking at me uneasily.

"And Jonah," I said.

He smiled slowly as if, after fourteen months, he was only now beginning to see a glimmer of who I was. "And Jonah," he said. "Only Jonah was a little different. Jonah was trying to flee the presence of the Lord. Not prepared to assist in scurvy tricks and trying to make a run for it. That's why he boarded the ship. Hell of a nervy thing to do, when you think about it." Chappel shook his head in wonderment. "Where did the poor bastard think he was going, anyway?"

"Tarshish," I said.

"But God had a little surprise for him."

I replied, "Jonah might have expected something of the sort. He knew Who was after him. He knew what he was up against. I always admired the way Jonah acted when God got His teeth in him."

All this time, Joy, his pale sweating face already showing his illness, was looking from one to the other of us as if we were dangerous lunatics. Chappel let a smile flicker at his lips, then snuffed it out. He mopped his plate with his last piece of biscuit, ate it, then threw one muscular sunbrowned arm over the back of his chair. "No, sir," he said convivially, "there isn't much the Good Lord won't put a man through once He sets His mind to it."

I took some time lighting my pipe, then, through blue smoke, said, "On the other hand, He'll never put a man to a trial without giving him the strength to endure it. Isn't that so, Mr. Chappel?"

The Englishman nodded. "So it's said," he allowed, tilting his head back and gazing up at the skylight to further consider this proposition. "But if that's true, a man's faith wouldn't be tested. Just his strength. And that way he'd get the idea he could get by just fine by himself, without God's help. And that's not what God has in mind. No, sir, not His style at all. He loves us too much to leave us in peace for a bloody minute." He looked at Joy. "Am I right, Matt?"

Matt Joy was distressed. He said quietly, "I think it's the heat talking. I'm going on deck."

"I'll go with you," said Chase, and he followed Joy up the companionway.

Chappel and I confronted each other across the table, both trying not to show how content with ourselves we were. After a moment he said, "I do hope we didn't say anything to offend him."

In spite of my new appreciation of the Englishman, I was determined to keep a distance between us. I asked him, "Do you discuss these lofty matters with the crew?"

He shook his head. "Most of 'em don't take much stock in religion, one way or the other."

"Coffin does, doesn't he?"

He looked at me warily, then said, "I guess you'd know your cousin's leanings better than I."

"Perhaps. Perhaps not."

"He's a fine lad. He admires you."

"Does he?"

"Told me so."

"In so many words?"

"He let me know. There's no mistake about it."

Dryly I said, "Then thank you for the information."

"I meant no offense."

"None taken. Only I think that it is you who have his confidence—and his admiration."

"We are friends," said Chappel with a trace of defiance.

"Of course," I said. "That is different."

"Different?"

We looked at each other in silence. Aloft there was a sudden crack of sail filled by a vagrant shift of air. I said, "I'm sure he told you that his father is dead."

"Killed by natives in the straits of Timor."

"So of course I have an added responsibility. A family responsibility."

"Of course."

"All the more since I hold his mother in high esteem."

"I'm sure with good reason."

Another silence. The humorous complicity that had arisen between us had faded when Joy had left us and was now replaced by unease.

Then I said, "Do you draw the line, Mr. Chappel?"

The question seemed to surprise him; then he smiled at me as if we were again the most understanding of friends. "I'm not a man of faith," he said at last. "So it doesn't matter." When he saw that I had taken in this remark, he asked, "And you?"

I puffed at my pipe, again feeling drawn to the Englishman —and all the more set on not betraying myself to him. I said, "Mr. Chappel, I want you to go on deck and tell the cook to sacrifice the pig."

By sundown a southerly wind had risen and the *Essex* was a ship again. As the skysails raked the Milky Way I took the altitude of Jupiter, and after going below to plot our latitude, returned on deck to con the helmsman on a new course. During the time I had been in the cabin the watch had changed. At the wheel when I returned I found stocky Charles Ramsdell, his dour face eerily lighted from below by the binnacle lamp. He turned to me without a word. Remembering his look now, in the light of subsequent events, I read in it an anguished awareness of being swept helplessly toward an unbearable fate. Yet at the time he must have been feeling no more than fleeting pangs of youthful jealousy. I ordered him to steer due west.

On the morning of the 12th of October the cry "Land ho!" was heard from the masthead. Off our windward bow, beneath a towering cloud, Hood's Island stood sharply on the crisp horizon.

5

Charles Island, Galápagos
22nd Oct., 1820

My very dear Mary,

Good fortune in the person of Capt. Abner Myrick, master of the *Mary Pinkham,* Sag Harbor, will bear this letter home to you. The *M. Pinkham* is homeward bound with 2,600 bbls having put in to these God-forsaken islands for the same purpose as ourselves, to provision with Galápagos tortoises. Myrick's report of the quantity and tame disposition of sperm whales to the westward on the Line is heartening. With a little luck we too may boast a full ship before long and find ourselves in the happy situation of Capt. Myrick, knocking down his tryworks and preparing his vessel to weigh anchor for home. Thinking of returning to you, my dear wife, and to our blessed Island, I must take care that these reflections do not take possession of me, for we still have casks to fill and must keep our spirits taut and trim for the work ahead. So I

must not let myself think (too much) of rounding Brant
Point, embracing you and walking arm in arm with you
up Main Street, and, best of all, hearing the bell in South
Tower through lacy curtains—not yet!

Our first anchorage in this archipelago was Hood's Island, one of the smaller of the volcanic isles which com-
prise it. It is a desolate place, whose only permanent inhabitants are seabirds, flamingoes, species of finches seen
nowhere else, iguanas, wild dogs, pigs, and the great land
tortoises which we have come here to recruit. Not a single
human except us intruders, and as I set foot on the rock-
strewn white sand I had the impression of returning a
million years in time to the planet as it must have been
before the advent of Man. In the shadow of the dead
volcano, under the inscrutable gaze of antediluvian reptiles, one is conscious of the wonder of life and the odd
condition of our species, which, alone among all creatures,
must reflect upon the meaning of it. The first afternoon,
after our tortoise hunt, I left the boat crews sprawled on
the sand and rocks to rest and climbed the side of the
volcano until I attained a ledge a thousand feet or so in
elevation, commanding a view of the blue lagoon where
the *Essex* rode at anchor and of the sea to the western
horizon. As I stood there contemplating the scene, I could
almost imagine that I was in the presence of the Maker of
All Things, and, on the chance, gave Him thanks for
bringing us this far in safety.

For seven days we collected the turtles, making a lively
competition of it among the three boat crews, until we had
loaded no fewer than 300 of them aboard the vessel, each
weighing between 50 and 100 pounds, stowing them in the
between-decks, in the hold, and giving others the freedom
of the foredeck. The catching of Galápagos tortoises is not
difficult, since they are slow-moving and, considering their

past experience with whalemen, remarkably unsuspecting. Two men approach the animal from one side and, seizing the shell, flip him on his back, in which position he is helpless. The protesting reptile is then dragged to a boat, ferried to the ship, and hoisted aboard. In the heat of competition among the crews an arduous task becomes an amusing recreation.

Here at Charles Island we are taking on still more tortoises, since I am determined to provision the ship sufficiently so that we can fill our oil casks before touching another port. My plan is to sail west on the Line, then, if need be, northeast to the Japan grounds, passing south of the Sandwich Islands, for I have resolved not to put in at Lahaina, since we are not sure how we would be received there and I am determined not to put the ship in any jeopardy. You may be sure that this plan will not be well received by our high-spirited third mate, Mr. Chappel, who professes a great affinity for the Fair Sex of any hue or quality, at whatever risk, but so it will be.

Capt. Myrick is, as I write, readying his ship for departure, so I must bring this letter to a close and see it delivered into his hands. I have written you of tortoise-hunting and whatnot when my fondest thoughts are of us, my dear bride, of our reunion and settling into a house of our own, which I hope we will do soon after my return. Do keep a "weather eye" out for a suitable dwelling *in town,* not pretentious yet with enough rooms for the future. Keep well, Mary dear, and accept the warmest salutations of your distant but most affectionate husband.

Geo. Pollard, Jr.

P.S. It may be some time before you will receive another letter from me. We will be on the high seas, a very small speck on the immensity of the mid-Pacific. The chances of encountering another New England vessel are not very great.

In recalling that cruise of the *Essex* I am trying to avoid, on the one hand, excessive indulgence toward its young captain and, on the other, excessive censure of him (as well as the occasional urge to disavow him altogether). My attempt is to let the facts speak, without twisting them to make them say what they ought properly to say. However, in the case of a passage in this letter the facts themselves are so presented as to leave, if unamended, a most imperfect impression of the writer. I refer to the picture of him climbing the volcano and, upon reaching a lofty promontory, giving thanks to the elusive Lord of Creation.

What happened in fact?

Fact one: The elevation of the promontory was not 1,000 feet but closer to 400. Indeed, the highest point on Hood's Island, according to the charts, is 650 feet.

Fact two: What he experienced there was not gratitude but something very different. Gazing down at his vessel in the lagoon and out to the blue open sea he felt an absolute faith in himself and his future.

Fact three: Not for a moment did he feel that he was in the presence of the "Maker of All Things." But, as always, free of Him.

So, are we to put the young mariner down as an incorrigible hypocrite?

Before reaching judgment let us take into account, first, that he did not know himself very intimately then and, second, that he knew his wife hardly at all. A thousand feet means very high, which is precisely where he felt he had been on the volcano, and what he wished her to know. As to the third assertion, that he

might well have been in the Lord's presence, here it would seem
difficult to rise to his defense (especially in the light of his recent
alliance with the irreverent Chappel), but again we must proceed with caution. What he is telling his bride is that on the side
of the volcano he experienced something so *like* being in the
Divine Presence that it might have been precisely that. He did
not discern then that the sense of the Lord's presence and that
of His absolute absence (which is to say, not the sense of His
being elsewhere but of His being nowhere) are so similar as to
be indistinguishable to Man's imperfect cognizance. We are so
accustomed to living on tenterhooks, not being certain of anything one way or the other, that any glimmer of revelation, be
it of God's existence or of His nonexistence, is greeted with
hosannas. For all my years of browsing at the Atheneum, I am
no more a philosopher or theologian than any of the old captains who gammed on North Wharf when I was a boy; I am a
nightwatchman; but the fires in my brain have burned away the
inner lids of my eyes, so that I see certain things that were
invisible to the young captain, dashing off his hasty note to his
bride.

6

On the morning of the 23rd of October we cleared Charles
Island and again steered due west on the equator, carrying all
sail under fair skies with a moderate northeasterly breeze. With
the good weather, an abundance of choice fresh food, and the
assurance of Captain Myrick that shoals of sperm whales
awaited us over the horizon, we should have been basking in

contentment, but such is human nature—at least such is *Nantucket* nature—that on the most halcyon days, when without a care in the world we turn our faces to the sun and close our eyes to capture its warmth and the cool of the wind, thinking of nothing whatever, it is precisely then that we suddenly find ourselves out of our element. From the moment we had weighed anchor I had sensed, without wishing to acknowledge the impression, that there was unrest aboard the ship. Chappel's unofficerlike conduct with the crew had worked its mischief, and his following, especially Billy Wright and Little Joe West, tried our patience with their covertly defiant antics. In the cabin the Englishman himself now presumed that an understanding existed between him and me that permitted him any foolishness. Joy's health had worsened; he suffered coughing fits and, though he bore his illness manfully, admitted to nightly bouts of ague. Chase, obliged now to shout threats and curses at the crew to maintain discipline, seemed to hold me responsible for the general disaffection. But of all on board, the most conspicuously altered in behavior was Owen Coffin. Ever since I had openly reprimanded Chappel, my cousin had turned moody and withdrawn, given to lonely contemplation of the horizon and listlessness in the performance of his duty. Coffin, who at the start of the voyage had been set apart by his fo'c'sle mates on account of his cultivated speech and gentle manners, had soon become a great favorite among them, appreciated for his candid nature and cheerfulness. Now he shunned all companionship, and I observed that he would not even look at Chappel and took care to stay out of his way. As for the Englishman, it did not take him long to notice the change in his young friend and, with no visible regret, to seek other company.

For a week we sighted no whales and the unease persisted. Our cargo of live tortoises had at first provided an amusing diversion for the crew, but at sea they quickly became a great nuisance, usurping the best lounging spaces and impeding movement across the deck, and finally became an oppressive presence. From aft their ebony carapaces resembled the shields of ancient warriors fallen in the field. Their mournful, snakelike heads lost their comic aspect. And since these lumbering reptiles were to provide us with our principal staple of food the large number of them was a constant reminder to the crew that we were still outward bound with no end to the voyage in sight.

I remember a conversation in the cabin during this restless time. After an evening meal Chase and I had gone on deck to take altitudes, then returned to plot our position on the chart, 0° lat. 108° 10′ west longitude. Chappel studied the chart, then tapped his pipestem on the Sandwich Islands, thirty-five hundred miles to the northwest, saying to me with an amused look, "Why not, Captain?"

Chase said, "Not safe. No American whaler's put in at the Sandwich Islands. No reason to think the natives there are any friendlier now than when they murdered Captain Cook."

"That was forty years ago," countered the Englishman. "Have a little faith in the perfectibility of human nature, Mr. Mate."

I said, "Why take the risk, Mr. Chappel? We have plenty of food and water."

Chappel leaned back in his chair, cupping his head in his hands, and gazing up at the skylight said, "They say it's the most beautiful place in the whole world." And adding reverently, "And that the women are the juiciest and most obliging to be found anywhere." Then very suddenly he sat forward and with a look of the utmost urgency said, "Captain, we must get to those islands before the missionaries."

Remembering that at Masfuera we had heard that a vessel was sailing for the Sandwich Islands with a cargo of Christian missionaries and their wives, I asked, "And why is that?"

"Because they'll corrupt the natives, that's why!" he replied vehemently. "Teach them to be ashamed of their bodies and sing hymns and wear hideous clothes. They'll forbid dancing and drinking and God knows what else. Why, they'll even teach the women chastity, for Christ's sake! They'll turn a bloody paradise into Boston on Sunday."

Chase said, "Maybe they'll also teach them not to boil Christians for Sunday chowder."

"You're thinking of the Black Islands," said the Englishman. "Melanesia. Fiji. Maybe the Marquesas. No reason to believe the Sandwich Islanders have a taste for long pig."

Chase said, "No reason not to believe it. Anyway, cannibals or not, they're born thieves and murderers. Human life means nothing to them."

"Perhaps," said Chappel, "but just think of the women." Then he turned to me and added, "Captain, we must consider the welfare of the crew. Men without women are in no condition to fight whales."

"A powerful argument," I told him, "but we touch at no port until we have a full ship. We'll sail west on the Line, north of the Marquesas, then northwest, passing a good five hundred miles south of the Sandwich Islands. Men with diseases are in no condition to fight whales either. We'll steer clear of island paradises."

"Pity," said the Englishman. "Great pity."

That evening I went on deck when Owen Coffin had a trick at the wheel. Off our bows there was a crimson sunset, and as the veiled sun neared the horizon it flared bright orange, and as it sank into the sea we seemed to be sailing on a river of golden light toward the pulsing rim of the star. By its last rays I saw that my cousin's face was sad.

"All well, Owen?" I asked him.

"All's well," he replied, as if the world were ending. From the fo'c'sle came a burst of brutish laughter.

"There's whales out there," I told him. "We'll be raising 'em soon and then we'll show the mate whose boat is faster, will we not?"

"We will," he said with an attempt at a smile. "We'll show him our wake."

After a moment I asked, "Will you ship again, Owen?"

He did not look at me but said, "I will—if you will have me."

No words of his could have moved me more, for I had come to believe that he bore a grudge against me. I said, "I would be glad to have you on my next voyage."

He was silent for a time, then, still not looking at me, said softly, "I thought I'd done something to displease you."

I said, "You had no reason to. If I've behaved coolly toward you, it was only not to show favoritism."

"You have treated me well. It is I who . . ."

When he hesitated I said, "You have done nothing wrong."

In the dying twilight he looked at me and I thought, He is my kinsman, almost as if he were my own son.

At that moment I felt the ship yaw. Coffin looked down at the compass, and his face froze. At once I realized what had happened. In coming on the first dog watch he had the duty, before relieving the steersman, of lighting the binnacle lamp. Somehow he had neglected to do so and in the oncoming darkness could no longer read the compass. Without a word I went to the lamp on the mizzenmast and with a taper carried a flame to the binnacle and lit the wick. As the boy eased the vessel back on her proper heading, I said again, "All well, Owen?"

"All's well," he replied.

By the lamp underlighting his lean features I saw that his

sadness had lifted, he appeared relieved and heartened; and so
I left him.

We sighted spouts the following day, lowered, and saved two
sperm whales with little trouble. During the next week we took
three more. On the 9th of November the barometer dropped,
the western sky darkened, and for more than a week we rode
out heavy weather, working westward through seas too rough
for lowering. On the 17th the sun came out on agitated blue-
green waves. At eight in the morning of the 20th, a fine day with
long blue swells to the clear horizon, the lookout at the cross-
trees raised the cry "Thar—blows!" and I rushed on deck to
behold the welcome sight of forward-angled spouts a mile distant off our leeward bow.

7

Helmsman, steer two points north'ard, if you please. Mr.
Chase, prepare for lowering."

"Boat crews!" The mate's quarterdeck bellow shook the crew
down from the shrouds and aft from the bows, where they had
been sizing up the whales, and they hurried to their boats, mine
starboard, Chase's and Joy's larboard. They came squinting
against the low morning sun, looking as eager for action as I
had ever seen them, for everyone on board knew that there were
enough whales in the shoal to fill the ship for the homeward
voyage. I felt a great exhilaration, and I saw that Chase, for all
his reserve, felt the same. Whatever we were to each other at

other times, now, with whales in sight, we were as brothers.

I said, "Good luck, Chase."

He smiled his slow smile and answered, "Good luck yourself, Captain."

The shoal was traveling at three or four knots on a southwesterly course. Now sailing west by northwest, the wind out of the east, we steered for a point a half mile to windward of the whales, so that when we lowered, the boats could run silently under sail and intercept them. Never on this voyage had conditions been so favorable.

When I judged that it was the right moment, I had the vessel brought around into the wind and hove to. When this was done I gave the order to lower, leaving on board Doc Thomas, the black cook, Chips Cole, the carpenter, and Willie Bond, the black who had replaced Mamula as steward. As my boat cast off and we raised the sail I called up to Thomas at the railing, "Prepare us a feast, Doc. Don't spare your best." The cook grinned and called back, "Jes' you bring me whales, Cap'n, I'll fix you a feed you'll ne'er forget."

My boat and Chase's ran abreast, Joy's following with Chappel in the bow, readying his irons. Behind Joy's boat the ship stood now to the southeast of us, almost a mile distant over the quiet sea, lightly ruffled by the wind, under blue sky; the whales dead ahead a quarter mile or so, six adults, of which two were large bulls, four females, two accompanied by calves. As we neared I signaled Chase that I would go after the larger of the bulls, leaving him the other, and all three boats then lowered their sails, unshipped their masts, and approached the whales from behind under swift, silent oars.

When we were about twenty yards distant I signaled my harpooner, Obed Hendricks, to stand and prepare to strike. At the same moment Chappel got up in the bow of Joy's boat, about to close on a large cow. In the second boat the mate had taken Ben Lawrence's place as harpooner and stood poised to strike his whale. I remember seeing Hendricks's arm cocked back, his broad hand locked around the shaft of the iron; all others' eyes were then on me, Ray, Reed, Weeks, Ramsdell, and nearest me Owen Coffin, smiling to show his confidence and courage. At that moment I felt ten times alive. No thoughts to homecoming, rose-covered houses, profits, reputation; my entire being was concentrated on the kill; all fear obliterated by the absolute act of will that we succeed. That perfect moment, the three harpooners poised, their barbs glinting in the sun, the boats in position to close on our quarry, I remember it.

I swung the boat toward the whale. "Strike, Obed!" I called out, and the harpoon arced through the air, sinking deep into the bull's black glossy side at the waterline. "Stern all!" I shouted, and the oarsmen responded as one, as I veered the boat away from the flukes that rose high and crashed down just clear of our retreating bow. Then as we backed and payed our line the whale sounded, taking coils from the tub faster than the eye could follow, the line smoking around the logger-head, slapping along the thwarts to the bow and drilling into the sea. I looked around and saw that Chappel had succeeded in striking the cow and was fast. Beyond, Chase was in trouble. He had struck his whale, but before Ben Lawrence could maneuver clear the flailing creature had hit the starboard side of the boat a glancing blow with his flukes. I saw Chase seize a hatchet and sever the line, to prevent his damaged boat from being pulled under. I called to him, "Hang on, Chase. We're cutting free." Hendricks had already taken up a hatchet, awaiting my order.

But at once the mate yelled to us through cupped hands, "No! Stay fast. We can make it to the ship."

Brave Chase. He ordered his men to strip off their jackets and stuff them between the broken planks. He then set a man bailing and taking his place at an oar began rowing eastward toward the vessel, now a little more than a mile distant. When I saw that he was staying afloat, I turned my attention to our own whale, still sounding, still taking line and showing no sign of tiring, bringing us farther and farther west, away from the ship. Joy's boat, dangerously low in the water, was being taken on a northwest course. I knew that when he reached the ship, Chase would put her off in our direction, so I had little care about being towed too far to leeward. To hearten us I called out to the harpooner, "Where are you taking us, Obed?" For answer he pointed to the northwest, where the remnants of the shoal had just surfaced and were swimming rapidly away. Our whale was then veering in that direction, bringing us abreast of Joy, flying through the lead-blue water after the retreating pack.

What took place during the next hour is best told from Chase's vantage point. For the facts and his impressions of them I draw upon my memories of what he told me in Valparaiso and in his *Narrative.*

By strenuous rowing and bailing, he and his crew reached the ship safely and hoisted the damaged boat aboard. He immediately ordered that the ship be brought about to bear westward, toward the two boats and the whales. Then, upon inspecting the damage to his own boat, he decided that a jury repair could be made by nailing canvas over the damaged planks. His choice was either to make that repair or else put in service the spare boat that was slung bottom up on spars over the quarterdeck, a task that would require extensive outfitting. His judgment was that the damaged boat, with its whaling gear rigged and ready, could be put in the water more quickly, so that he could rejoin the chase. Though no man could have known it at the time, this decision was to be—I am convinced—the proximate cause of our catastrophe.

Carried on the easterly wind, the clatter of hammers could be heard more than a mile to westward.

Chase and his crew had half finished their work when Tom Nickerson at the helm called out, "Sperm whale off the weather bow!"

Chase ran to the railing and saw a huge black bull about eighty-five feet long lying still in the water a hundred yards from the ship, his head toward her.

As the mate watched—hesitating whether to lower his partially repaired boat in pursuit of the creature—the whale spouted, then sank from sight and seconds later broke the water a ship's length away headed directly for the vessel at a rate of about three knots, the ship then making about the same speed. Chase yelled to Nickerson, "Put her hard up!" hoping to let the attacker pass under the bowsprit, but it was too late. The words were hardly out of his mouth when the whale struck the starboard bow with a violent jar that brought the ship up as if she had hit a rock, and for a moment she trembled like a living thing. Some of the men had been thrown to the deck. Others clung to supports. They looked at one another in perfect amazement, unable to speak. The whale was then passing under the vessel, grazing her keel. Chase got to his feet and saw the whale surface alongside the ship to leeward and lie still, apparently stunned by the force of the blow. It remained there about a minute, then suddenly swam away from the ship and sounded. The mate had by then recovered himself and, concluding that a hole had been stove in the bow, ordered the pumps rigged and manned. The whale surfaced again about a mile to leeward, now in convulsions, enveloped in the white foam his violent writhing created around him, and smiting his great jaws together as if maddened by rage. After a time he started off at great speed across the bows of the ship, to windward, in the direction of the boats and the retreating shoal. By then Chase had realized that despite the working of the pumps, the bow of the ship was settling in the water, and he turned his attention to readying the boats, the half-repaired one and the spare, for embarkation. Just then he heard Ben Lawrence cry out from the forward hatchway, "Here he comes! He's making for us again!" Chase turned to see the whale, about a mile distant, almost directly ahead, bearing down on the ship at great speed and with what seemed to the mate, in his words, "tenfold fury and vengeance in his aspect." As it neared the ship it was traveling at such velocity, about six knots, and with such violent thrashing of its tail, that surf flew in all directions about him. Chase, still possessed of a desperate hope of saving the ship, shouted again, "Hard up!" but the vessel had not fallen off more than a point when she took a second blow directly under the cathead which completely stove in her bows, so that the sea now flooded in too fast for the pumps. Again the whale passed under the ship, went off to leeward, and was seen no more.

Realizing that the *Essex* was doomed, Chase ordered the pumping to cease. He sent a man below to retrieve two quadrants and two Bowditch navigators, while he himself took the compass from the binnacle. With the bow settling rapidly now, he decided to abandon the damaged boat and launch only the spare. Seizing a hatchet, he cut away the lashings that bound her to the spars and called on those near to take her as she came down. They did so and bore the boat on their shoulders to the waist. As the boat was being readied, Chase sent below again for charts and the log book, and for my trunk and his own, but by then the cabin was half flooded and only my trunk was retrieved. Rapidly now, the ship was going over on her beam ends; the boat was hastily put in the water and all nine men aboard jumped in her and pulled clear of the ship. They were scarcely two boat lengths from her when she fell over and settled into the water.

. . .

At this moment Joy and I, still fast to our whales, were being towed in an arc to the north. It was Obed Hendricks who first observed that something was wrong. Standing in the bow, he looked back to where the ship had been, and the look of wide-eyed terror on his long, craggy face froze my blood.

"Oh, my God!" he cried. "Where is the ship?"

I stood and scanned the sea in disbelief. Had we in the excitement of the chase so lost track of time and distance as to have been towed out of sight of the vessel? It was impossible. The sun was where it had been. Visibility was clear to the horizon.

"Cut free!" I ordered, and Hendricks seized the hatchet and with a blow cut our tether to the whale. I then looked across to Joy's boat and saw that they too were now aware of the mysterious disappearance of the ship and were also cutting loose. As we rowed toward where the vessel had last been seen, I remember thinking, "What *trick* is this? What monstrous *game* is being played against me?" My boat crew, Coffin and Ramsdell nearest me, searched the sea with each pull of the oars, then looked to me for explanation—while I fought to retain my judgment in the face of the incomprehensible disappearance of my ship.

When we came in sight of Chase's boat and the wreck, no one spoke at first. Then, as we neared the dismal scene, I felt as if my blood were draining out of my body, and I called out to the mate, "My God, Mr. Chase, what has happened?"

He replied, "We have been stove by a whale." And we brought our boats together and he told us what had happened.

For several minutes we were all stunned and could not act; then I told Chase that we must attempt to reach supplies of food and water. We boarded the wreck and with only the hatchets from the boats cut away rigging and masts so that the ship might right herself, for only then could we scuttle the deck planks to reach stores in the between-decks in the waist. With strength drawn from desperation we accomplished this labor in an hour; and when the masts were cleared the vessel did right herself sufficiently for us to cut through the deck. We recovered six hundred pounds of hard bread, all the kegs of water we dared load on our boats, and several tortoises. From a locker we also obtained a couple of files, two rasps, about two pounds of boat nails, a small canister of powder, ball, and two pistols.

As night approached we made a line fast to the wreck and moored our three boats to the leeward, setting a watch to free us should the wreck begin to sink. With the coming of darkness the wind, which was from the southeast, rose and the sea became agitated. Our discomfort was intense. We could not sleep. We were too confounded to speak, and moans, stifled whimpers, despairing prayers, curses, were the only human sounds heard in the wind. My thoughts kept returning to the whale, which Chase had been certain had acted in vengeance. Once, toward morning, I drifted into sleep only to be awakened at once by a vision of the gaping jaws of the whale closing on our boat and by my own cry of terror.

Nov. 21.

Clear dawn, strong breeze holding from the SE, rough sea. We had not yet formed any plan of what to do, but pulled up to the wreck and clambered over it, searching for useful articles, but more because we could not yet accept the fact that this wretched raft of timbers that had been the *Essex* could no longer shelter us. By afternoon we collected ourselves a little and, setting a watch on the stump of the foremast to look for ships, we went to work stripping the light canvas off the wreck and fashioning sails for our boats. Using light spars, we rigged each with two masts, to carry a flying jib and two spritsails. The waves by then were continually breaking into the boats, and, fearing that our provisions would be spoiled and that the boats would founder, we secured some light cedar boards and built up the sides, about six inches above the gunwales. The work was not completed by sundown, and as we tossed about in the darkness of that second night the full horror of our predicament gained possession of my mind. I could not believe that the loss of my ship, my hopes, perhaps all our lives could result from the blind rage of a rogue whale. There had to be some hidden cogency to the catastrophe. It could not be that we were victims of *nothing,* for that would be unbearable. Then, on that second night, with the southeast wind whining through the blackness, with my companions moaning in despair, I determined that, like old Captain Coleman and all the other Nantucket men who had faced their hour of great peril at sea, I was not about to die as long as anything could be done about it. For the first time in two days, I slept.

Nov. 22.

Brisk SE wind, clear skies. At sunrise we again hauled up to the wreck, which under the constant pounding of the sea was beginning to break up. Casks had bilged in the hold, and oil spread over the sea all around us. We completed the making of sails and nailing the cedar siding to the boats and at noon were steeled to leave the wreck, though in what direction, toward what landfall, what hope of salvation, we still had not determined. I took an observation and calculated our position, then directed that a council of the officers be convened in my boat, Ramsdell, Ray, and Weeks exchanging places with Chase, Joy, and Chappel for the purpose, leaving Coffin and Hendricks as an audience to our deliberations.

I said, "Our position is latitude zero degrees thirteen minutes north, longitude one hundred and twenty degrees zero minutes west. We have been carried by the wind and current west by

northwest of where the whale struck. A mere twenty-five hundred miles on that course would bring us to Mr. Chappel's
paradise."

"We'd never beat the missionaries now," said the Englishman ruefully.

"Nor the winter typhoons," I said. "The *konas.* An open
boat wouldn't stand a chance."

"With luck we could slip between them," said Chappel.

Then, looking at me, Chase said, "Doesn't look like we can
lean too hard on luck."

Meeting his gaze, I said, "Luck or not, whatever we do we'll
do it together. Our lives depend on staying together."

"Agreed," said Chase.

"Agreed," said Joy.

"Couldn't ask for finer company," said Chappel with a wink
at Owen Coffin that brought a faint smile to the boy's lips.

I opened a Bowditch navigator, studying the lists of Pacific
islands and their positions. I then said, "My friends, here is our
situation: west by northwest—the Sandwich Islands, twenty-
five hundred miles, favorable winds and currents—then *konas.*
North—the coast of Mexico, contrary winds and currents—
impossible. East on the Line—the Galápagos—there too, wind
and currents against us. South by southeast—the Easter Islands, not much of a landfall in a hell of a lot of ocean—and
a very uncertain reception from the natives."

"Not so very," said Chase grimly.

"South by southwest—Henderson Island and Ducie Island."

"Uninhabited, possibly uninhabitable," said Chase. "And
almost never visited."

"But islands all the same," said Chappel. "Blessed Henderson. Blessed Ducie. I kiss your uninhabitable earth."

"Southwest—the Marquesas, the nearest of all, a thousand
miles. We could run with the trades, perhaps a month or less."
I glanced at my cousin, seeing his look of trust and remember-

ing his father's fate, and adding, "But again, what do we know of the natives there?"

"Nothing good," said Chase.

"Beastly stories," said Chappel.

Then Joy, who had been combing his mind to remember something, spoke up suddenly. "And Pitcairn? The *Bounty* mutineers' island. Where is Pitcairn?"

"Englishmen!" said Chappel ardently. "An island inhabited by Englishmen! An Albion in the Pacific. Oh, where is Pitcairn?"

I searched the Bowditch for that island, but to my dismay found that it was not there. I said, "I believe it lies to the south and somewhat west of Henderson, but where exactly—"

"Anyway," said Chase, "they live outside of English law. How would they receive us?"

"Most cordially!" Chappel assured us. "With tea and music and their native wives. Though cutthroats, they are gentlemen."

I then said, "Without knowing its position, we'd best forget Pitcairn. We must choose the best course according to what we do know. Mr. Chappel, what is your opinion?"

The Englishman reflected a moment, then said, "You know where I'm for going, Captain. As for *konas,* we risk meeting squalls in any direction we sail."

"Joy?"

"I say the Marquesas. Perhaps the stories are exaggerated."

"Chase?"

The mate was silent, then said, "It's true we can meet foul weather on any course, but the captain's right: in this season the *kona* storms can be depended on, and they're murderous. As for relying on the hospitality of natives, I say we'd best not, except as a last resort. I say we steer south. Say to the twenty-fifth parallel, where we'll pick up the variables."

"And then?" said Joy.

Chase hesitated, then said, " 'Course, there's always a chance of being rescued."

"And if we're not?"

"Then we work east."

"East to where?" asked Chappel.

When Chase looked at me, I answered for him. "The coast of South America."

"My God!" said Chappel. "That's—three thousand miles!"

"Four thousand," I corrected him.

Part Three

IN THE OPEN BOATS

1

Nov. 22, 1820

A whaleboat is a frail thing. A man too. We were twenty men in three whaleboats, divided as follows:

The Captain's Boat
George Pollard, Jr.
Obed Hendricks
Brazilla Ray
Owen Coffin
Samuel Reed (black)
Charles Ramsdell
Seth Weeks

The First Mate's Boat
Owen Chase
Benjamin Lawrence
Thomas Nickerson
Isaac Cole
Richard Peterson (black)
William Wright

The Second Mate's Boat
Matthew P. Joy
Thomas Chappel
Joseph West

Lawson Thomas (black)
Charles Shorter (black)
Isaiah Shepherd (black)
William Bond (black)

The distribution of six men in Chase's boat and seven each
in the others was owing to the fact that the mate's boat, the
spare, being old and patched from several stavings during the
cruise, was the weakest of the three. All were heavily laden with
bread, water kegs, tortoises, and sundry supplies and gear, so
that they rode perilously low in the water.

By half past twelve that day, with an easterly wind rising, the
sky darkening, the sea running high, I decided that there could
be no advantage to staying with the wreck any longer, and,
ascertaining that Chase and Joy were prepared, I gave the order
to set sail on the course we had determined, south by southeast.

"No matter what, we stay together," I called out as the wind
filled our sails and we put the remains of the *Essex* astern of
us, pointing into smoky scud to the south. That afternoon, in
each boat, we busied ourselves tending sail and securing our
stores, yet, despite our activity, I felt anguished sailing away
from the wreck, nor was I alone, for we all cast longing looks
back at what had been our ship, as if she could suddenly be
whole again and the attack of the whale a bad dream, until at
four we lost sight of her.

The first night a full moon stood in the eastern sky, roving
behind clouds. We kept our course together very well, and I
remember our voices calling through the wind.

"Should we set lanterns to be seen?"

"Too much breeze."

"Is that a ship?"

"Where?"

"To windward."

"It's a cloud."

"All right, Mr. Joy?"

"All right, Captain."

"Mr. Chase?"

"Took a sea. Bailing. All right."

Nov. 23

Wind moderate. Seas still heavy. For the first time since setting sail, rations of bread and water were distributed, equally to each man in each boat: a half-pound biscuit, a half pint of water. The first night, when fast to the wreck, we had drunk copious draughts of water, believing our supply sufficient for any contingency; but now, figuring distance, winds, currents, and no rescue, we judged that with the trade wind, on the course we were now lying, we would require twenty-six days to reach the latitude of variable winds and thirty more to make the South American coast; so I fixed the bread and water allowance at a sixtieth of our total supply per day, believing that if we only stayed afloat, this stringent rationing would see us through the worst that could befall us.

That night, in the lighter airs, we hoisted lanterns so that we might be seen by a passing vessel and so that we would not separate in the darkness. Bone-weary, I could sleep only fitfully, my thoughts torn between hope and fear.

Nov. 24

At sunrise—the first since our departure from the wreck— our wretched little flotilla sailed abreast, about six fathoms apart, Chase's boat to leeward of me, Joy's to windward. Chase and his crew had the worst of it, since besides taking occasional seas, his boat leaked and a man had to be set bailing night and day.

And that was not his only difficulty.

At about eight o'clock, closing the distance between us, his face grim, Chase said to me, "Captain, we have a thirsty man here." He nodded to the bows of the boat, where the black, Peterson, sat wide-eyed, trembling all over. "Caught him with the bung in his hand." With that I ordered the boats to lower sail and heave to, and when we were joined I opened the tin box I had taken from my trunk containing two pistols, ball, and several canisters of powder. I passed one pistol, with powder and ball, to Chase, the other to Joy, then I drew the musket from the stern and said, "Rationing will be strictly enforced." Chase and Joy loaded their pistols. Peterson was shaking with fear. I then said, "Every man will be given an equal chance. Food and water will be shared equally. From now on, the punishment for theft or attempted theft of food or water will be death."

Chase, Joy, and I then put away our weapons, keeping them near at hand. Peterson, who had thought he was a dead man, called out, "God bless you, Captain! God bless you, Mr. Mate!" We then hoisted sail with the feeling of having met our first human crisis with humanity and resolve.

Nov. 25

I am recalling these events from a combination of direct memory, rough notes I made in the boat on the pages of my Bowditch, and Chase's *Narrative*. My notes for this date say only, "Wind ESE strong. Bread damaged. Chase's boat repaired."

How little those words convey of that arduous day!

The rising wind was forcing us on a course west of south, though how far west we could not tell exactly, since, without glass or log line, we had abandoned the idea of keeping a longitudinal reckoning. We only knew that we were being driven steadily farther from our goal and closer to what we feared were cannibal isles—the Marquesas and the Tuamotu archipelago. That same unkind wind was spraying wave-tops into the boats, so that by the gray dawn light we discovered that part of the bread in all three had been soaked.

Chase, however, was in more serious trouble. By eight o'-clock his boat was rapidly taking in water through a leak in the bottom, the water already shipped making it difficult to locate the opening. Chase informed me of his plight, and we again hove to and joined our boats. While four of his crew bailed frantically, the mate and Ben Lawrence felt the bottom for incoming water.

One thought was in all our minds then. If Chase's boat foundered, Joy and I would each have to take three more men on board, thus reducing our chances of staying afloat in even moderately high seas to almost nil. Yet we could conceive of no other choice. Even in that alarming situation the threat to us was still abstract, and our thoughts still those of civilized men.

From our boat Obed Hendricks discovered the sprung streak in the lee bow of Chase's, about six inches below the waterline.

"Heel her over," I called to Chase, taking a hammer and nails. He at once ordered all his crew to the weather gunwale while I maneuvered the stern of my boat alongside the bow of his and, taking nails one by one from my mouth as the boats threatened to crush my arms, I managed with a few blows to secure the streak as snugly as if Chase's boat had been careened on Brant Point.

Any satisfaction we might have felt over this success, however, was engulfed by the awareness of how near this accident had brought us to annihilation and how vulnerable we remained. By luck we had retrieved nails from the wreck, without which we would have given conclusive proof to the adage that without a nail a kingdom is lost.

By that evening Joy's state of health had worsened, and I put Chappel in charge of his boat so that Matthew could have a chance to rest.

Nov. 26

Wind abated and hauled out to ENE, enabling us to hold a more favorable course. We took advantage of the respite to dry our clothes and also the bread that had been wet. That afternoon Ramsdell accidentally knocked a biscuit overboard and I reprimanded him for it, more severely than I intended. The truth is that I felt an aversion toward Ramsdell—all the more because I could find no satisfactory reason for it.

Nov. 27

Wind veered back to E. At noon Chase and I calculated our latitude to be only 3°15′ S, and we could reach no good guess of our longitude. We considered whether to fall off and take our chances on reaching an island in the chains to the southwest, but our fears of hostile natives or of sailing through the archipelagos into the empty reaches of the South Pacific determined us to hold to our original plan.

Nov. 28

A night of terror. The wind had hauled further to S, the sea became tempestuous, and after nightfall we could barely make out the other sails, Chase's ahead of me, Chappel to leeward. At about midnight, with Hendricks tending the sails, I had just fallen asleep in the bottom of the boat when I was violently jarred awake. My first thought was that we had run aground. Then in the darkness I could make out Hendricks's frozen eyes fixed on the water to windward. Brazilla Ray was repeating over and over, "Madre de Dios! Madre de Dios!" I sat up and perceived the dim sheen of a huge fish passing astern, then turning and making for us again. I yelled to Chase, whose boat was the nearer, "Chase! We are attacked by a fish!" At once the mate put about, but by then the creature was bearing down on our lee bow and, opening its jaws, struck the boat a second, even more violent blow. I seized the spare sprit pole and with that frail weapon tried to ward off a third and then a fourth attack, but without success, until at last of its own accord the fish swam into the blackness to leeward. We enjoyed no relief from the fear that had seized us all, for as Chase's boat approached us, Coffin and Ramsdell called from the bows, "Captain, we're stove! We're shipping water fast!" Under the impression that we were foundering then and there, I shouted orders to transfer our provisions to the other boats, then went forward to inspect the damage. I found that we had indeed stove, but above the water-line, so that the leak was controllable. I then ordered the trans-fer of provisions to cease, called my crew astern to keep the bow high, and set Ramsdell and Ray to bailing. Thus, taking turns at the buckets, we passed the rest of the night, in constant apprehension that the fish, or another of its kind (we concluded that the attacker was an orca, or killer-fish), might return and finish the work. With no prospect of sleep, too shaken to con-verse, we had ample opportunity to relive the cruel complicity of disasters that had befallen us and to speculate on what lay in store.

Nov. 29

At first light we laid to and I and my crew repaired our boat, nailing thin boards on the inside of the stove bow. We replaced what provisions had been transferred and resumed our course, the wind being a little more favorable.

By then we had begun to suffer painfully from thirst—all the more because we had consumed the partly dried, sea-soaked bread before it spoiled. Had we foreseen the consequences of eating this already salted, briny bread we would never have touched it. We all experienced the torture of raving thirst, which could not be quenched even for an instant by our little allowance. Yet I dared not increase the ration. Our extreme suffering began this day, as if announced by the orca.

That afternoon a shoal of dolphins surrounded us, recalling the bright-hued escort that, seen from her lofty quarterdeck, had seemed to welcome the *Essex* into the Atlantic. Now we were meeting their fellows under different circumstances, and I had the impression from the curve of their mouths as they leaped that they were laughing at us. Indeed, I am certain that we presented an exceedingly comical spectacle to them. Here we were, twenty individuals of a species supremely unsuited by nature for the element in which we found ourselves; eight black, twelve white, variously dressed, some in blue shirts, some in red, others in black jackets, some with black hats, some with cloths tied at their heads—in three *boats*—and if there is anything that must excite the risible faculties of a dolphin it would be that clumsy contrivance in which men bob on the surface of the sea. I don't think that their humor was unkindly meant. They must have thought that since we had ventured so far into their world we must have had good reasons for doing so—not guessing what our reasons were. I even think that had there been an island nearby they might have guided us to it, for the pure fun of it. We tried to catch them with a hook tied with a white rag for a lure; and playing our game, they would rush at the rag, then swerve away at the last minute, convinced by then that we were complete fools. They stayed with us all that day, then in the evening about six o'clock, with a leaping salute, left us for other entertainments.

Nov. 30

Pleasant weather, the first since leaving the wreck, moderate favorable wind. Our thirst and hunger were now intense, and at one o'clock that afternoon Chase proposed that we should slaughter a tortoise in each boat, there being six remaining in all. I agreed, and hoarse cheers greeted the decision. In my boat I officiated as butcher, severing the beast's head, detaching the yellow breastplate, and with our one large sharp knife dividing the meat, being careful to save every drop of blood in the carapace. About a gill was collected and emptied into a cup. I passed it to Hendricks, saying, "A swallow per man till it's gone, those who favor it." Hendricks drank and passed the cup to Ray, who touched it to his lips, then with a shudder passed it to Ramsdell, who drank and gave it to Coffin, who also drank, then passed it to Weeks, who unhesitatingly refused and passed the cup to me. A swallow remained, which I drank off like medicine. We then made a small fire in the carapace and cooked the meat, enjoying a rude yet exquisite banquet which for a time restored our bodies and spirits. On this day we found ourselves in latitude 7°53' S, about 480 miles from the site of the wreck.

Dec. 1–2

Continued fine weather brought temporary forgetfulness of our situation. Raging thirst revived our memories.

Dec. 3–5

Mares' tails announced a worsening of the weather, and by nightfall the sky was overcast. About ten, in deep darkness, Chase and I discovered that Chappel's boat did not respond to our calls. We hove to, and Chase raised a lantern at his mast. After searching the dark for some time we saw an answering light a quarter mile to leeward. We ran down to it, and reaching the strayed boat, I called out, "What's wrong, Mr. Chappel? I thought you liked our company?"

"Nothing personal, Captain," the Englishman called back.

Yet it was not so light a matter. Indeed, it seemed all-important to us that we stay together. A primal need for comradeship now that we were at the mercy of the wind and waves had surprised us with its force, being far stronger than any such feelings we had known on the ship, when even in times of peril we had felt on equal terms with the sea. Constantly in our minds was the thought that if one boat was wrecked, its provisions lost, then humanity would constrain us to take on board the survivors, share our last crumbs of bread and drops of water, dooming us all, almost surely, to a horrid end. And now, never far from that thought was the question whether *if it came to that* we would submit to that fate or whether as the survivors clutched at our gunwales we would not beat them back into the ocean to die.

Logic argued for separation: we would eliminate the delays of night searches for each other and, more important, we would extinguish the dreadful specter of becoming either the victims or the assassins of our comrades in the other boats. Nor was it easy to stay together. On dark nights it was enough to let our attention stray for an instant for a boat to drop out of sight. On the 5th, Chase vanished, and we located him only after he fired his pistol twice.

It was the mate who, when we were hove to after finding him, first uttered the alternative suggestion. "If we go our own ways we'll make better distance," he said to me, though without much conviction but rather because he felt bad about delaying us. Just as he spoke, a westering cloud revealed the full moon, and with the sails down we could all see one another clearly: Joy, his face pallid, in the bows of the third boat, Chappel in the stern, Joe West and the four blacks all looking at me intently; Chase and his crew also; and in my own boat those in my special care, Hendricks, Ray, Ramsdell, Coffin, Weeks, and Reed, all waiting for my answer.

I said, "We stay together—if we can. But if a boat gets lost at night we wait till first light to search. Agreed?"

"Agreed," said Chase.

"Chappel? Joy?"

"Agreed," said Joy weakly.

"And we'll all meet in Liverpool," said Chappel.

Dec. 8

This afternoon the wind set in from SSE and by midnight had increased to a gale, bringing torrents of rain, violent squalls in quick succession, forcing us to unship the masts. We attempted to catch fresh water in the sails, but the little we collected was briny from the salt encrusted in the canvas. Sharp flashes of lightning illuminated our craft clinging to the face of towering black waves under silver sheets of rain, seeming wrapped in fire. Without sails, masts, or rudders our boats were completely unmanageable, and all that terrible night we were driven we knew not where nor how far; and by the dark dawn, having slept not at all, we were too dispirited to care about anything, each of us having striven to abandon himself to destruction. Seth Weeks sat near me clutching his head as if to shut out all awareness of where he was; Obed Hendricks, who had been bailing, passed the bucket to Brazilla Ray, who took it without interrupting his invocations to the Mother of God; Reed sat rigidly in the waist; Coffin and Ramsdell lay in the bows in each other's arms for warmth and comfort; I sat astern repeating in my mind the litany "You will survive"—willing myself to believe it.

Dec. 9

By afternoon the gale began to moderate a little, and we made efforts to get a little sail on the boats, setting double-reefed mainsails and jibs, but on the swells could get no accurate compass reading. Just before setting, the red sun broke from between the mountainous waters and the low, boiling clouds, blazing in our eyes. We were headed due west.

Dec. 10

On our southward course again. Hunger and thirst created an almost uncontrollable temptation to partake freely, just once, from our stocks; but the same cravings warn of the supreme agony of having *nothing,* so we continue to subsist on our meager ration. By then, thoughts of satisfying our hunger and thirst, especially our thirst, crowded out all others, even those of rescue. As guardian and dispenser of provisions, I had become alienated from my crew.

That afternoon we overtook a small shoal of flying fish, four of which flew into our mainsail and dropped into the boat, one just at my feet. I seized it up and began to devour it alive, head, scales, wings, everything—until I felt Reed's iron grip at my wrist, and reluctantly I shared what was left with him. At the same time Hendricks and Ray were struggling for possession of another fish, which they, too, reluctantly divided. Ramsdell had caught yet another, partly eaten it, then offered the rest to Coffin. Weeks seized the fourth, but as he took it to his mouth it slipped free of his hold and into the sea.

No one spoke afterward, but each of us was aware how fragile the law of sharing that we lived by had become. Only Ramsdell had voluntarily obeyed the commandment, and he no doubt not so much by constraint as in friendship. I think that no one, even poor Weeks, blamed anyone else; we all knew the hunger which had momentarily banished scruples; but Ramsdell—he of all people!—had resisted and voluntarily shared with his friend. In any event the law was weakened, especially by my own instinctual disobedience of it, and henceforth I could no longer depend on its authority but only on its enforcement to overcome the cravings that could at any moment change us into wild beasts. Now wherever I moved in the boat I wore my loaded pistol, and when I slept it was never without my head or my legs resting on the food chest.

Dec. 11–14

We made slow progress in light airs and calms, under hot sun. On the 11th we killed our remaining tortoises and made a fine feast of them, which invigorated us considerably. Then on the 13th we were blessed with a change of wind to northward, which brought relief from the heat and permitted us to make all sail to the east. Our hopes of deliverance revived. We supposed that we had cleared the westerly trade winds and reached the variables, but, alas, it was not so. The night of the 14th the wind died and we were beset by a perfect calm.

Dec. 15

Our sufferings on these windless days almost exceeded belief: burning heat, hunger, thirst, and despair all combining to torment what life remained in us. With our water supply alarmingly diminished, I halved the ration, with no objections, since we all equally dreaded the prospect of having none. We experimented with holding salt water in our mouths, and our own urine, but only aggravated our thirst. To seek relief from the rays of the sun, Hendricks, Coffin, and I lowered ourselves over the side to cool our bodies, only to find that we were too weak to haul ourselves back over the gunwales, but needed the help of Ramsdell, Ray, and Weeks (who did not swim and had stayed aboard) to clamber back. When in the water we found that a species of small clam had attached itself to the hull. Finding them to be a delicious food, we collected all we could, and I divided them into seven little piles, which we quickly consumed.

Our latitude was then 21°42'S. Longitude unknown.

Dec. 16

Dead calm. I took an observation at noon and found that overnight we had lost ten miles to the northerly set of the sea. Chase confirmed my findings. This unexpected setback disheartened me, and for the first time I found no strength to resist what by now seemed to be the fated certainty that we perish. All that afternoon I remained dispirited. Owen Coffin must have read my thoughts; he looked at me often with great concern, then toward nightfall, to my utter surprise, he said quietly, "Captain, we must challenge the other boats to a race."

I couldn't believe my ears. Then I laughed until I choked.

Coffin said, "We must do something to change our luck. We can't just quit."

"He's right," said Obed Hendricks.

"Madre de Dios," said Brazilla Ray.

I signaled the boats to converge, and, using oars, we did so. I then announced, "Mr. Chase, Mr. Chappel, the captain's boat hereby challenges you to a rowing race!"

Chase fixed me with a narrow look, no doubt thinking that I had gone mad. Chappel said, "To Valparaiso, Captain? Or should we say Rio?"

I said, "Coffin has said that we must do something to break our luck. He says we can't just quit. I agree with him, and so does everyone in this boat. We can't just wait for the wind, we must go after it."

Chappel said, "I'm afraid we cannot."

"And why so?" demanded Chase, suddenly taking to the idea. "We're half sunk and we accept."

"Because of Matt," said the Englishman. "He's sick as hell and can't be tossed about."

Matt Joy, who lay on the seat amidship, then half rose and in a hoarse voice said, "No, Tom, we accept. Here, boys, ease me into the bows and out of your way. We accept and we'll win, too."

"Then you're on, Captain," said Chappel with a grin. "A race for the bloody wind."

Coffin looked at me with a smile and said, "We'll show 'em our wake, won't we, Captain?"

"By God, we will, cousin," I said.

Of course, as races go it wasn't much. The miracle was that anyone could pull an oar at all; and there we were, twelve of us at a time, all who could, each taking a turn until his strength was gone, pulling in slow, ragged strokes through water as still as Hummock Pond, in the cool of the evening, a soaring red twilight abeam of us, as Chappel sounded out a verse now and then to keep his crew together.

> At the Blackwell docks we'll bid adieu
> To lovely Kate and pretty Sue;
> Our anchor's weighed and our sails unfurled
> And we're bound to plow the watery world.
> Hurrah, we're outward bound.

We rowed for almost three hours, the pain of the exertion distracting us from despair, until only a few could still manage an oar. Chase, with his leaking boat, was far behind. Chappel was abeam of me when I called it off, declaring a draw.

Dec. 17–20

At dawn the next morning a light breeze sprang up, causing us almost frenzied feelings of gratitude and joy. We sailed on course for three days until, on the 20th, Hendricks, standing in the bow of my boat, suddenly yelled out, "Land! There is land!"

We had found the wind.

2

All three boats descried the island almost at once, and a cheer went up. I remember Brazilla Ray raising his outstretched hands to the sky and with closed eyes repeating his thanks to the Virgin.

It appeared at first as a faint ultramarine peak in the haze to leeward, with, as we approached, a low white beach and a high, rocky escarpment. Consulting my Bowditch, I determined that it must be Ducie Island, lying at 24°41′S latitude, 124°40′W longitude, a paradise basking in the sea, our deliverance. Yet as we ran down for it my wracked brain began to imagine that it might be populated with savage beasts, cannibals, one-eyed humans, men with heads of birds.

When we landed on the sandy beach I disembarked cautiously, musket in hand, Chase and Chappel with drawn pistols, confronting only the cries of birds from the hills beyond, as the gentle surf lapped at our feet. Then Chappel dropped to his knees, kissed the sand, raised his emaciated arms, and with tears in his eyes cried out, "Blessed, blessed Ducie!"

For an hour we lay on the beach, recovering our strength; then we set forth, unsteady on the firm ground, in small groups or singly to search for food and, far more urgently, water. There was no council of officers, no orders, no plan. Without a word being spoken we all somehow understood that the strict law of equal sharing that applied at sea would not apply here, but rather each would forage for himself, sharing his bounty according to the circumstances. Believing ourselves abundantly provided, we were a free society again. Chase trapped a fish in a tidal pool, killed it, ate part of it, shared part with Cole and Nickerson, who were nearby, and brought the rest to Joy, who stayed by the beached boats, too weak to reconnoiter. Chappel, Wright, Weeks, Coffin, and Ramsdell went into the hills, where they found colorful tropical birds which, being unacquainted with any enemy, could be seized with bare hands from their perches in the trees. The blacks from Chappel's boat gathered small crabs from the rocks. Brazilla Ray and Sam Reed found growths of edible peppergrass. Joe West caught several small fish with a hook and lure.

That evening we built fires and made a copious feast of roasted birds, fish, and peppergrass—but no water had been found, and, with the coming of night, the great joy we had experienced that morning had dimmed.

By the dying fire Chase said, "The damned truth is that if we don't find water we're worse off than before. Getting nowhere, with less chance of rescue here than at sea, and when our water's gone, that's it."

Chappel then said, "There must be water. How does the grass grow? What do the birds drink? There's got to be water."

I said, "We'll search again tomorrow. If we find none we'll put to sea the next day at first light. Agreed?"

"Agreed," said Chase.

"We'll find water," said Chappel. "I can smell it."

Dec. 22

We spent the morning combing the island for signs of moisture. Then about three o'clock a shout went up from the shore beyond a rocky point about a quarter mile from the boats. We converged there to find Chappel and Charles Wright dancing in a circle. The spring they had discovered rose from a crevice in the flat rock, the surfaces of which composed the face of the beach. One after the other my comrades took their fill, my cautions to drink slowly falling on deaf ears. In my turn I drank a little, then a little more every several minutes, as life and hope flooded through me. The Englishman, who now wore a headband of blue, yellow, and red feathers he had fashioned for himself, was beside himself with delight. Turning from Wright, he took Coffin's hands and pranced around the rock, skeletal now, his amber hair flying, his brown eyes bright and wild, calling out to me, "What did I tell you, Captain? We found water! We've come through! We've bloody come through!"

Then Joy, whom we had momentarily forgotten in the excitement of the discovery, crawled up on the wave-worn rocks above us, having somehow dragged himself the distance from the boats. Coffin quickly took up a half-filled keg and carried it to him. Joy did not drink at first. He looked at me steadily—until I understood and nodded. Then he closed his eyes and said, "Thank you, merciful Father." Then he drank.

We then hastened to fill our kegs, for we perceived that at high tide the spring would be submerged. That night, restored, we debated our possible courses of action in the light of the new discovery. Chappel was in favor of setting up housekeeping on the island, building lookout towers, preparing signal fires, awaiting rescue.

"I was born on an island," he said. "I am partial to islands. If Crusoe could survive on a tropical island, then I damn well can too."

Chase said, "How long could we find food? We've already taken all the birds we can find. We can't live on peppergrass."

Chappel looked at Joy and said, "The Good Lord will provide, won't He, Matt? At least fish from the sea?"

"Where they seem quite happy to stay," said Chase, who had been fishing from shore with a hook all morning with no success. "I vote that we stay just long enough to repair the boats. A few days, maybe. No more."

"I agree with the mate," I said.

Dec. 23–25

On this occasion Chase proved to be the better prophet. In the few days we had been on the island we had all but exhausted the food supply of unwary birds, hatchlings, eggs, crabs, even peppergrass. On the 24th, a whole day of foraging produced less than enough to satisfy our hunger. By then the boats were as well repaired as they ever would be, and in the afternoon, after making some computations, I called a parley.

I said, "A thousand miles east by southeast is Easter Island. I say we make for it."

"But what do we know of it?" asked Chase. "Is there food and water there? Is it inhabited?"

"We don't know," I told him. "We've got to take our chances."

Chappel then pounded the sand with the flat of his hand and said, "My dear chaps, I'm taking my chances right here. Dear Ducie's good enough for old Tom."

"You'll die here," said Chase.

Chappel smiled as if he hadn't a care in the world and said, "Then by St. George I'll die on English soil. I hereby claim this bountiful island in the name of the King."

"I'm for putting to sea tomorrow," the mate said.

Joy said, "Sail for Easter Island on Christmas."

I looked around the intent faces of the others, then said, "We put to sea tomorrow morning. Mr. Chappel is staying. Who is staying with him?"

Billy Wright raised his hand. Then slowly, with an anxious glance at me, Seth Weeks raised his too. The blue sea lay waiting beyond his fingers. No one else. I then saw that Owen Coffin was undecided.

The Englishman saw it too. Gently he said, "Owen?"

Torn by conflicting feelings, the boy looked at him, started to speak, caught himself, then turned to me and said, "I'll take my chances in the boat."

By evening Chappel, Wright, and Weeks had built a crude shelter of branches, above the beach, and they spent the night in it, apart from the rest of us, who slept by the boats. Early in the morning I wrote a brief account of the fate of the *Essex* and our situation and intended course, placing it in a tin box and that in a wooden box, which I nailed to a tree, in case the three who were remaining should die before the visit of a ship. I then ordered that firewood be collected, and with Chase chose three flat stones and had one placed in each boat to serve as hearths for cooking fires, should we catch fish or birds and need to preserve the meat from spoiling. When we were ready to sail, Chappel and his companions had not come down to the beach, so Chase and I went up to them. I carried the musket, which I had decided to trade for Chappel's pistol, the larger weapon being, I judged, more suitable for his needs, the smaller for mine. We made the exchange, then I told him that if we were rescued or reached land we would send help as soon as possible and wished them luck.

For once Chappel's wit had deserted him. Solemnly he wished us luck too, and we all shook hands. Seth Weeks was in tears. It was clear that the Englishman was impatient for us to leave. He may have feared that Weeks or Wright might undergo a change of heart; but more than that, I think he sensed as we did that a bond had been broken that now left us strangers. Having chosen different courses, we were no longer companions in a common trial but in a sense rivals for the prize of life, even, it seemed, enemies. Yet Chappel, at the end, just as we were turning away, with a comforting hand on

Weeks's shoulder, called out to us, "See you in Liverpool, gentlemen."

On the beach, when we looked back, the three were gone. We launched our boats, Hendricks taking Chappel's place in the third, and with a fine breeze from the northwest we set sail for Easter Island.

3

Dec. 25–Jan. 2, 1821

With fair wind, sufficient water, and a supply of birds and small fish which we cooked over fires, we were for the first week as comfortable as could be expected, and hopeful. On the 30th the wind hauled out to ESE, directly against us, but on the following day came to northward again, and we resumed our course.

Jan. 3–9

On the 3rd we encountered heavy squalls from the WSW, accompanied by dreadful thunder and lightning, that threw a gloomy and forbidding cast over the ocean and greatly lowered our spirits. We consumed the last of the cooked birds and fish and began again on our short allowance of bread. Then, on the 4th, we discovered by dead reckoning that we had sailed south of the latitude of Easter Island and that, with the wind holding ENE, we would not be able to reach it. We then decided that we had no choice but to set a new course for the nearest easterly landfall toward which the wind would let us sail, ESE to Juan Fernández Island off the coast of Chile—a distance of twenty-five hundred miles.

Jan. 10

On this calm, hot, hazy morning Hendricks called out to me that during the night Matthew Joy had become delirious and was very sick. Since there were then seven in the third boat and five in mine, I ordered that the invalid be placed in my boat, where he could be a little more comfortable. This was done and we settled him as best we could, as he moaned and tossed from side to side. Toward midday he was quieter and seemed to rest easily; then he opened his eyes, raised his head, surprised to find himself where he was, then urgently said, "Captain, I must be with my own crew."

"You're sick, Matt," I said.

"I'm all right," he insisted. "I must be in my own boat."

Unaware that for weeks his boat had been in the charge of Chappel and now of Hendricks, Joy pleaded with me until, certain that he could not live much longer, I called to Hendricks, "Obed, Mr. Joy will take command of his boat again." Hendricks understood at once, and Joy was eased into the stern of the third boat, where Hendricks handed him the mainsail sheet.

"How far to Easter Island?" asked Joy then.

"A day, sir," said Hendricks. "Maybe two."

Joy nodded, smiled, then his eyes turned upward and he fell forward into Hendricks's arms and was dead.

The next morning Joy's boatmates sewed him up in his clothes and secured the cooking stone to his ankles. We then brought the boats to and prepared to bury him in the sea. All looked to me for something that would pass for a Christian ceremony, knowing how Joy had set store by such matters. For a moment I looked to Coffin, but this time found the words myself, such as they were. I said, "Our shipmate Matthew Joy is dead, and if he is entering the Kingdom of Heaven for eternity I say that his short life was still a voyage worth the making and done in seamanly fashion to the end. And I say too that the fact that that voyage is over doesn't take a damned thing away from it. His suffering is done with. God knows what's ahead for us. Let's think of Matt and, by Christ, let's all take strength from his damned bravery and his damned faith and—Oh, God damn it, boys—over the side with him!"

Joy's boatmates then committed his body to the deep, as they say, and the ceremony was over. We stood again on our course; but the loss of Matt Joy cast a pall over our feelings for many days. I still remember him as an uncommonly good man and have sometimes wondered whether his virtue had anything to do with his being taken first.

Jan. 12

We had the wind from the NW, where we wanted it, and it rose steadily until by afternoon it was blowing a gale, and we had to take in sail and run before it. Never had we made such distance. By evening thunder shook the sea; lightning flashed all around us; the rain came down in cataracts. Chase, Hendricks, and I rode the waves like men possessed, exulting in the fury of the storm that sped us on our course. Our one apprehension was that we would lose one another, so we sailed as close together as we dared and kept constant watch. About eleven it was blowing and raining as if the heavens would separate. In the eerie light of receding lightning I saw Chase's boat on the crest of a wave ahead, then turned to find Hendricks just behind me to leeward; but when I looked again for Chase's boat it was gone. I held our ESE course, thinking that the mate might have hove to ahead, or that at worst by daylight we would rejoin him. At dawn Hendricks and I searched the green waves as if our very hopes must bring Chase's boat into sight, but in vain.

4

Jan. 14

On this chill gray morning Hendricks, his boat about a ship's length to windward of us, held up the keg that had contained his bread supply and overturned it to show that it was empty. The moment we had dreaded was upon us. The third boat was without food. Ours had enough for five or six days—for us alone. Were we to share equally with the other boat? What law, precedent, or instinct was to guide me? By noon Hendricks had asked for nothing. I had offered nothing.

That afternoon another visitation of dolphins distracted us from our dilemma. As they played around each boat, Hendricks and I rigged makeshift harpoons from knives and sprit poles and attempted to kill one, without success. That night we in our boat forewent our bread ration and, as the wind freshened from the north, I was many times tempted to fall off our course and leave Hendricks and his crew to their own fate; but great as this temptation was—disguised as a noble duty to my own crew—I could not bring myself to do it. At midnight Coffin relieved me and I managed to get some sleep.

Jan. 15

By the first pink streaks of dawn abaft I awoke to see my cousin staring to windward, a look of horror on his lean youthful face. I sat up. Ramsdell, Reed, and Ray were also staring speechless across the heavy sea. The third boat was about two ship's lengths from us, rising on the crests, then dipping out of sight. At first I could not make out what was happening in it. Then, as the rays of the rising sun raked the wave tops, the boat was suddenly presented to our sight on the slope of a wave. The body of a black man lay across the thwart amidships. Hendricks, using a boarding knife, was extracting the heart. William Bond was in the bows retching over the side. The boat then dropped below a wave. When it reappeared, Hendricks was drinking from the heart as skeletal arms seized up at his hands.

I am now summoning long-sequestered memories, with little help from Chase's *Narrative,* even though his experiences after his separation from us were—up to a point—similar to our own. I still kept a rough log in my Bowditch, the entry for the 15th reading, "Lawson Thomas died. Consumed for food in the 3rd boat. Fairly heavy swells. Wind NNE."

My log does not show that I had begun to dream of banquets.

Jan. 16–20

By this time we were too weakened to distinguish clearly between present terrors and imagined ones. The night of the 17th began for me with a nightmare. I was taking late supper with my Aunt Nancy in her cozy kitchen on Broad Street. In the dream there was a teasing question about whether we were related. The table was laden with delicious food, chowder, a roast of some sort, bread and butter, pies and puddings, none of which we touched because—that was the terrible question in the dream: why did we only look at each other, never touching the food? Only then did I realize that a third place was set at the table. And then, outside in the dark, a shadowy figure passed the windows. Nancy reached for my hand as if to reassure me that there was nothing to fear. Then the kitchen door burst open and a man's figure filled the entrance. It was Hezekiah, his head battered and bloody, glaring at me.

I remember the dream because over the years it has recurred.

I started awake, but no sooner had I fought free of the nightmare than in the sea all around us I heard cavernous blowing sounds that I recognized at once as whale spouts. I prayed that this was a continuation of my dream, but it was not; we were in the midst of a shoal of cachalots.

We clung to the gunwales to keep in balance in the swirling wakes of the whales, drenched by their warm spray, fearing at every moment that one would nudge us to a watery death; but in a few minutes they parted company with us, having inflicted no damage.

For the rest of the night I stayed awake, then slept at dawn.

Jan. 21

This morning we consumed the last of our bread. Only a few gills of foul water remained. Hendricks, who during the butchering of Thomas's body had kept a distance from us, then drew near. Having separated the limbs from the body and thrown the torso overboard, he and his crew had then to cook the yet uneaten meat or it would soon spoil. The only cooking stone was in our boat, theirs having served to bury Matthew Joy decently.

If words were exchanged between the boats, I don't remember what was said. Our throats were parched, our stomachs feeding on themselves, minds benumbed, only a shrewd rage to live governing our actions; what was done was done by communal assent, by swift hands, our eyes averted from one another.

We prepared a fire, roasted the meat, then shared it between the boats, in each of which it was divided equally. For the first time since leaving the wreck I slept soundly through the night.

Jan. 23

(My notes continue the story clearly enough.) "Chas. Shorter died in 3rd boat, shared by 2 boats. Wind NNE."

Jan. 27

"Isaiah Shepherd died in 3rd boat, shared by 2 boats. Wind hauled to NNW."

Jan. 28

"Samuel Reed died in 1st boat, shared by 2 boats. Wind held NNW."

The death of Sam Reed affected me deeply. He was then nineteen, a big, simple-hearted boy of mingled African and Portuguese blood, docile but with a will of incredible strength, as he proved that day. At about eleven, on that fair morning with a fresh favorable wind, he said to me, "Captain, *I beg your pardon,* but I don't want to live no more." I tried to hearten him, as did Coffin, but Reed had made up his mind and there was no way of changing it. When Ray told him that it was a sin to take his own life, Reed replied, "Ain't takin' it, just lettin' it get took." Then, suddenly fearful, he looked to me and asked, "It's all right, ain't it, Captain? Ain't no sin, is it?"

"No," I told him. "It's all right." Ray said nothing more.

So Sam Reed lay down in the bows and closed his eyes. He lay there all afternoon. At sundown, with hardly a sigh, he let his life be taken.

Over the years I have sometimes wondered about the fate of the blacks in my charge. Of the seven who signed on the *Essex,* only Mamula, who had left her in Tecamus, may be presumed to have survived. All the other six died in the boats, and with the exception of Joy (who was sick from the start of the voyage) they were the first to die. Throughout our ordeal they had received the same rations and treatment as the whites. And it

might be thought that their pigmentation better adapted them
to endure the tropical sun. Yet (save Joy) they all died first,
whether by chance or not I do not know. Was there some
reason? Was it perhaps because of some inherited spiritual
injury from the Middle Passage and bondage? Or because,
benefiting from a purer religion, a stronger faith in the hereafter, they clung less desperately to life in this world? Or because they were, with their heat-absorbing pigmentation, more
vulnerable to drying out? I have no answer.

Jan. 29

This morning a squall overtook us, and we unshipped masts
and abandoned ourselves to the wind and the waves. When by
afternoon the storm began to moderate, we found that Hendricks's boat was nowhere in sight. Coffin, Ramsdell, Ray, and
I were now alone, weeks from the South American coast, without food or water.

Feb. 5

No one of us suggested it. It was not necessary. The question
had been whether anyone would weaken and die, as the blacks
had done, before our need became unbearable. Now, on this
day, by the time the midday sun was beating down on us hunger
was gnawing at our very reason, and our desperate glances at
one another announced that the time had come to decide which
one of us must die to keep the others alive a little longer. There
was no wind, and under a sky that seemed filled by the pulsing
sun the boat rose and fell gently on the blue-green swells. How
to decide? Whatever else, I told myself, it must be done fairly
—by lots, each of us four given an equal chance. If not, we
would all succumb to unspeakable savagery. Dimly I remembered tales I had heard as a boy on the wharves, of castaways
eating their dead, of drawing lots to determine who would be
killed, and the names of ships, *Drot, Medusa,* whose crews had

been obliged to resort to a custom of the sea as ancient as ocean voyaging. What ruled me then was the feeling that what was happening was *determined* and that I, as captain, was responsible for letting it unfold as it must. I was sitting on the decking in the stern, Coffin near me on the sternmost thwart, Ramsdell and Ray on the tub oarsman's thwart, just forward of him. I took the pistol from my sea chest and set it on the thwart beside my cousin, within reach of all. No one spoke. I then tore a page from the Bowditch and folded and tore four strips of equal width from the margin, three of them about two inches long, the fourth one an inch. I held up the short strip, saying, "Whoever draws this gives his life for his shipmates. Then we'll draw again for who does it. Agreed?"

All three nodded assent.

I then turned my back and arranged the strips in my hand so that four equal ends appeared. I turned again, and because he was nearest offered them first to Coffin.

He hesitated a moment, then drew the short strip.

I looked at him, frozen in horror. I had prepared myself for my own death but not for his. I started to speak but could find no words. I watched his face compose into resignation, and quietly he said to me, "Tell my mother I love her. Tell her how I died."

"Owen—" I said, but he shook his head sharply, and I realized that he was telling me urgently that what had been begun must proceed as we had agreed, without delay or doubt, that the giving of his life must happen as if it were decreed. With trembling hands I tore one of the remaining strips in half, arranged them, and offered three even ends to Ray. He drew a long one. My heart pounding, I offered the last two to Ramsdell.

He drew the short strip.

He stared at the pistol a moment, then said, "I cannot. I will change places with you, Owen."

Firmly, in an anguished voice, Owen Coffin said, "No. You must do it, Charles. And quickly, too. I forgive you and God will too."

When Ramsdell started to reach for the pistol, I became frantic and, seizing the weapon myself, I cried out, "Owen, if you don't like your lot I'll shoot the first man who touches you! I will take your place!"

With perfect calm, as if he were already beyond suffering, care, or human tie, he replied, "I like my lot as well as any other. Quickly, Charles, quickly." And he lay across the thwart with his head on the gunwale. Ramsdell then took the pistol from my hand and shot his friend through the temple.

5

We subsisted on Coffin's roasted flesh until on the morning of February 11 Ramsdell and I found Brazilla Ray dead, and we lived on his flesh until it was gone. After that our scant remaining strength began to fail rapidly and, though the weather held fair, we could barely manage to keep the boat on our ESE course. Our burned, bearded faces were hollow-eyed; sores kept our lips parted. By then hallucinations, dreams, reality had become one. I saw dolphins, but when I tried to lance them they became girls in bright-colored dresses running, laughing, across a summery Nantucket moor. I ran after them but soon found myself alone on the highest place on the Island, Altar Rock.

All my forces were now expended in the struggle for the possession of my reason, against the sun, against the immensity of the sea, against whatever power, real or imagined, threatened to destroy it. Even the cravings of hunger and thirst were now less urgent than the preservation of my sanity. One evening, about the 16th or 17th, Ramsdell lay down in the bows and when I asked him if he was all right he said, "Goodbye, Captain. I won't be seeing the dawn."

I went near him and pleaded with him, telling him that with every hour as we approached the coastal waters rescue was more likely and that he must hang on. I was in great fear of his dying, for I sensed that alone I would quickly slip into madness and a lonely raving death. Whatever had gone before, I now desperately needed Ramsdell—as he needed me—*alive.* He seemed to understand this and spoke no more about not seeing the dawn.

We were by then too weak to be any threat to each other.

Feb. 18–23

I have no memories of the following days, until the 23rd, and then only vague ones of voices, powerful hands lifting us into a boat, onto a ship's deck, then below into bunks. I would learn that as I was being taken from our boat, the strongest seamen from the whaleship *Dauphin* of Nantucket could not pry loose the bones I held locked in my arms.

Part Four

HOMECOMING

1

Zimri was his name. You will find it in the Book of Numbers, which tells how the original Zimri was impaled with a Midianite woman by a javelin hurled by one Phineas which thrust through them both. That, and the fact that the Lord, being pleased by Phineas's deed, stayed a plague from the children of Israel, is all that is certain. Clearly Zimri made a serious mistake in bringing the Midianite woman, as he did, into the sight of Moses and the children of Israel. You wonder why he did it.

This Zimri was Zimri Coffin, master of the *Dauphin*, about thirty-five years old then, and, being of a different branch of Tristram's tribe, only a distant relation to Owen. When his crewmen eased me and Ramsdell over the bulwarks onto the deck I knew him at once but, at the time, could not put a name to that beard-rimmed round face with sky-blue eyes set in consternation. Though we were known to one another on Nantucket, he at first did not identify us. And little wonder. We lay there gasping in the sun like sea monsters hauled up from the deep, our ulcerated bodies skeletal, the bones breaking through the skin, our lips thick with sores, our clothes in rags. At last one of the Nantucket lads looking on cried out, "My God, that's Charlie Ramsdell!" And Zimri Coffin came closer to me and said, "George Pollard? Can it be George Pollard from Polpis?"

The next thing I remember was awakening on a bed in a cabin of some sort. Captain Coffin sat beside me; another, heavy-jowled man wearing a black reefer coat watched me from a desk chair. For a moment I had no idea where I was or how I had come to be there, and I was filled with alarm. Zimri Coffin, sensing what was the matter, put his rough hand to my brow and said, "Rest easy, Captain Pollard. I'm Zimri Coffin and you're berthed in my office on board the *Dauphin*. This gentleman's Aaron Paddack, master of the *Diana,* on board for a gam. We were cruising for whales east of St. Mary's Island where we fished you up this morning. Date's February twenty-third, 1821. Here, now, have a go at this."

And with his own hands he fed me a gruel of rice.

When I had eaten a few spoonfuls, I lay back in exhaustion. Captain Paddack said, "Damn me, Pollard, looks like you've been through hell."

"Time for that," said my host.

"How's Ramsdell?" I managed to ask.

"Pretty low," said Coffin. "But he'll pull through, and you will too if I have anything to say about it. Damned if I fish you up just to throw you back again."

"What the devil did happen?" asked Paddack.

"Time for that," said Coffin again, though with less insistence.

"We were stove by a whale."

"Your boat?" demanded Paddack.

"Our ship. The *Essex.* "

The two captains looked at me in silence.

"Sunk?" asked Zimri Coffin.

"On the Line. One hundred and nineteen degrees west."

Paddack whistled softly. "When?"

"Twentieth of November."

Zimri Coffin made a mental calculation. "Then you been in the boat—more'n ninety days."

"Ninety-one."

"What about provisions?" asked Paddack.

"We had bread and water for a time," I said, as a wave of dizziness hit me. "There were two other boats," I said with difficulty. "We were separated. No word of them?"

"None we've heard," said Zimri Coffin.

It was growing dark. He lit the lamp over the desk. Paddack said, "You say you had bread and water for a time."

Both men stared at me in silence, hardly breathing. I remembered that an item of human bones stood between us. Sheltered from wind, sun, and wave, I felt that I was now adrift in a new and threatening element. Again vertigo overcame me and I lost consciousness.

When I came to my senses, Zimri Coffin and Paddack were speaking softly to each other. On deck seven bells sounded. Paddack was saying, "Wonder if he's off his head?" And my host replied, "Poor fellow might be better so." Then they perceived that I was awake, and broke off. I sat up, suddenly filled with a pressing need to tell these good men everything that had happened, as if to pour out my story would lighten its burden.

They listened spellbound as I rasped out the tale. I told them of the whale's attack, our council in the boats, our first struggles and hardships. I amazed myself by my lucidity and coolness. I told them of the three who had chosen to remain on Ducie Island, urging that the news be conveyed as soon as possible to the American authorities in Valparaiso so that a rescue might be undertaken. In describing the death of Matthew Joy I faltered, but recovered myself and in relating the first uses of the dead for food I spoke as unemotionally and incisively as if I were recounting a maritime incident to an underwriter. I was bent on explaining the events to these experienced and judicious whalemen in the clearest possible light, confident that they would understand the extremities to which we were driven. Then, as I began to tell of the lottery and of the execution of

Owen Coffin, I found that my whole body was shaking uncon-
trollably.

"It was the only thing left for us to do," I said, trying to
conceal the trembling from the two captains, who were staring
at me in alarm. "It was the only fair way to give some of us a
chance to live a few days more. It was that or die, all of us, an
awful death, perhaps barbaric, become animals. You see, by
then—" I broke off, aware that I had been speaking more and
more rapidly—*reasoning*—to distract my auditors from my
violent shaking. Then, summoning all my will, I went on, "We
all agreed. We were all prepared to die. When Coffin drew the
short paper I offered to take his place. Ramsdell did too. Owen
refused. You see, he was determined to die like a man. And he
did! By God, he did!"

Then the cabin was filled with a sound like the howl of a
dying animal. I remember the captains watching me, frozen, as
I realized that the ungodly sound in the cabin was issuing from
me and that I had no power to stop it.

Zimri Coffin sailed for a week after whales in the company of
the *Diana*. The fair weather held, but not a spout was raised.
Thoughts of the fate of Chappel, Wright, and Weeks weighed
on me, and, still weakened and unsteady, I was increasingly
impatient to reach Valparaiso. Coffin, however, was not prepared to leave the cruising grounds and would not touch at St.
Mary's Island, which in the year since the *Essex* had been there
had become a stronghold of royalist pirates. He assured me that
we would soon be raising a ship bound for Valparaiso, but one
balmy day followed another with no sail but the *Diana* in sight.

On the fourth day after our rescue, Ramsdell and I were both
able to come on deck. That first meeting on board the *Dauphin*

was an unsettling one. I asked the boy how he was feeling. He lowered his eyes, then slowly looked up at me.

"I wish to holy God I'd taken Owen's place," he said in a broken voice.

"You offered to," I told him. "You offered to in good faith, and he refused."

Suddenly his eyes filled with tears. "Did I?" he said defiantly. "Is that what is called good faith? Or was I damned sure he'd refuse, same as he refused you?"

"You mustn't blame yourself. He wanted it to be as we agreed. He wanted to die an honorable death."

Ramsdell laughed dryly, then smiled at me. "Well, we didn't stand in his way, did we?"

Anger stirred in me. I said, "You were prepared to take his place. So was I. He wouldn't go back on his word. We must remember how it really was."

He looked at me a long time, then quietly said, "I murdered him. That's how it really was. He was the only friend I ever had, and I murdered him. I wish to God I'd died in his place."

Shaken, I fairly shouted at him, "It was not murder! We had no choice! We drew lots! We followed the custom of the sea!"

He stared at me in disbelief. "The custom of the sea?"

"No man alive can say it was murder."

A slow, terrible smile transformed his face.

"No dead man either."

I found nothing to say. After a moment he turned from me and went below to the steerage. I went to the bulwarks and stood looking out to sea, eastward to a line of fair weather clouds.

On the morning of March 3 a sail was raised, and by midday the vessel hove to a ship's length to leeward of us. She was the Nantucket whaleship *Two Brothers.* I recognized her master as he swung down into a lowered boat, Captain George Worth, a massive bear of a man in his late sixties, a broad-brimmed black hat clamped squarely on his white-maned head. It was said of Worth that in his career he had sailed a million miles, taken tens of thousands of barrels, all without losing a man. His seamanship and knowledge of whaling craft were unmatched, and ashore as well as at sea his judgment on any matter generally settled the argument. As Zimri Coffin greeted him in the waist —speaking intently and nodding in my direction—I suddenly felt apprehensive, realizing that Captain Worth's assessment of my conduct following the loss of the *Essex* might well predict the character of my reception on Nantucket.

At the cabin table with Zimri Coffin at its head, Worth and I facing each other, I repeated the story, this time keeping myself in control, and yet under Worth's steady gaze, my conversations with Ramsdell fresh in mind, I heard myself recounting the events in a manner calculated to disarm criticism—and I was certain that Worth was hearing my recitation in the same way.

When I fell silent he puffed slowly at a blackened briar pipe, then said, "Can't see what kept you from running with the trades and currents to the Sandwich Islands."

"We feared the winter *konas.*"

"And the Marquesas?"

"We feared the natives."

"Pitcairn?"

"It's not in Bowditch. We didn't know its bearing."

"Who proposed the lottery?"

I remembered the desperate, emaciated faces of Owen Coffin, Ramsdell, and Ray looking at me. "We all knew that one of us had to die. I proposed the way of deciding. The lottery was accepted by all of us."

Zimri Coffin said, "Surely that will be understood ashore."

Looking at me steadily through drifting strands of blue smoke, Captain Worth replied, "Damned little will be understood ashore."

At this, Zimri Coffin appeared distressed, protective of his prize catch. "Worth, you can't mean that these brave men who have suffered so much will be brought to some sort of lubberly judgment?"

"Hell no," said Worth. "Not if you mean an inquiry or a criminal indictment. They won't take that on themselves. You can bank on that." Then, his eyes still fixed on me, he added, "Damned little will be understood—and nothing will be settled. Ever. Best get used to that, Pollard."

Dauphin, Diana, and *Two Brothers* cruised together, providing one another security against both pirates and the navy of the new Chilean government, which at that time had a habit of impounding neutral vessels suspected of having dealings with the royalist enemy. The weather had worsened, and by late afternoon on March 5 two separate rain squalls stood on the fiery western horizon. A fourth vessel was then sighted bearing for us from the north. After some apprehension the ship was identified as another Nantucket whaler, the *Hero.* Then, as she hove to, we saw that from her mainmast she flew the black pennant signifying death or distress.

Obed Starbuck had not slept in two days. In the *Dauphin*'s cabin, rain starting to hammer on the skylight, Zimri Coffin, Paddack, Worth, and I listened as that young man about my own age, the first mate and now acting master of the *Hero,* related what had befallen his ship.

On February 26 the vessel's master, James Russell (a cousin of the former captain of the *Essex*), had rashly put in at St. Mary's Island, taken a whale in the bay, and cut it in. On the morning of the 27th two boats from the mainland port of Arauco came alongside and ordered the captain to go ashore and see the governor. The captain complied, supposing that only a formality was in question, not yet knowing that the "governor" was in fact the royalist pirate General Benavides, and the men in the boats members of his private army of looters and murderers. The captain and his crew were detained ashore, while three armed boats approached the ship, fired on her, then boarded and took possession of her. During the next three days the pirates looted provisions, oil, loose gear, and personal property, including the captain's trunks. They then cut the *Hero*'s cables, taking all her boats except one. With the vessel drifting toward the beach, Starbuck and the remnant of the crew quickly set sail and, owing to a favorable wind, managed to elude the boats launched to retake her. He then decided to make for Valparaiso to seek help.

"I had no choice," the distraught youth continued. "I couldn't rescue the captain and his men from an armed garrison, and I was damned if I'd surrender the ship to those renegades."

"You did what had to be done," said Worth.

"We'll see you provisioned for the run to Valparaiso," said Zimri Coffin.

Then for the first time Starbuck fixed his attention on me, no doubt struck by my cadaverous aspect and unable to account for my presence.

"You're George Pollard," he said. "Master of the *Essex.*"

"I am George Pollard," I told him.

Then Zimri Coffin told him our story.

In the sallow light in the cabin, the rain now driving in sheets above our heads, Obed Starbuck stared at me incredulously, indeed with a look that made my own flesh crawl.

"Damnable thing," he said at last. "Damnable."

I asked, "When do you sail for Valparaiso?"

"At first light. I must sleep first."

"Will you take Ramsdell and me? I must send help to my men on the island."

Starbuck hesitated, still looking at me in disbelief. Zimri Coffin put his hand on my shoulder and said, "You're better off here till you've mended a bit. Starbuck'll have all he can do sailing shorthanded. He can get help on its way to your men."

"You understand?" said Starbuck.

"Yes," I told him.

"What island?"

"Ducie."

"Ducie," he repeated, then looked at me a last time, nodded to Coffin and Worth, then in great agitation rushed up the companionway as if it were a relief to be going on deck in a driving rainstorm. Zimri Coffin followed him.

I was badly shaken by the encounter. Captain Worth seemed to read my thoughts when he said, "You'll have to get used to people not seeing you for the pictures in their heads."

I looked at him without replying.

"Main thing is not to let yourself become what they see."

I reflected a moment, then said, "I won't."

"You'll have to get by on your own—more than most of us do."

"Will any owner give me another command?"

"Want one, do you?"

"More than anything. More than anything in the world."

"Figured you might." He pulled at his pipe, then said, "I'd say there's a fair chance. Those fellows are businessmen. They believe in odds, and the odds are that you've had your share of trouble for the rest of your life."

For another week we cruised in company with the *Diana* and the *Two Brothers,* raising no whales. Then on March 12 Captain

Worth came on board and informed us that on the following morning he would be sailing for Valparaiso for provisions and, if we wished, would ship me and Ramsdell as passengers. I was heartened by the news. Zimri Coffin, however, seemed sorry to let us go.

"Take good care of 'em," he told Worth. "They're still pretty shaky."

"Don't fret, Zimri. I won't let anything happen to your babies."

"Goodbye then, Pollard. And good luck to you."

"You saved our lives," I told him. "I'm grateful to you."

"Won't hear a damned word of it," he said gruffly. "It's a fair trade for the reputation I'll have in my old age. 'See that fellow,' they'll say. 'That's old Zimri Coffin, same what fished up the captain of the *Essex*.'"

With light winds from the southeast, the *Two Brothers* was three days beating down to Valparaiso. On the south wind I could smell the land before I saw it. Then slowly, out of the morning haze the blue coastal hills appeared, then the headlands that formed the north-facing bay, and finally the town: the presidio, parade grounds, custom house, warehouses, wharves, and above on the hillsides sand-and-mustard-hued dwellings with gardens. As we worked in on short reaches, the smell of land, of earth and grass, gave way to the aromas of human settlement, of cooking, laundry, wood fires, cordage. There were two vessels at the wharves and more riding at anchor, among them four whaleships. We turned into the light breeze and dropped anchor two ship's lengths from the largest ship in the port, the U.S. frigate *Macedonian*.

At her taffrail, waving to me, was Chase.

2

As Worth and I were being rowed to the *Macedonian,* I experienced a feeling of intense well-being and an abnormal acuity of the senses. The sky was the bluest blue, the water the greenest green, the air pungent with life. I was not yet aware that my condition was an early symptom of a sickness that was then stealthily invading me. The sudden sight of Chase, alive and safe, and the assurance that through him help must be on its way to Ducie Island produced an easing of my spirit's struggle that left my body defenseless.

Worth, I discovered, was acquainted with the commander of the *Macedonian,* Commodore Jacob Downes.

"Spit-and-polish Navy," he told me. "Thinks whalemen are the scum of the seas. Worse luck, he's the ranking American authority in Valparaiso at the moment. Lately it was Commodore Ridgely of the *Constellation* till he sailed for Coquimbo. The consul finished his tour and lit out over the mountains for Rio. New consul's overdue and God knows where. So it's Downes, which is worse than nothing. Ridgely's a damn good man."

It was Sunday, and because it was the Sabbath the officers and all hands on board the commodore's flagship wore dress whites. The deck had been holystoned bone-white. Spars gleamed with varnish. Bulwarks and cannon shone glossy black in the sun. Brightwork glittered. A bosun's pipe shrilled and a petty officer conducted us toward the quarterdeck, where Commodore Downes awaited us. He was a tall, fleshy officer of fifty or so, his narrowed eyes shaded by a gold-encrusted fore-and-aft hat. In his arms he cradled a large white cat of a long-haired breed. A step behind the commodore stood a commander and two lieutenants, arms locked behind their backs. Around and above us were a number of sailors and petty officers who had found reasons to gather near the quarterdeck or climb in the mizzen rigging for a look at the castaways.

A little apart from the officers, dressed in blue dungarees and a white jacket, stood Chase, as gaunt and burned as I. I went to him and seized him by the shoulders.

"Thank God, you're alive," I said.

He smiled and said, "Seems we made it, Captain."

"Your crew?"

"Only Lawrence and Nickerson."

"Hendricks?"

"No word yet."

"Chappel?"

Before he could answer, the commodore, slowly stroking the white cat, replied for him: "Captain Pollard, I am pleased to inform you that before his departure for Coquimbo, Commodore Ridgely arranged for the rescue of Mr. Chappel and the other two who were left on the island. A merchant vessel bound for Australia. If they're alive they'll be saved—and at minimum public expense."

In the commodore's cold eyes and set features I could feel his contempt. Never in my life had I felt such contempt.

"I am grateful to Commodore Ridgely," I said, warning myself to batten down my temper.

Just then, from forward, a signalman approached one of the lieutenants and whispered something into his ear, at which the lieutenant whispered into the commander's ear, and the commander squared himself, approached the commodore, and whispered into that august ear.

Downes then frowned and announced, "Gentlemen, I have just been informed that Captain Russell of the whaleship *Hero* and his boat crew have been taken prisoner by General Benavides at Arauco. Most unfortunate, of course. Damned nuisance, in fact. Never would have happened if Russell hadn't put in at St. Mary's. Every shipmaster in the Pacific knows about Benavides."

"Russell was fast to a whale," I said.

The commodore examined me in pained surprise.

"That whale, sir, was in waters controlled by a murderous renegade with a small army of heavily armed cutthroats."

Worth said, "Then why, sir, hasn't something been done about heavily armed cutthroats controlling the cruising grounds of American whaleships?"

The commodore continued stroking the cat with smoldering calm until that animal, sensing trouble, suddenly shot from his arms.

He drew a weary breath and said, "We are on station here to assure the political stability of the region, gentlemen. We are here under the orders of the Secretary and President Monroe to deter any foreign intervention which might threaten the new government of Chile. We are not here to make war on pirates." And though he didn't utter it, his next thought was plain enough: Nor play nursemaid to reckless blubber-hunters.

I said, "So Russell and his crew remain prisoners?"

"We have no authority to enter General Benavides's territory, if that is what you're suggesting, young man."

Worth intervened sharply: "I'd venture a guess you've no orders not to. I doubt that it's the intention of the Secretary and the President to let American citizens on lawful business be locked up by pirates. Damn it, man, what are these guns for?"

Then, when the commodore turned red and began to breathe

heavily, Worth inquired, "Is it a question of public expense, sir?"

Speechless now, the commodore looked at me, and I turned to Worth and said, "Surely not, Captain. I'm damned surprised you'd suggest such a thing. I'm sure that the commodore has far better reasons not to run afoul of Benavides."

Commodore Downes drew himself up and declared, "Gentlemen, the *Macedonian* sails for Rio on Monday at first light. Our tour of duty is completed here, and we are not about to engage the government of the United States in foolhardy adventures."

"There, you see, Captain Pollard?" said Worth. "There's your reason. Vessel's completed her tour of duty and ain't about to go looking for trouble. Captain Russell's and his crew's families will certainly understand that."

That set-to must have proved to Commodore Downes's satisfaction that Nantucket whalemen are not gentlemen fit to share the seas with the Navy, which he was determined to believe all along anyway. We didn't let him down. While that incident didn't reflect much credit on anyone concerned, it was a revelation to me. For the first time I had confronted a mainlander who expected a Nantucket whaleman to behave with the servility befitting an outcast from human society. With the help of Worth I disappointed him, but I did not forget the lesson.

I don't remember leaving the *Macedonian.* Worth told me afterward that I'd held on until we were back on the *Two Brothers,* then become delirious and lost consciousness. Of the next several days I have only random memories. My first clear recollection is of awakening in a comfortable room with windows overlooking Valparaiso harbor. Owen Chase was seated in a rattan chair, gazing out to the horizon.

Hearing me stir, he turned. "How are you feeling, Captain?"

"Where are we? What day is this?"

"Consul's house. Tuesday. You've been very sick."

Chase told me then that after the departure of the *Macedonian,* Worth had arranged to settle me here, under the care of a Chilean physician and the Indian housekeeper, who lived in the house with her young son. Worth had then put to sea again in the hope of filling his ship, though not before parleying with the master of the Nantucket whaleship *Eagle,* who had agreed to ferry Chase and the other *Essex* survivors around the Horn and home. I alone was to remain in Valparaiso.

"Worth insisted you were in no shape to go to sea, and that I should see to it that you stayed ashore until he came back for you. Said something about keeping a promise to Zimri Coffin and that he'd ship you home himself on the *Two Brothers.* You've a friend there, Captain. He admired the way you stood up to the commodore when you were damn near dying on your feet."

"Then I can thank Commodore Downes for something."

"Peacock!" spat Chase, then bitterly he said, "Anyway, didn't make any difference, his not going for Russell and his men."

"They were released?"

"Shot. About the same time we were on the *Macedonian.*"

In my half-roasted brain I could picture the firing squad, the execution, but could summon no grief for dead men I had never known. I had none to spare.

Then Chase asked, "You'll stay on?"

I nodded. "Can't disobey Worth. Besides, I don't want to go back like this. We'll need all the strength we've got once we're 'round Brant Point." We fell silent, then with difficulty I said, "I guess you heard how Owen Coffin died?"

"Starbuck."

"It was awful, Chase. Damned awful." I hardly got the words out before I burst into tears, burying my face in my hands. Chase came to the bed and put his hand on my shoulder.

When my sobs eased a little he said, "You had no choice. I'd have done the same thing. Damn near did too, but the Lord provided."

I looked at him feeling as if after a youth together and seven years at sea in close quarters I was seeing him truly for the first time. "I'm grateful for that, Chase."

He smiled and said, "We just had a little bad luck."

Fever swept through me. "That's all?"

"That's all."

"Chase?"

"Captain?"

"You said on the day of the wreck that the whale came at the ship with purpose."

"I'm sure of it."

"I've thought a lot about him."

"He's not been out of my mind long."

"An old squire with his best days long past."

"Traveling out of the herd."

"But not far. He could hear their singing and their screams when our irons bit into them."

"And our hammering when we worked on the boat."

I nodded. "He'd had all he could take."

"Yes."

"And that's all?"

The mate reflected a moment, never taking his eyes off me, then said, "Even if there was anything more to it we'd never fathom it, so what's the use of thinking about it?"

Before Chase left he gave me a letter that an outward-bound whaler had left with the *Eagle.* I recognized Mary's fine hand. Then he said, "By the way, seems I'm a father."

"Congratulations," I told him, then scanned the letter in my hand. "Seems I'm not."

"Stay with you if you like."

I knew he meant it. Moved, I said almost roughly, "Thanks, my friend, but you hurry back to Frances and that young one of yours. I'll be all right. I'll be sending the housekeeper's boy with a letter for Mary before you sail."

We shook hands, and he started to leave. In the doorway with the glare of the bay behind him, the *Eagle* riding at anchor, he turned and with a wave said, "See you in Liverpool."

Then he started down the stairs to the dusty street.

Though we could not bring ourselves to speak of these matters then, I was to learn that Chase and his fellow survivors had also, after our separation, endured extreme suffering and horrors. On February 8, Isaac Cole had died in convulsions and, at Chase's suggestion, been butchered the following morning and, over the next few days, consumed. After that food was gone, Chase considered following the same dread custom that we had resorted to, but before this became necessary was rescued by the brig *Indian,* out of London, on February 18, six days before Ramsdell and I were taken on board the *Dauphin.*

3

46 Centre St.
June 14, 1820

My very dear husband,

I write you on this June day which you may (or may not) recognize as being the anniversary of our marriage.

Last Saturday I was very pleased to receive a letter from
you through the courtesy of Captain Stevens, who was
good enough to deliver it to me personally. He assured me
that when he left you at St. Mary's Island you were in fine
health and spirits and, though I should not turn your
head, he said that you are very highly regarded throughout the Nantucket whale fishery, especially in view of your
age, and I can assure you that this report made me proud
indeed. I hope that by the time this reaches you Mr.
Chappel will have mended his impertinent ways and that
Matt Joy will have improved in health. After much
thought I decided not to tell Nan that he was not better
since such news could only worry her to no avail, and I
can tell you that whatever we may say and how brave or
untroubled we may appear, Nantucket whalemen's wives
do worry, and rather a lot too if you must know. Of
course, I promptly transmitted to the other Nancy your
high commendation of Owen, and I think that she is now
a little more reconciled to his having gone to sea, and
showed pleasure upon hearing your words of praise,
which I read aloud to her. Your little niece Ann is becoming a very engaging young lady with a gentle yet strong
nature not unlike her brother's and none of the contrari-
ness of so many eleven-year-old females. As she has a high
opinion of you she was proud to hear that Owen is acquit-
ting himself well.

Now I must delay no longer in telling you the *great news*
—praying that you also will find it to be so and not blame
me for taking a step which, were you not at sea, we would
have taken together. You wrote me to "keep an eye out"
for a house of our own in town, and I did! I obeyed your
instruction to the letter except—are you comfortably
seated? Is Mr. Chappel behaving himself?—I did not stop
there. In a word, I found the perfect house for us and I

bought it! It is the old Brock place on Centre, only you must imagine it completely reshingled, repainted inside and out, the oak floors sanded and varnished, and furnished (at least partly), as it now is. I am writing these lines at a desk by the upstairs front window, praying very hard that you will love our new home as much as I do, or half as much would be quite enough. Do you forgive me? Perhaps you are saying to yourself, "My G-d, what is there to forgive? What a clever creature I have married!" I do hope so.

In any case, whatever you may think (such important things as houses require much reflection to be seen in their proper light), you may be sure that I did not proceed without the advice and approval of every member of my family and of yours and of half a dozen friends. Joists and beams were pricked and found sound. And though the price was not cheap ($1,900), Father gave proof of his belief in the soundness of my choice by making us a loan free of interest and repayable at our convenience to the amount of $2,700, which more than covered the price, the refurbishing, and sundry costs.

Oh, now I have such trepidation! I am amazed at my temerity. I do love this dear house, very much, but if you do not like it too I could easily put a For Sale sign in the window (with good reason to expect a profit) and walk away from it. Please like it. There are still the questions of the weathervane and the brass knocker. Otherwise it is ready for your return. There is a west-facing second bedroom and a small borning room on the upper floor, which alas have not been needed yet but, if God is willing, will be in the future. Whatever your thoughts you must have no concern about the loan if it should happen that your present voyage does not prove to be as successful as you would wish. Father knows the risks of whaling and will

not expect repayment until it is no burden to us—perhaps
when a freshly painted sign will be nailed over the door
of a Straight Wharf countinghouse: Geo. Pollard, Jr., &
Sons, Whale-Oil Merchants.

Stay well, my dear husband, and know that you are in
the constant and most affectionate thoughts of your wife

Mary Pollard
(of 46 Centre Street)

I went to the window and stood staring out across the harbor.
For the first time I understood clearly that the ambitious young
captain who had sailed the *Essex* out of Nantucket eighteen
months before no longer existed. The Pacific had swallowed
him. He was another human being now, with no past but a
single appalling story. How would Mary, in her new house, so
full of plans for the future, respond to that tale which was
already being borne around the Horn?

How would the Island?

How would Nancy Coffin?

I went to the washstand, poured water into the bowl, and
scrubbed my hands. In the cracked brown mirror I noticed,
behind me in the doorway, the housekeeper's six-year-old son
watching me with widened eyes. Seeing that I had observed him
he turned and was gone, and I knew that for the rest of his days
he would retain a memory of the American who had consumed
his kinsman.

I looked again into the mirror, trying to know the stranger
in it.

4

Valparaiso
March 22, 1821

My very dear Mary,

By the time you read these lines you will have learned
of the loss of the *Essex*. Though our sufferings were extreme I am now recuperating (though more slowly than
Chase and the other two returning on the *Eagle*), and my
greatest concern is now about the grief and pain that these
reports must be causing you. It is a sad irony that I who
have wished only to offer you happiness must bring you
distress instead. I shall be coming home on the *Two Brothers* when that vessel returns to this port in a month or so.
As you know George Worth, you will know how fortunate
I am in having such a benefactor. He has taken my predicament to heart and is assisting me both materially and by
his kindness, by his sound good sense, and—not the least
—by his assessment of my future career. It is his opinion
that I will be given another command, since it will be
perceived that the calamity resulted from no fault of
mine.

The news about the house pleases me very much, especially since for three months I did not think that I would
ever see the inside of any house again, much less our own,
and I do commend you for your enterprise. In view of
what has happened I will be obliged to depend upon your
father's generosity in carrying the loan for an unknown
time—though, as I am not at ease being in debt, this will

be an added spur to repairing my fortunes as soon as possible. For now, I look forward most eagerly to attaching a weather vane to the roof and a brass knocker to the door.

As you may imagine, the experiences in the boats have wrought changes in me. I am much thinner and my skin is burned and mottled, but with every day these conditions are improving, so that by the time we meet I expect that I will not make so very alarming an impression. I accept what happened as the work of a Providence which I no longer attempt to fathom, and leave it at that. Please know that you are in the constant and most affectionate thoughts of

> Your Husband,
> Geo. Pollard, Jr.

5

To the east and south of Nantucket lie dangerous shoals—Old Man, Tuckernuck, Rose and Crown—which have claimed many vessels and many lives. To the west, between Muskeget Island and Martha's Vineyard, lies a maze of shifting shoals and serpentine passages. Only from north by northwest is our Island accessible to ships, through a narrow, tide-dredged channel, and God help the unknowing shipmaster who would venture into this labyrinth without a native pilot. Even Nantucket captains have no easy time of it, since for years the passage has been sanding in, and returning with a full whaleship has usually meant lightering part of the cargo ashore, an expensive and exasperating procedure. From my years of blockade-running and whaling, I thought that I could sail these waters blindfold, but on the 21st of August, when the lookout at the masthead of the *Two Brothers* raised Great Point lighthouse, I was so troubled by apprehensions of what awaited me ashore that I felt certain of nothing. What reception awaited me? Would I in fact be offered another command? Was I sure enough of myself to accept it?

The lighthouse rising and falling off our lee bow in the light of the mild rose dawn seemed threatening, the shoals too near.

George Worth, standing with me at the taffrail, seemed to sense the drift of my thoughts, for by then, after almost three months at sea together, we had become friends, like father and son should be but seldom are. He said gruffly, "Just remember, now, you ain't done with whaling 'less you want to be."

"I hope to hell you're right."

"Oh, I'm right. You're too good a whaleman to beach for no reason."

"No reason?"

"No good reason, damn it! I thought we'd done with all that." When I didn't answer, he scanned the horizon north, to windward. "Make out Monomoy?"

I followed his gaze until I saw the distant pink lighthouse at the southern tip of Cape Cod. "Dead abeam," I told him.

He suddenly clapped his hand on my shoulder and said, "Ain't had the best luck so far, but you got eyes like a frigate bird!"

By ten o'clock we had put Great Point off our lee quarter and beyond the long white sandspit of Coatue and the rises of the moors beyond the harbor I made out the four windmills and the two steeples of the town. As we rounded into the mouth of the channel I waited for Worth to bring the vessel into the wind and signal the lighters. Instead he held a course bearing on Brant Point, closing the distance to the shallow bar.

"Taking her across?" I asked.

"No," he told me. "You are."

I looked at him in surprise, hearing the rush of water against the bows.

"What's ailin' ye?" he said sharply. "We got the wind and the tide, and you can read this channel better'n anyone. What's ailin' ye?"

I took the helmsman's place at the wheel. For a moment I felt as if the strength were ebbing from my hands and that I had no power to prevent the ship from running aground; but then, feeling her response and making out the curve of darker green that marked the center of the channel, I steered the *Two Brothers* across the bar with, I judged, about six inches between her barnacles and the bottom.

"See?" said Worth, pleased as could be, as we rounded into the harbor and full view of town. "Warn't nothing to it, was there?"

"I thank you for that," I said, relinquishing the wheel to the helmsman.

"Thank me, do you? Why, Hell's fire, you just saved me and the owners the lightering fees and a half-day's work. See, I couldn't have done what you just did. Ain't got the eyesight for it anymore."

The bell in South Tower was striking twelve. The slow, wavering peals told me that I was home at last, and suddenly I was filled with trepidation. I felt that I was not yet ready to part company with the sea. A dozen ships stood in the harbor, others at the wharves. I saw that many new houses and commercial buildings had been built since I had left. Then I saw the crowd.

They had come down to the waterfront, they stood silently

on the wharves, they lined the beach between Brant Point and the ropewalk. Boys were perched on roofs. Others were approaching the ship in dinghies and sailboats. There must have been two hundred silently watching as Worth brought the *Two Brothers* to anchor off Old North Wharf.

Sensing my feelings, my benefactor said, "Now remember what I told ye. Don't let 'em see what they come to see. You don't have to take your hat off to nobody on this Island."

I remember that first step off the top of the ladder on the wharf. I felt unsteady, determined not to show it. I knew almost everyone there, and no one spoke. Some met my glance steadily, others looked away. Those seconds seemed endless. Then Owen Chase pressed through the throng and shook my hand.

"Welcome home, Captain."

"Thank you, Mr. Chase."

Tom Nickerson and Ben Lawrence then came up to me. Young Nickerson, very moved, said in a voice for all around to hear, "We're glad you're back safe, Captain. We owe our lives to you and the mate."

I shook their hands warmly. Then I realized that one of the survivors from the boats was not present.

"Ramsdell?" I said to Chase.

"Still pretty low," he told me softly. "Keeps to himself."

"You've made a report to the owners?"

Chase nodded. "Gideon Folger's awaiting yours tomorrow. Wants you to get some rest first."

Then the crowd was making way for someone. A woman in a gray bonnet and full-skirted gray dress was hurrying toward me. For a moment I was not certain that it was Mary. In two years she had changed, was no longer a girl but a woman now, a little rounder in the face and not so slender, with a set look to her, a determined look. In the boats, in the Pacific vastness that obliterated time and memory, I had sometimes tried to recall her face and her voice, her presence, but could not. She, this stranger, my wife, came to me to be embraced, and I embraced her. We looked at each other in silence, watched by a hundred pairs of eyes, until I knew that what I had dreaded to see in her face was not there. Then she smiled and was my bride again.

"Welcome home, Captain Pollard," she said.

"Glad to be home, Mrs. Pollard."

Brother Bill sat up on a wagon with a freshly painted sign, "H. Riddell & Son, Dry Goods." I was to find that he dressed for Sunday every day now, so that no one would forget his importance. If there had been any doubt that we had outgrown our childhood friendship, it was gone now. He greeted me with a muttered welcome and a look as if I were contaminated with plague. I thought, Don't let yourself become what they see, and I thanked him heartily and was about to help Mary up on the wagon and climb aboard myself when that surprising lady said, for all around to hear, "If it suits you, Captain, we'll walk up Main. I've some errands to do."

"Suits me fine," I said.

So, with a part of the crowd straggling after us, we walked hand in hand up the wharf past rows of greasy black casks to Water Street, over to Main, and up the center of town, people watching from doorways and windows, Mary making it plain with the set of her head and her firm stride that she was pleased her husband was home, that nothing that might have happened in the Pacific Ocean made the least difference to her, and that she'd be mightily surprised if it did to anyone else. At Miss Macy's shop, she bought a spool of thread. At Jenkens's grocery, a tub of butter.

At the new brick bank we turned down Centre, Mary nodding to acquaintances as she chattered to me about the recent weather, who had died, who had married, who had bought or sold property, until at the stroke of one we stood before the two-storied clapboard house at the corner of Quince, the old Brock place, now ours.

"Do like it," she said.

Inside, the house smelled of fresh paint. There were white curtains on all the windows, hooked rugs on the shining floors, a sofa, chairs, tables, and on the wall the framed sampler Mary had embroidered as a child with the legend "God Bless Our Home" and the alphabet. Talking a blue streak about what had still to be done, what fixed, what changed, this way or that, she led me through the little dining room to the large kitchen with its capacious brick fireplace, high mantel of blackened oak, back again to the living room and up the stairs to the front study (where I am writing now) to our bedroom adjoining it, with a white counterpaned bed, white curtains. Near the head of the stairs we passed a small rectangular space without curtains or furnishings.

"And this?" I said.

"The borning room."

We looked directly at each other for the first time since we were alone together. Again I searched for a sign of revulsion in her face, and she knew that I was, but in her warm brown eyes I found only caring and compassion. More than anything I wanted this woman's love and to give her mine, but I felt distant from her, out of my element, as helpless as when I had lain gasping on the deck of the *Dauphin*.

"You've heard everything?" I asked.

She nodded. "Owen Chase came here. He wanted me to hear it straight from him first. It was good of him."

"Chase is a good man."

Reading what was in my face, she said, "You're a good man, too, George Pollard. And don't you forget it."

"Not everyone would agree. Ramsdell doesn't."

"I feel sorry for that boy," she said. "Even though it was done fairly, he must feel as bad as if it wasn't." Then she said, "Chase said it was done fairly."

"As fairly," I said, "as such a thing can be done."

"Everyone on the Island understands that."

"Does Nancy Coffin?"

"That woman!" she said bitterly.

"She has cause."

"She has no right to say the things she has."

"One can understand."

"She has no right to judge what God alone can judge."

"I'll call on her tomorrow. It was Owen's last wish."

Suddenly her eyes were full of fury. "If it's judgment you want, you'll find it in that house."

"It was Owen's last wish."

"Go to her, then."

I felt then that the love of this woman and the comfort of this house were farther than ever from my reach.

That afternoon, after our dinner, my parents and sister Susan paid a call. It was a difficult visit. We sat in the parlor. My mother's eyes were full of accusation. I warned you, she seemed to be saying. My father, who had fallen from a ladder and injured his back, spoke of his accident at length, as if to assure me that misfortune is man's common lot. Then my mother asked me if I had heard about Betsy.

Wary of her tragical look, I said I had not.

"Left the Island. She and Tom moved to Hudson, New York."

"When?"

"Month, maybe," said my father.

A silence followed. Out of pure kindness my poor sweet sister then said, "Wasn't to do with you, George. They were fixing to leave anyhow."

I would learn that though Susan had been told about the loss of the *Essex,* she had no idea of exactly what had happened in the open boats. She knew for a certainty that something was going on in that kitchen that was not right, but she couldn't guess what it was, and as she looked from one still face to another, she suddenly burst out, "Why aren't you just happy he's home?"

During that visit, Mary had busied herself in the kitchen. She was on good terms with my father, but not with my mother. When my family had gone, I found that she had heated a cauldron of water in the fireplace.

"We'll wash the ocean off you," she said.

We set a copper tub by the fire, and I enjoyed my first proper bath since Valparaiso. After that we went upstairs. The bedroom could not be darkened against the midafternoon north light. When I had lain with her after our wedding, in a back bedroom of the Pleasant Street house, it had always been at night, in darkness, both of us careful not to be heard by her family. Our lovemaking had been furtive, and we had promised ourselves such privacy as we had now. I came to my wife in daylight, in our own house, apprehensive from months of wondering what her feelings would be toward me now, whether revulsion or, worse, a steeling of herself against revulsion. I had been fearful of our first intimacy. I need not have been.

I slept. When I awakened, it was dark. I was alone in the bed. I had no idea where I was. I felt sudden cold terror. There was no sea-motion, no sound. Valparaiso? I wanted to cry out, but could make no sound. Dreadful moments passed until I remembered my homecoming. The silent throng at the wharves. Mary. The curfew sounded. Nine peals, followed by fifty-two more.

When the last died away I arose and went to the window, looked down Broad Street to the fifth house on the left, Nancy Coffin's, and to the dark, beyond, where the waterfront began.

Tomorrow I would make my report to Gideon Folger.

Then I would call on Nancy.

In the street someone was approaching. Lanternlight announced a nightwatchman, making his rounds. As he drew nearer I saw that it was a gangly man dressed in black. He looked up at me and by the lantern's glow I recognized the burn-twisted, noseless face of Silas Bench. He grinned at me, raised the lantern in a mock salute, then turned down Broad. Only then did I observe that the left sleeve of his jacket was empty.

Downstairs I found Mary at her embroidery work.

"I let you sleep," she said.

"I'm obliged," I told her. I went to the window and looked out into the dark street. I said, "I see Silas Bench is on the night watch, shy an arm."

She nodded. "Sperm whale."

I sat opposite her. After a silence I said, "Worth thinks I'll have another ship."

She put down her work and looked at me sharply. "And why wouldn't you, for Heaven's sake? Wasn't your fault what happened out there."

"That what people think?"

She frowned. "Them with the brains God gave 'em. Besides, those owners aren't fools. They know you'll pester whales to the end of Creation to show this Island what you can do. You'll have your ship."

"I hope you're right."

"So do I," she said, taking up her work. "Wouldn't want you fidgeting around this house for the rest of my days."

I smiled at her then. "I do like this house, Mary. It all just takes some getting used to."

"Take your time," she said. "And don't fret. You'll have your ship. You'll have whatever you're set on. You're too stubborn not to."

"George Pollard—and Sons?"

"Sons too—God willing."

Then I let a thought out that I would have done better keeping to myself. I said, "Can't let Chase get too far ahead of us."

Mary twisted her mouth the way she does and said, "Having a family's not a contest, Captain Pollard."

Figuring then that I might as well be hung for a wolf as for a lamb, I said, "Good thing, too."

To my surprise Mary burst into tears, the first time I'd ever known her to. I went to her and tried to comfort her. Through her sobs she said, "I want a child so bad, George. So bad."

Only then did I find out how much I wanted one too.

About ten, Mary went up to bed and I went out for an amble in the town. I had a purpose; I wanted to find Silas Bench. A halfmoon stood over South Tower, and I started that way. I wanted to know what Bench thought about our experiences in the Pacific. I knew him to be a ruthlessly honest man, and I wanted his view of what had happened, how it struck him. Remembering the usual paths of the night watch, I figured that he would most likely circle Academy Hill to Gardner Street, then over to Main and down to the center of town and the wharves. I went over Centre and up Main, intending to intercept him. But for a glow here and there at a curtained bedroom window, the bluish moonlight, the streets were dark.

I walked on, my legs still fighting the unyielding ground, past the Meeting House to the corner of Pleasant Street. There, beyond the Riddell house, I saw Bench crossing with his lantern, disappearing into the maze of lanes in the direction of the harbor. I doubled back down Main, walking rapidly now, on a parallel course. At Orange I caught another glimpse of him, crossing near South Tower. Now we must surely converge at the wharves. I mentally prepared myself for the encounter. Without fear of anything or hope of anything himself, Bench was a man to reckon with. As a younger man I had measured myself against him, formed myself out of what he saw in me that would serve me as a whaleman. I needed him now.

But where had the man gone?

At South Water Street I stood waiting to see lanternlight in the darkness by South Wharf. When none appeared, I walked down South Water to that wharf, where two whaleships and a coastal schooner out of Boston were berthed. I looked out to the end of the pier. There, silhouetted against the silvery water, I saw him. He stood motionless, gazing out at the harbor, the ships at anchor, the blackness beyond.

But where was his lantern?

I guessed he had extinguished it so as to admire the beauty of the night.

I swear I did.

I walked out on the pier. When I was about twenty paces from him I called out, "Bench."

The other turned quickly. It was Charles Ramsdell.

I froze. Ramsdell stared at me, his eyes widening. We confronted each other in silence, then he said, "Can't you sleep neither, Captain?" Before I could answer he demanded in an anguished voice, "What do you want of me now?"

"Nothing," I told him. "I thought you were someone else."

"I'd give a lot to be someone else."

"You mustn't blame yourself."

"Should I blame you?"

"If it will help."

He shook his head, smiling bitterly. "Oh, you are so—*fair.*" Then, perhaps feeling that he had gone too far, he said, "You never did like me, did you?"

Determined to be honest, I said, "I took special pains to treat you—fairly."

"You didn't approve of my friendship with Owen, did you?"

"I was hardly aware of it. How would I not approve of it?"

"And were you—hardly aware of his friendship with Mr. Chappel?"

He smiled as he saw that his insolent question had touched me. I replied, "For the sake of Owen's memory and your own sake, I'd stow such thoughts as those. They make no sense and do you no credit."

"They made sense at sea. There was nothing wrong with his friendship with Mr. Chappel, until—"

"Until what, exactly?"

He was breathing hard, barely able to control his voice. "Owen—felt that he had done wrong. You—made him feel so. That's why—he—"

"Go on."

In a croaking whisper he said, "That's why he was willing to die!"

Seized by fury I said, "That's a damnable lie! Owen accepted his fate as it had been fixed by lot. He died like a man. He did not give his life to appease anyone. And you are no friend of his to say such a thing!"

As I fought my anger, the young man seemed to gain control of himself. It struck me then that he was deliberately trying to goad me into doing violence to him. He said, "Perhaps I knew Owen better than you, Captain. He cared very much for you. He would have done anything to have your good opinion of him —and he did."

Hardly knowing what I was saying, I demanded, "And did you kill him for my good opinion of you?"

With an anguished twist of his head he looked up into the darkness. After a long time he said quietly, "I killed him because it was decided by lot." I then felt compassion for him, and I said, "It's not wrong to have lived, Charles. We must both accept Owen's gift." And when he did not reply, I added, "God's gift."

He looked at me a moment, then his eyes blazed in bitter triumph, hearing that I had spoken falsely.

I turned and left him.

I never did find Silas Bench that night.

6

The next morning was warm and pleasant, dull sunlight, hazy sky. I set forth for Folger's office on South Water Street, eager to relate my story of the cruise. Though Ramsdell had not been requested to make a report, after my encounter with him I suspected that he might have already circulated an account of the tragedy that would set it in a false light, and I was anxious to correct any such wrong impressions. My concern (I truly believed then) was that Owen Coffin not be dishonored by Ramsdell's troubled recollections. I hoped that Nancy Coffin would not misconstrue what had happened. For somehow, at sea, I had formed the notion that she would accept the death of Owen, the manner of it, with courageous resignation—understand!—as a Spartan mother might accept the loss of a son fallen on the battlefield. Even Mary's warnings had not dislodged this mad idea. Could I have secretly supposed that my aunt, having transgressed communal laws herself, might the more readily have accepted the news from the Pacific? Could I have assumed that a bond still existed between us that even that report had not broken? Nothing is impossible. There is no exaggerating the capacity of a young whaleman to shut his mind to the feelings of a woman.

Only as I passed Nancy's house on the way to Folger's office and found all the shutters drawn in the middle of the morning did I have any inkling of the reception that awaited me there.

Three men were seated in Folger's small office when I entered. Folger at his desk; Mr. Ransome, the Boston underwriter's Nantucket agent; Zenas Coffin. As I entered, the three broke off their conversation and stared at me, so that for a moment, in the strong flat light filtered through cobwebbed windowpanes, they sat frozen as if they were sitting for a portrait. Gideon Folger was a tall man of about sixty years, with silken white hair, gentle worried eyes, a set jaw. He was known throughout the Island as an honest, fair-minded man, a Friend, whose conscience could never fault him for having sent out an ill-provisioned ship, and who was known to provide tidbits of fine foodstuffs for his officers and books of the edifying sort for his crews. If I have until now avoided describing him, it is because I never knew quite what to make of him. There seemed to be a war within him between his finer feelings and his commercial ones, a struggle which ran against the Nantucket grain and was unnerving to whalemen. He seemed to be acutely conscious of the physical risks and hardships of whaling while denying that they existed. I should have realized that if ever there was a Nantucketer disinclined to hear of horrors at sea, it was the owner of the *Essex*. But I was too anxious to tell my story to perceive such a thing.

A very different sort of man was the other shipowner in that tableau. Zenas Coffin was then in his late fifties, in poor health, with graying hair, a pale complexion, and the fierce blue eyes and ample jaw that ran in the Coffin family. In his prime he had been a whaling master almost the equal of Worth, and he was still the best pilot of Nantucket waters. His will was absolute; his opinion unshakable; his love for his family, his driving devotion to the Island of his birth were all-consuming; and at that time—and ever after—no man understood the whaling industry, the world markets for its products, and the trading opportunities for its ships better than Zenas. The Coffins were reputed to be standoffish and clan-proud, and Zenas was that, but one always knew where one stood with him, and that morning, surprised to find him in Folger's office, and remembering his offer on Sheepshearing Day, I was very anxious to learn what his view of me might be now.

Ransome was a thin, frail spike of a man, about forty, a former Bostonian who in his long residence among us had earned a reputation for businesslike dealings and little else. I had never taken to the man. He seemed not to accept the fact that he was born an off-Islander and, though he might live here all his life, would die one. He possessed a mainlander's notion of social distinction according to birth and wealth. He was deferential to our Quaker gentility, scornful to those he thought inferior to him. So it was now. He looked at me as if he figured that his struggle for esteem was somehow advanced by what he took to be my fall from grace. He seemed to be flattering himself that he was entitled to speak for the Island about me, thinking, "You have risen far and fast, young man. You were on your way to amounting to something. And now look at you."

As I say, I had never taken to the man.

"Good morning, Captain Pollard," said Gideon Folger with a careful smile.

"Good morning, gentlemen," I said, as Zenas Coffin with a push on his ivory-headed cane rose to his feet.

"Here, Captain," he said, "sit yourself down. Just leaving."

"Do stay, Zenas," said Folger in a tone of urgency.

"I've no business here, Gideon," he replied, "except to tell Captain Pollard what I already told him. When we've a master's berth open, it's his for the asking. My offer still holds."

"Thank you, sir," I said.

"Friend," he corrected me.

"Friend."

With a brisk good day he left us.

When I turned again to the other two, the underwriter's agent appeared disappointed, Gideon Folger unnerved.

"We won't keep you long," said the latter. "Just a few questions to satisfy Mr. Ransome's people in Boston. We've already heard the facts from Mr. Chase."

I said, "Mr. Chase was not in my boat."

Folger, alarmed, looked to the agent for assistance.

"Our only concern," said Ransome, "is the loss of the *Essex.*" He took out a notebook and applied a pair of steel-rimmed spectacles to his nose. "Mr. Chase reported that on the twentieth of November, 1820, in latitude zero degrees forty minutes south, longitude one hundred and nineteen degrees west, that vessel was struck and sunk by a large sperm whale. Is that correct?"

"It is."

"What cargo did you carry at the time?"

"Eight hundred and fifty barrels of sperm oil. Eighteen months' provisions."

He consulted the notebook again. "Then you stayed in the boats, moored to the ship, for two days."

"To the wreck," I said.

"Then on the second day you left—the wreck."

"The third day."

"That is, after the second night?"

"Correct."

"She was afloat when you left?"

"Foundered. Breaking up."

"Did you see her sink, Captain Pollard?"

Gideon Folger watched me anxiously. In a voice the agent had not heard before I said, "The wreck was awash. Sinking.

There was no question of salvage. Only of our lives, Mr. Ransome."

Taken aback but still protective of his self-importance, he said, "I'm quite certain that Boston will understand that, Captain." And to the owner he said, "I think we have everything we need from Captain Pollard. I have the necessary documents to establish the value of the ship and her outfit, and I'm confident that full valuation will be paid."

I said, "Lives were lost, Mr. Folger."

"We're all very aware of that, Pollard," said that gentleman. "Devastated, in fact. The miracle is that any of you survived." Again he looked to the agent for aid.

"We are insurers of hulls, sir, not of lives."

To Folger I said, "There could be claims."

Once again the agent replied for him. "Though not an attorney, I venture that Mr. Folger and his partners have little to fear from claims. In such matters it is the master of the vessel who has absolute authority and absolute responsibility. The assumption, Captain, is that you and your officers did your best to prevent loss of life, against impossible odds. You then observed—customs of the sea—customs rarely practiced, to be sure, but customs nonetheless. If anyone were to be liable, it is not the owners but yourself, sir: however, I can assure you that you are not in any actual jeopardy. Rarely have courts interfered involving the discretion of officers in dealing with maritime emergencies. As for Mr. Folger, no one would dream of holding him or his associates responsible for what happened under your command."

I said, "Then no one has anything to worry about."

"I did not say that, Captain Pollard. I was referring only to the disposition of courts."

"We are devastated, of course," repeated Folger, "but hold you in no way responsible, Pollard. You did everything humanly possible. I agree with Mr. Coffin that you should have

another ship, and if I had one to give you you'd have it at once."
He hesitated. "Now, is there anything further that we require
from the captain, Mr. Ransome?"

"Nothing whatever. The claim will be settled and the whole
matter forgotten, I trust, as soon as possible."

Angered, I said, "I do not intend to forget Matt Joy"—I
looked directly at Folger—"or Owen Coffin or the others."

The owner appeared stricken. "Pollard, if there is anything
I can do," he said. "Anything within reason."

I stood before the frightened man. "Sir, none of it was within
reason. It wasn't then and it isn't now."

Then, without a glance back, I turned and left the office.

When I knocked at my aunt's door that afternoon, my cousin
Ann opened it. Dressed in black, very pale, she looked at me,
and in that first instant I saw the shadow of horror that crossed
her face. Then, as if she had rehearsed it in her mind, she came
to me and kissed my cheek as she had always done.

"Please come in," she said in a hushed voice.

The parlor was very dark, heavy curtains drawn across all the
windows. Nancy, also in black, sat in a wing chair near the cold
hearth, staring at me as I entered. As my eyes grew accustomed
to the dusklike gloom I saw how she had aged. Her hair, in
disorder, was now almost white, her face was pale, puffy, and
lined, her hands and head trembling, her once-lively eyes dull
and fixed.

"Nancy—" I said, as if saying her name could bring back the
young woman I remembered.

The clock on the mantel ticked indifferently. Beside it now
stood three small oval portraits, of Hezekiah, Edward, and
Owen.

Ann said, "Greet him, Mother."

My aunt remained silent, then her eyes suddenly blazed.

"Murderer!"

"Mother!" cried Ann in an anguished voice.

"Go upstairs, child."

Ann hesitated, then turned and darted up the stairs, the last two steps creaking loudly.

I said to the woman in the chair, "I've come because Owen's last words were to you. He wanted me to tell you that he died bravely, as he surely did."

She looked at me, her head wavering. At first I thought she had not understood. As if to herself she repeated, "Bravely?" Then in fury she cried out, "Bravely? You murdered my son!"

I heard Ann's quick steps on the stairs, she ran into the room, crying "Mother! He's suffered too. We must pray for him as we pray for Owen."

"Pray for him?" said my aunt. "Pray for this murderer? He has my curse."

Ann, stricken, tried to protest. I said gently to her, "I'm leaving."

"Go to the devil!" said Nancy Coffin.

7

I was shaken by my aunt's condemnation. I had not felt that I had committed a crime. I had not felt like a murderer. I had come to love Owen Coffin like a son, and to me his death was an irreconcilable loss, a horror still beyond my comprehension, but I had not thought of it as murder. Until that visit I had held to the story that I had poured out to Zimri Coffin and Worth after I was pulled from the sea: the necessity of a sacrifice, the

agreement to the lottery, the fairness of it, Owen's brave accept-
ance of his fate, that passionate accounting, which now, with
my aunt's accusation ringing in my ears, was again called into
question, as it had been by Charles Ramsdell. Was I, then,
guilty of a horrendous crime? As Worth had predicted, no
formal questions would be asked by Island or Massachusetts
magistrates, no inquiry convened. In the days that followed, the
glances of the townspeople, their silences, the bitter memory of
my aunt's denunciation, my own unsettled thoughts made me
long to be hauled before an authority before whom I could call
the other survivors as witnesses (even Ramsdell—I could answer him too!) and be found innocent or guilty, to be absolved
of wrongdoing, or spend the rest of my days in captivity brooding over the ins and outs of my case. It was not to be.

During this time Mary did her best to show the Island that
nothing had happened. We took evening strolls along the sandy
lanes of the town, attended one of her father's auctions, paid
calls, received visitors, and on Sunday attended church on
Academy Hill with the family.

As for Henry Riddell, he had made clear his views toward
me from the moment the news of the *Essex* had reached Nantucket. In a familial act of faith he praised my courage and
seamanship and defended my conduct.

"Such things are bound to happen, don't you see?" he would
say. "Can't be helped. Don't change the fact that George is the
best young whaleship master on this Island. He'll be another
Worth before he's done. Just wait."

And George Worth also continued to speak out for me. Early
in September, having turned seventy, his vision failing rapidly,
he announced his decision to retire from whaling.

"Won't miss the stink of blubber, you can be damn sure of
that," he told everybody, and nobody believed him, of course,

but nobody said so. Then one morning, soon after the word was out, I ran into him on Main Street and he invited me over to his house on Orange for a gam. We settled in the front parlor. The sister was not home, but expected. He fired up his black briar pipe, puffed, then looked at me through the smoke.

"Still set on whaling again?" he demanded.

"More than ever."

"Why?"

"Wouldn't have thought you'd ask that, Captain."

"Have you asked yourself?" he pressed me. "Have you dared ask yourself?"

"To earn a living," I said. "It's the only trade I know."

He nodded. "And that ain't even the half of it, is it?"

I said, "It's what Nantucket men do."

"To prove we add up to something, eh? Hell of a way to be somebody, ain't it?"

"It's not just that—and you know it."

"I guess I do, at that. It's in your blood or it ain't, and if it is there's no getting rid of it. Ever." He looked around the snug little parlor, then at me again. If I had my good eyes back, I'd be shipping again myself. Sea's spoiled me for shore life." He laughed dryly. "Damnable way to go out of this world." Then urgently he said, "Will Folger give you another ship?"

"Said so, but he has none now. Might have just said it. Zenas Coffin said the same, and I believe him, but he's not short a master either."

With an odd glance at me, Worth set his pipe in an ashtray by his chair. "Come outside, George," he said. "I've a little something to show you."

He hoisted himself to his feet. I followed him back through the kitchen, out into a scraggly little garden at the edge of the bluff, with a sweeping view of the harbor.

"See the *Two Brothers?*"

I looked for that vessel at her anchorage. Then I saw that she was now tied up at Old North Wharf, carts, wagons, dockhands swarming at her waist.

"Outfitting," I said.

"She's yours."

Worth was a widower with one living child, a son who had married young, left the Island, and bought an apple orchard in upper New York State, and was hardly a son at all to him anymore. I remember that moment in the ragtail little garden overlooking the harbor well. In a single instant I found that I had a ship again, a career, a future—and, it seemed then, the whaleman father I had always wished for. And from the look of him I suspected that Worth felt that he had a son back.

"If it's what you want?" he said, suddenly wary.

"It is. And I thank you."

Gruffly he told me, "Wasn't nothing to it. Owners know what a whaleman you are. Didn't have to twist their arms much."

"Wasn't the mate to be master?"

Worth nodded. "Eben Gardner's first-rate. You're lucky to have him. But he's young and he'll have his day. This is yours. So let's splice the main brace."

He clapped me on the back and we went back into the kitchen, where he poured rum into two glasses, raised his.

"To the new master of the *Two Brothers*—fair winds and a full ship!"

The vessel, I learned, was to sail in three weeks. Mate Gardner and Worth's two other officers, Second Walt Barrett and Third Jim Coleman, had signed on again, as had about half the crew, the replacements having already been recruited.

"How will they feel about sailing under Pollard of the *Essex*?" I asked Worth point-blank.

The captain examined the contents of his glass, then looked at me with what was the closest he ever came to a smile. "Truth is," he said, "I get the feeling they kind of take to the idea. They know you're a fine seaman and handy with an iron, but it's more than that. See, I think they figure sailing with you gives them a sort of—importance."

8

Within a few days, all Nantucket knew that I had been chosen as captain of the *Two Brothers*. That appointment was a far more convincing sign of my innocence than exoneration by a court would have been. If I was still watched and whispered about, I was not aware of it.

The following evening, Chase paid a call on me. We sat in the parlor, both uncomfortable.

"Congratulations," he said, very downcast. I could see that something was troubling him.

"You'll have a ship soon yourself," I said.

"Maybe."

"If the *Two Brothers* was short a mate, you'd have one now."

He looked surprised. "Why, I thank you for that, Captain. But you've no need of me. I hear Eben Gardner's a fine whale-man."

"So Worth said."

We fell silent. Then, abruptly, Chase said what he had come to say.

"I'm publishing an account of our voyage."

I said, "So you'll tell everything?"

"What happened, happened. We should have nothing to hide."

"Hiding is one thing, making a penny dreadful of it is another."

"Isn't it better to tell it as it was than as it would be imagined?"

"Will you plead our case, then?"

"Damn it!" he said then. "You have a ship, I have a hungry family!"

So the true motive was out. I surprised him, saying, "I wish you success with your project, Chase."

Sheepish now, he said, "And I wish you a greasy voyage, Captain."

"Mark my words, we'll be racing ships soon, not boats. And, by God, I'll—"

"Show me your wake? Just try it."

Smiling, we shook hands, and he left. I remember wondering how he would tell of what had happened in my boat.

Mary received the news of my new command without surprise. "What did I tell you? And here you haven't even put up the weathervane."

"I put the knocker on the door."

"Guess I'll be waiting a couple of more years for the weathervane."

So, less than nine weeks after my return I was to sail again, bound for the richest habitat of sperm whales on the planet, the Japan grounds. A week before sailing, on a gray rainy morning, I convened my three officers in the ship's cabin to acquaint them with the plan of the voyage. By then I knew them well enough from our acquaintance on the return from Valparaiso to have formed an opinion of each man. Eben Gardner was, at twenty-three, a lean, silent, settled youth. All business. None of Chase's ruminating watchfulness. If he resented my selection as master, he didn't show a sign of it, then or ever.

Walt Barrett, also twenty-three, was Eben's follower, emulating him as best he could, trying to make up by sheer will and courage for what he lacked in natural grace. I understood him well.

Jim Coleman, twenty-one, was an agreeable youth, brave and willing, who made heroic efforts that morning not to imagine what had happened in my whaleboat.

Of course, the question had lingered in my mind as to their opinion of me as master of the *Two Brothers.* They had known me as a fellow Islander all their lives. They knew my reputation as a whaleman. They knew that I had Worth's confidence. But these men had seen me as a gasping skeleton clutching the femurs of my dead shipmates, and that impression, with all the images that it must have set turning in their minds, set me apart from them. So I came to the cabin on that dismal morning wondering whether my officers were sailing with me with a willing heart. I need not have worried. Worth had been right. From the first, they seemed to take a certain pride in shipping with me. They sensed my determination to succeed. And if my presence on board presented an added hazard, these Nantucket boys seemed only gratified for the opportunity to prevail over it.

The night before our departure I slept fitfully. In the small hours I dressed and went out into the cool fall night for a last stroll through the town. At the corner of Centre and Main I encountered Silas Bench, making his rounds. He held up his lantern and seeing who it was said, "Up late, Captain."

"Early," I told him.

"No matter. It's night. Choice time for a man to be alone with his thoughts."

"Yes," I said, wishing to be on my way.

"Always knew you was a private sort of person," he said. "Knew it right off."

"I remember."

"And I knew something else."

I waited.

"You wasn't born to have it easy in this life, no more'n me."

Part Five

THE
SECOND VENTURE

1

I remember my feeling of well-being when on the 8th of October, 1821, a crisp, fair day, we cleared the harbor and set our first course for the Azores. Being in possession of a ship again had refreshed my spirits, and I felt ready for any challenge. Throughout the cruise to the Western Isles the weather held fair. I held frequent boat drills, and by the third week the half-dozen green hands were as fit and eager to engage whales as any of us. I felt restored. Anyone from the *Essex* would have been amazed at the changes in me. From the beginning I had resolved to avoid any intimacy with my officers and crew. I would not again let myself be ensnared in the webs of personal entanglement that beset men on a long voyage. I showed myself to be calm, even-tempered, distant, leaving small infractions of discipline to be dealt with by my officers. When, off the Azores, we raised our first whales and took three, Eben Gardner afterward was moved to say that I fought whales "like Cap'n Worth done when he was spryer."

Into the South Atlantic the cruise continued without a hitch. We doubled the Cape with little trouble. In the Pacific we took more whales. From Valparaiso I wrote home.

2

Valparaiso, Chile
April 4, 1822

My dear Mary,

   A successful voyage thus far with 840 bbls. in our
hold, and yesterday we arrived in this port to be greeted
with most excellent news. Commodore Ridgely, now
head of our navy's Pacific station, has informed me that
the rescue of Chappel, Weeks, and Wright was effected
and that all three are now safe and sound. Beyond doubt
they owe their lives to the commodore's prompt action
in arranging that a Sydney-bound English ship, *Surrey,*
Capt. Thomas Raines, put in at Ducie Island. When
found the three were near death from starvation and
could not have lasted much longer. On board the *Surrey*
they recovered, reaching Sydney in fair health, and are
last reported to be sailing for England, where Chappel
will no doubt kiss the precious earth he expected never
to see again. By now the parents of Weeks and Wright in
Barnstable will have been informed of their sons' deliverance. As for the third boat, there is now scant hope that
any aboard it will be found alive. So the final chapter of
the *Essex* story is written and the book closed. As for
me, I feel like the Phoenix born again from his ashes. I
am thankful to you for your strength and affection and
to your father and Worth for their trust. Those of my
present crew—including Mate Gardner—who saw me
pulled from the open boat more dead than alive can

scarcely believe that the spray-eating whalehunter who leads them onto the backs of cachalots is the same man. From this port we will work slowly northward to the coast of Ecuador, then west to the offshore grounds (passing near the grave of the *Essex*) and then west northwest skirting the Sandwich Islands to the Japan grounds. Convey my greetings to your family and mine and all our Island friends.

> Yr. affn't husband,
> George Pollard, Jr.

On the Peruvian grounds our luck held. Our try-pots blackened the sky. In the boats I felt inspired, exulting in each kill. Near the site of the wreck of the *Essex* we left the Line and sailed northwest.

3

Was it within my power to avoid what happened on the night of February 11, 1823?

Judge.

We had been holding a course parallel to that chain of small islands, rocks, and reefs that extends a thousand miles west by northwest of the Sandwich Islands. With the wind out of the northeast, we were to leeward of that ill-charted archipelago and considered ourselves to be in no danger. At noon of the

10th, Gardner and I took observations, finding ourselves due south of a rocky island named Gardner Pinnacles after a kinsman of his. That afternoon, with surprising swiftness, the wind hauled around to the northwest and the western sky began to darken ominously. We made short sail and by the next morning, under a thick, scudding sky, were beating against a gale out of the west. Being now to windward of the chain, with no sign of the storm abating, I altered our course to northeast, intending to clear the lee of Gardner Pinnacles, putting the archipelago between us and the wind. Our chart showed an unobstructed passage some hundred miles wide between Gardner Pinnacles and La Perouse Pinnacle in French Frigate Shoal. At noon of the 11th the mate took another sighting, which placed us on that new course, though owing to the reduced visibility we knew that the observation was subject to a larger-than-usual margin of error. As the gale increased we took in our waist boat, turned up our quarter boats, and at five in the afternoon close-reefed the fore and main topsails and took in the mizzen topsail and foresails. At seven we doubled the watch.

"Breakers to leeward!" came the cry from the masthead.

"Helm hard a-weather!" I shouted over the gale, and at the same instant the vessel struck, seemed to float her length away, swinging into the wind, then struck again, shattering the entire stern beneath us. We clung to whatever handhold we could as the sea made a road over us and the ship quickly filled with water. I and part of the crew then unlashed the overturned quarterboat and righted it while the mate and the others did the same with the waist boat, and in driving rain and swirling waters we succeeded in launching both boats with all hands aboard, eleven men in each. We pulled clear of the wreck and joined together. We had each oars, a sail, a compass, a Bowditch, the drenched clothes on our backs, no water or provisions except two small pigs that had floated into the mate's boat. It was pitch-black, rain falling in sheets, then letting up for a moment so that we could hear breakers. Since we had no idea whether we had struck on a reef or an island, or what lay around us, I gave the order to pull to windward and lie off the wreck so that in the morning we might ascertain our situation and perhaps obtain provisions. Just then a heavy squall came on and we separated, seeing no more of the mate's boat, soon finding ourselves near a reef that roared tremendously, then observed phosphorescent waves of yet another reef, to leeward. We shipped a quantity of water, which we bailed constantly, and several times were near sinking, being then beyond fear, hope, despair, or faith, animated only by the rage to elude extinction that we share with all creatures. When the long-wished-for dawn began to break, it revealed a most dismal scene: fields of sheeny slate-gray rocks pounded by huge breakers encompassed us. As the light increased we saw at a distance to the north what we took for a ship. We set our sail and made for it, but soon found that the supposed vessel was a high rock, rising fifty feet out of the sea and with breakers all around. We then headed south and soon made out what this time was certainly a ship and which we presumed was the wreck. It appeared to be driven on the rocks of one of three small islands that lay beyond a chain of reefs extending far to windward. Resolving to attempt to cross the reefs, we sailed to leeward and found a small opening, eight or ten feet wide, and dropping sail, we called on our last reserves of strength and rowed through it, reaching the lee shore of the easternmost island. This island was small, appearing to have once been larger, for we found the stump of a huge tree with roots fast to the ground. We observed turtles, sea birds, several sea elephants. When we had made our way to the highest elevation, about eight feet above the beach, we discovered that what we had taken for the wreck was in fact a ship at anchor to the lee of the neighboring island. As the

wind held strong and we were too exhausted to attempt the
windward crossing, we made desperate efforts to be seen, waving our arms and tossing our shirts into the air, but to no avail,
and as we watched helplessly the vessel got under way and was
soon out of our sight. We then lay down and made ourselves
as contented as possible with our lot. About noon the cook, a
young New Bedford black, noticed that the pig that we had
taken on from the mate's boat had strayed toward the shore,
and he went after it, returning at once with the news that the
ship we had abandoned hope of ever seeing again was now hove
to at the lee of our island. We at once went to our boat,
launched, and rowed hard. At one o'clock we were on board the
Nantucket whaleship *Martha,* Captain John H. Pease, where
we found Eben Gardner and all ten of his boat crew safe, having
been rescued earlier that day. And so, as far as could be known,
our misfortune depended on an inaccurate observation of the
cloud-screened sun, faulty charts, and the extreme force of the
west wind, and our salvation on the meandering of a pig.

4

Captain Pease, four months out, ferried us to the port of
Honolulu, where I arranged for the homeward passage of my
crew, then early in April secured a berth for myself as passenger
on the U.S. Brig *Pearl,* Captain Chandler, bound for Boston.
On April 16, Chandler brought his vessel to the island of Raia-
tea in the Leeward Group of the Society Islands in order to
repair a leak in the hull. On that afternoon we tied up in the
languid port of Uturoa under the crags of Mount Temehani,

sacred to the ancient Polynesians, and soon the sound of hammering below decks was shattering the tropical peace. On deck there was more commotion when a boat brought on board two young Englishmen, who were boisterously greeted by acquaintances of theirs, my fellow passengers the Reverend and Mrs. Chamberlain, American missionaries returning to Boston. This spirited reunion took place in the waist while I was taking my ease alone on the afterdeck under a canvas rigged for shade. From his dress one of the visitors appeared to be a missionary himself, while the other young man was unidentifiable except by his gentlemanly attire and an observant manner that distinguished him from the vigorous savers of souls. He soon took notice of me and, finding me already watching him, smiled uncertainly, looked away, glanced, until there could be no doubt that something about the figure lounging on the afterdeck, in that out-of-the-way harbor under the holy mountain, had stirred the young man's curiosity. I watched him as he took the first opportunity to inquire about me from the Chamberlains and then, their reply having overcome any reticence he might have felt, to approach me.

"Captain Pollard," he said, "my name is George Bennet. May I sit with you?"

I gestured to a chair near mine. "You are welcome to," I told him.

He was about twenty, slender, with dark-brown hair, a lean, handsome face, calm yet intense brown eyes. He told me that he was a Londoner, traveling for his health and—he added with a deprecating smile—his "improvement." He was journeying with the Reverend Tyerman, as his assistant, in order to discover if he himself, in his words, had "a calling to serve the Lord." When he had thus introduced himself, he then asked me about the recent misfortune which the Reverend Chamberlain had alluded to. To this day I cannot explain what it was about this particular young man, a complete stranger to me, that

caused me to speak as freely as I did with him for the better part
of an hour. I suppose that at that time, under the impression
that I had put the *Essex* experiences behind me while I had not
in fact even begun to come to terms with that calamity, much
less the second one, I was ripe for a willing ear. Under that
awning I delivered myself of the story of the *Essex* from her
departure under my command, her cruise, her sinking, to the
drawing of lots; yet again, as on board the *Dauphin,* I found
myself incapable of giving words to my recollections of the
sacrifice of Owen Coffin. Again I began to tremble until at last
I said, "I can tell you no more of that—my head is on fire at
the recollection!"

The young man spoke little, but I knew that he was hearing
my story with understanding and compassion. Then, calmer, I
told him of the loss of the *Two Brothers,* and even as I spoke
I began to comprehend for the first time the finality of my
misfortune. I ended my tale saying, "Now I have lost that vessel
too and am utterly ruined. No owner will ever trust me with
a whaler again, for all will say that I am an unlucky man."

To that, this kind young stranger said something that I would
never forget. He said, "Perhaps, sir, you will in the end gain
more than you have lost."

We must have spoken further, but I have no recollection of
what else was said. He then left the vessel with Reverend Tyerman.

Yes, I did consider not returning to this Island. Who would not,
under the circumstances? At Uturoa it became clear to me that
there would be no more voyages, that my Nantucket whaling
career was over. After George Bennet left the *Pearl,* in that
drowsing Polynesian harbor under the mountain, a place supremely unsuited for practical thinking, I struggled to assess
my prospects and chart a new course. If I did return to the

Island, there would be pressures on me to move with Mary to the Polpis farm. Henry Riddell might make a place for me, under son Bill, in his dry-goods and auction business. But as neither outlook appealed to me, I turned my thoughts to larger, if vaguer, horizons. With daring, anything was possible. My fellow Nantucketer David Whippey had won the confidence of a Polynesian king and now lived as a white regent on his own Pacific island. Other ex-whalemen were prospering in the China trade. Pelts and sandalwood. I could sign on a foreign merchantman, even a sealer or a whaler, provided that no one knew my story. There was the mainland, with its cities, rivers, and the western territories, where enterprising men could make fortunes, it was said. All that was necessary was to venture, take the first step, trust myself to chance.

Yes, in Uturoa I did consider not returning to the Island, though at heart I must have known that I would go back. It would have been unthinkable to leave Mary alone on Nantucket with an absent husband with such a story attached to him, and worse to settle her in some outlandish place before I could provide for her. But something else too was drawing me back, an attraction which on that afternoon, after Bennet had left, I could feel but not define, certain only that it was not the allurement of home comforts, but a challenge as compelling and dangerous as had once been the call of the sea.

At three o'clock the leak was repaired and the *Pearl,* with her Nantucket-bound passenger, set sail for the Horn and Boston.

Part Six

THE NIGHTWATCHMAN

1

As I had surmised in Uturoa, my whaling career had ended on French Frigate Shoal. Though I was not openly blamed for the loss of the *Two Brothers,* I was not exonerated either. There was simply no determination. On the morning of my return to the Island on the sloop *Susan Ann* of Boston, the owners heard my account and Eben Gardner's without comment, but it was plain that I would never again be offered an officer's berth on a Nantucket whaleship. I sensed that the feeling prevailed that I bore a fatality more dire than bad luck, an unnatural onus that could not be squared with the laws of chance. The Island's commonsense view of me now was that I was a Jonah.

Mary once again received me as if nothing had happened that should make any difference to anyone. I even wondered, in the parlor after our supper, whether she understood the consequences of this second disaster. I asked her whether she knew that I would not have another ship.

"Of course I do," she said. "Now maybe I'll get that weather-vane up."

"Been doing some thinking," I told her.

Stony silence greeted this news.

"Been thinking about settling off-Island."

"Hope you got it out of your system."

"There's nothing for me here now."

She nodded as if she had expected as much. "George Pollard," she said, "you're no mainlander."

Seeing that I was still not convinced, she said, "You're home, and folks'll get used to the fact as soon as you do. Meantime, I don't want to hear any more about moving to the continent. A man who can take on the whole Pacific Ocean doesn't need to run away from the place he belongs."

The next morning I borrowed my neighbor Will Pease's bay mare and rode out Polpis Road. I had two visits to make, the first to the farm.

Mary had warned me, but I was not prepared for the changes there. The barn roof was falling in. The house badly needed painting and shingling. The porch sagged crazily. Everything—corn, tomatoes, beans, peas, squash, melons—needed tending. The terns' screeches told me that if this had ever been my home it was not anymore.

I stepped up on the porch. Susan came to the open kitchen door. Thinner now, she wore a patched brown dress, and her ginger-colored hair was uncared for. For a moment, the morning sun behind me, she saw me as a stranger. Then she ran into my arms.

"I've no pearls for you," I told her.

"That's all right, George," she said, looking me over at arm's length. "I'm just glad you're home and won't be killing more whales."

She drew in her breath as if she had said something wrong.

Gently I said, "I didn't know you felt like that about killing whales."

In confusion she said, "I always tried not to—for you."

In the kitchen my mother, thinner too and more careworn than I remembered, turned from the stove and came toward me, wiping her hands on her apron. I embraced her.

"Will you be staying for dinner?" she asked.

From the parlor I heard my father's voice. " 'Course he will, Tamar. What kind of a question is that?"

My mother looked at me as if he hadn't spoken.

"I'll stay for dinner," I told her. "Then I'll be going on to Sconset."

For answer she sniffed, as if to say, "I'd have thought as much."

I went in to see my father. He was stretched out on a narrow brass bed, an heirloom from the Bunkers. Though he was pale and still, I realized how much raw life there was in him even when he was ailing. He managed a smile, tried to sit up, grimaced in pain, eased back.

"Worse than before?"

"Not always. Glad you're home, son."

I sat in a chair near him. "Looks like you could use some help around here."

In the doorway my sister said, "Oh, yes, George. We've been waiting for you—since we heard."

Her voice trailing off, she looked anxiously from my father to my mother for the confirmation that once again she had in some inexplicable way done something she should not have done.

In the kitchen a pot clanged down on the range.

My father said, "Susan only meant to say we're glad you're back. We know you have your own life now."

I smiled at him, regretting that I had never let myself be close to him.

"You're right, there," I told him. "My life's mine again."

"Best way," he said. "Not the easiest, but the best."

I nodded. "I'll lend a hand with the harvest."

My mother stood in the doorway. "How will the harvest be sold?"

"I'll be fit enough Thursday," insisted my father.

Susan was looking at me expectantly. "Remember the good times we used to have in town, George?"

My mother said, "A whaling man don't take vegetables to market."

I turned to my father. "I guess a couple of Polpis men can manage all right."

2

By then, George Worth had given his snug house on Orange Street to his sister and moved to a fishing shack on the wind-swept bluff of the village of Sconset, commanding the Atlantic. There were rumors that living alone was beginning to get to his mind.

That afternoon I knocked at the door of the shack.

"Who's there?" demanded a familiar gruff voice.

When I said my name, I heard grunts and scraping furniture, then the door opened.

I hardly recognized him. He wore a full white beard now, his huge head was balding, his body shrunken and stooped; his eyes were glazed over and seemed to stare past me. In little more than a year he had become an old man.

" 'Bout time you hauled yourself out here," he said. "Come aboard."

The one room he lived in was no bigger than a ship's cabin. A kitchen space at one end, a rumpled cot at the other, a round table with three chairs by a wood stove in the center, a chest of drawers under one of the ocean windows, his sea chest by the door. The only decoration was a small painting on the rough whitewashed wall of a young girl bundled in a fur muff and hat and coat under falling snowflakes. Navigating mostly by feel and memory, my host located a bottle of rum and two glasses and planted them on the table, motioning me to a chair.

"Ain't much," he said, "but it suits me. Had my fill of sitting around with them beached wrecks in town. I can't see to play cribbage anymore. I've heard all their lies and, what's worse, they've heard all mine. 'Least out here I can hear the breakers and the wind."

He poured a couple of fingers in each glass and raised his. "To greasy voyages and safe returns," he said. We drank. Then I said what I had come to say.

"I let you down."

"Stow that," he said. "What happened?"

Using a saltcellar for French Frigate Shoal, a spoon for our course, a knife for the wind, I told him how the *Two Brothers* was lost.

"Could have happened to anyone," he said. "I'd speak for you again, but it wouldn't do any good. Owners are set against taking another chance on you. Idiots, all of 'em." Using his fingers to locate our glasses, he refilled them, reflected a moment, then asked, "What's ahead for you?"

"The farm, for now. They can use some help."

"Then what? You're no dirt scratcher. Never was."

"Thought I might ship out of New Bedford or Sag Harbor, but it seems they've heard of the *Essex* there."

His glazed eyes sought mine, then he spoke quietly. "They've heard of the *Essex* wherever men speak of ships."

"Thought of going to the mainland. Mary's set against it."

"She's dead right. What would you do with yourself? Skipper a steamboat on the Hudson River?"

When I hesitated he said, "Strikes me your toughest fight's still ahead of you"—he raised his finger to his temple—"here!"

Then he pointed to the floor. "And right here on this Island. The sea kind of takes care of you, in its way. Ashore you're on your own."

We gammed and drank away most of that afternoon. In his long career he had formed a generally low opinion of that class of men he called "the owners," but which I understood comprised a larger segment of humanity than the proprietors of ships.

"It's ledger entries to them. They don't know the real cost of them clean candles and fine white oil. We do. We know the price men pay for it, by God! To kill whales there's got to be fury in your arm and fire in your heart or you're dead, your men with you. You don't strike whales for the damned oil. You've got to love the hunt and the kill till you've precious little love for anything else. You've got to stand up to what no man was meant to stand up to while every other bluewater sailor considers you the scum of the seas! You've got to go through Hell and come out the other side with faith in yourself." He crashed his fist on the table. "That's where the real fight is!"

He broke off, adrift, found his bearings on another tack. By then, the reddish sun was at the western windows and the rum was doing good work on us both.

"Day'll come when they fish whales with rockets fired from ships' decks. Glad I won't be here to see that. What kind of whalemen could pride themselves on such work? By then our breed'll be long dead and gone." Then he cried out, "By the Eternal, George, I don't envy 'em! They'll be born damned and won't know why!"

One other thing Worth said that day stuck in my mind. Even though I was three sheets to the wind, I remember it. Out of the blue he had reached over and clapped me on the shoulder and said, "By God, George, you'll be lord of this Island yet!"

When I left the shack, the rum bottle was empty, the sun was setting, and I owe my safe return that night to the good judgment of Pease's mare.

For three days I worked at the harvest from dawn to dusk, sleeping in my old room overlooking the Inner Harbor. In that time I don't believe a waking hour passed that I didn't think of Thursday, regretting my impulsive promise. To me, who had twice surveyed the town from my own quarterdeck, the prospect of delivering provisions to ships such as I had commanded, yes, and dreamed of owning was, as the day approached, increasingly unpleasant. Each night in that house I had nightmares. Before dawn on Thursday, I dreamed that under my Centre Street window the nightwatchman had stopped, but when he raised his lantern I saw that it was not Silas Bench but Hezekiah Coffin, his face bloody and broken, staring up at me. From the deck of the *Essex* I saw the whale making for the ship, as Chase had seen him, felt the vessel shudder from the blow, watched him make off, veer back, turn, shake the sea in fury, begin his second run. I was dancing with a young Nancy Coffin at Sheepshearing, but as the fiddle played and we turned gracefully on the grass, in my arms she became an old woman with hatred in her eyes. On the quarterdeck John Mamula was backing away from me, on the eight walking legs of a spider. And as each vision gave place to another I was drawn helplessly toward some ultimate horror. My frozen hands offered the straws to Owen Coffin. Water lapped at the bows of the boat. Ramsdell held the revolver to Coffin's head. Desperate to save my kinsman, I led him up a rocky mountainside. At the summit, under low, still clouds, was a clearing in the center of which was a gray flat rock. Everything was gray. Owen looked at me, bewildered, trusting. Then, as I watched helplessly, he laid his head down on the stone. I wanted to cry out, but I could not move or speak. A shot cleaved the blue sky. His bright blood spilled into the sea.

I awoke howling. A figure stood in the doorway. Shaking, I stifled my cry.

" 'Bout time," said my father.

He came into the room.

"Guess I was dreaming," I said, still trembling.

"You got cause to dream—and holler too. 'Bout time you did."

"I thought I was over it."

"You're not, and you won't be until you stop fighting it off. Something like that's bound to get to you. Best let it."

I felt a rush of affection for this man I had hardly let myself know. I said, "Time to get started for town?"

"No need," he said. "I can manage easy."

For just an instant I felt relief. Then I was overcome by uneasiness. I asked myself, What are you afraid of? Can it be that you went chasing after whales just to meet Nantucket on your own terms? Have you stood the worst the Pacific could give you to still be gallied by a damned village? I thought, This is the fight Worth meant, only beginning.

"I'm going with you."

"No need."

"Yes, there is."

His smile came slowly. "Susan'll be tickled," he said.

It was a radiant warm day, freshened by shifting airs, a hint of autumn. The three of us hitched the roan to the loaded wagon, and with Susan between me and Father I drove out to the Polpis Road and turned west. Soon, beyond the rise of moor, the two steeples came into view, the four windmills on Popsquatchet Hills turning grudgingly. At the milestone we heard nine wavering peals of the South Tower bell.

The road passes close by East Mill. There, at the rise where the sand rut becomes cobbles and starts down, the whole town heaves into view, the steep, shingled roofs, brick chimneys, wharves, masts, blue water to the spit of white sand that forms the harbor. Ponderously the four wood-framed canvas vanes of the mill swept over our heads. The creaking of wooden machinery, the grinding of the giant stones, these sounds stirred my uneasiness, my countryman's fear of the town.

Down New Dollar Lane and onto Main I drove, standing up, Nantucket-style, sennit hat back on my head, nodding greetings to passersby, draymen, wagoners, shopkeepers, letting one and all know that if the sea had played a few tricks on me it had not gotten to my pride, that I was home to stay and with no apologies to anyone. I greeted everyone I knew, some I didn't. Gideon Folger and Gilbert Coffin on the steps of the Pacific Bank, Jim Starbuck, Sam Jenks, Bill Folger, even Caleb Mitchell as he drove past me in his fancy chaise looking up at me in surprise. At Centre Street we picked up an escort of six young boys on the prowl for adventure. Recognizing me, they took up our pace, walking abreast of us down past John Folger's house, Miss Macy's shop, Riddell's dry goods, Cromwell Bernard's tailor shop, Miss Cary's boarding house, across Federal Street and past the Merchants Bank, William Hadwin's office, Zenas Coffin's three-story building, the gambrel-roofed warehouses at Union Street, through the press of wagons, carts, drays, bearing hemp to the ropewalks, spars to the wharves, canvas to the sail lofts, boxes to the candleworks, casks of oil to the refineries, past South Water Street, past the blacksmith shop where Amos Paddack had set his anvil clanging as he forged a lance while his son Ben ground an edge on an iron, past Whale Street, the boys following us right out Straight Wharf and up alongside the whaleship *Alexander,* where we were going.

There, to the clatter of caulking mallets and screams of winches, the boys, various idlers, and the outfitters had the privilege of watching George Pollard, Jr., former master of the *Essex* and the *Two Brothers,* loading baskets of vegetables and

kegs of pickled cucumbers on board the *Alexander,* as if nothing was the matter.

I was in the highest spirits. The boys were staring at me as
if to see if I had blood on my lips. I felt a freedom I had never
known before. Susan, sensing the change in me, was happy. My
father sat on a bench gamming with friends, watching me with
a look of satisfaction.

Suddenly, in a single movement, the boys darted off toward
the end of the wharf. I looked up. A great white stern-wheeler
was leaning round Brant Point. Everyone followed the boys out
for a better look, for a steamboat was a rare spectacle in those
days. I stood with my father and sister watching as the vessel
righted to an even keel and made for Old North Wharf. Then
a white plume rose from the smokestack and an amazing sound
shook the harbor. Susan clapped her hands to her ears, as the
gulls on pilings and roofs took to the air. The sound echoed up
the Inner Harbor and back. Mallets stopped, only the clang of
the anvil and the churning of the reversing paddle wheel filled
the silence that followed. The boys watched the marvelous
vessel, rapt, oblivious now of the ex-captain of the *Essex.*

3

That autumn my father's back improved, and, with the harvest
on, I did not return to Polpis. In October I was employed as
an assistant to my neighbor William Pease, a surveyor, who was
then engaged in platting the commons on the western end of the
Island. On his box wagon we traveled grown-over lanes and
ruts, braving bees, mosquitoes, poison ivy, sumac, jounced over

rolling moors that reminded me of the sea, ran lines through thickets, by ponds and hummocks, along bluffs above the sweeping beaches, returning late with the gray-rose twilight behind us, hearing the faint bell from the town.

The pay was small, but I valued Will Pease's company. About my own age, tall, lean, he spoke little, saying only what needed to be said and nothing more. Having never gone to sea, never married, his whole life was the Island, and I learned from him, as I had never let myself learn from my father, that a landsman may acquire an independence of spirit as strong as any seaman's. He kept a journal every day, entering receipts and expenditures, where he went and whom he met, and anything else that caught his attention. But his curiosity stopped at the shoreline. His interest in the mainland and the rest of the world appeared to be nil. Never in our rambles together did he ask me about the *Essex.*

I was sorry when in December the survey was completed and he had no more work for me.

In that month Mary's father offered me a clerkship in his Main Street store. With misgivings, feeling no calling for the work, I accepted. For six weeks I kept accounts, served customers, received merchandise at the wharves, until it became clear to both Henry Riddell and myself that whatever the Lord wanted of me it was not to be a shopkeeper. The quarterdeck, it seems, is not a good apprenticeship for the stockroom. My resignation was accepted as cheerfully as it had been offered.

From February to April of 1824 I was without regular employment. I fished with my father, dug peat for fuel, roamed the moors and beaches, visited George Worth in Sconset, and generally engaged in that Nantucket pastime known as *rantumscooting;* that is, going from one place to another with no special purpose. In late April, for the first time, I found the courage to open the water-stained Bowditch navigator in which I had kept the rough log of our ninety-one days in the open boat. The penciled entries (alongside and in between the columns of islands and coordinates) were brief and stark. They stirred memories.

Nov 25   Wind ESE strong. Bread damaged. Chase's boat repaired.

Nov 28   In the night attacked by a large fish. Damage repaired. No sleep.

Dec 8   Gale. Violent squall. Thirst. No sleep.

Dec 20   Raised Ducie Island 24°4'S 124°40'W. Great relief. Our hopes refreshed.

Jan 11   We bury Matthew Joy in the sea.

Jan 15   Lawson Thomas died. Consumed for food in the 3rd boat. Fairly heavy swells. Wind NNE.

Feb 1   Owen Coffin shot.

It was at this uncertain time in my life that I resolved to keep, like Pease, a journal of my observations. I bought a notebook with a mottled black-and-white cover for that purpose, making the first entry on April 29, 1824. Reading over these early entries today I find that they offer few hints to the storms that were raging in me at that time. The April 29 item, with its false leads to my state of mind, is particularly deceptive.

April 29, 1824.

A clear, cold Sabbath. Attend the North Church service with Mary, her father, mother, brother Bill, to please Mary (more truthfully, to avoid displeasing her). Reverend John Mooers officiates. Nancy Coffin and Ann occupy their pew two ahead of ours. Nancy looks ravaged by grief and elixir. Ann appears pale, unwell, sad. Mary says that since the death of Edward, Nancy will not let her out of her sight, keeping her a prisoner in that gloomy house. Reverend Mooers tells us that suffering is caused by opposing the will of God. He says that the undeveloped man will suffer until he attains consciousness of God. He says that suffering activates the three great principles of spiritual growth— faith, hope and love; that the beauty of morning is known because of the darkness of night, that sorrow and suffering are forever making channels of joy, even as winter storms make channels through the Bar. As we leave the church Ann tries to speak to me. Nancy hurries her away. No one explains to Reverend Mooers that winter storms cause the Bar to shoal.

This afternoon I walked to Brant Point to watch the *Alexander* weigh anchor and clear the harbor. For the first time I begin to understand what it will be like to spend the rest of my life on this Island.

I must find employment this week.

Who could imagine from this entry the turmoil I was in then? I was reconciled to nothing. The confidence that I had felt the day I drove the wagon to town had left me, and I was more invaded by self-doubt than ever. Nowhere in that church, in the Bibles in our hands, in the Reverend Mooers's words, in this world was God present. Far from lifting my spirits, the sermon cast me down. I thought, Dear Lord, if you exist, is it your will that I live the rest of my days as an outcast on this Island, deprived of peace, ordinary dealings, friendship, love, faith? No answer. God is mum. Damnation, what is the sense of this life of mine? Where can it lead but to madness? Lord, I am guilty

—surely you will permit me to be guilty? I have lain with my mother's sister. I have killed her son, my kinsman and all but a son to me, and eaten of his flesh. I am the guiltiest man on earth. Will you agree? Is it too much to ask? Anything but this silence.

And so on. Church was no place for me. I did not truly seek God to pull me through. It was only words, play-acting. I was on my own, and knew it.

The reference to the "death of Edward" is to the fact that Nancy's other son was lost with all hands when his vessel was caught in a hurricane off Barbados. So, all of her men had now perished at sea, leaving her alone with Ann.

May 1.

To Polpis this morning. Replaced two rafters in the barn. Found father much improved. On to Sconset in the afternoon. Geo. Worth is, in his own phrase, "slipping his moorings" and knows it well. It is painful to witness his efforts to keep his thoughts on course and his memory alive. Once, for a full minute or so, even as he was talking to me he could not remember who I was. I grow dim in his mind.

The diarist is still shying away from the truth. In that meeting with Worth I felt in fact that, despite his momentary lapse, the old man was seeing past all my disguises to a part of me that I was hiding even from myself.

May 4.

Silas Bench is dead. He succumbed yesterday morning to consumption, said to have been induced by the noxious

effluvia of night air. He was an excellent whaleman, and
that is about all anyone knows of him. He leaves no family
on Nantucket, no estate, and few impressions but of his
twisted face and twisted humor. I learned from Peleg
Crosby of the watch that I was thought by some to have
been Bench's closest friend on the Island.

The Coffin ship *Lydia* sailed today for the Pacific.

To Coatue with Pease for quahogs. Mary concocted an
excellent chowder which the three of us enjoyed this evening.

May 16.

The question of gainful employment must be resolved.
I am determined not to remain a dependent of Mary's
father. In conversation on Old North Wharf with Peleg
Crosby of the watch, he suggested that I apply to the
selectmen for Silas Bench's place on it. I was taken aback,
having never envisioned myself engaged in such a menial
occupation. "Why not?" I said to Peleg, not to offend him,
his proposal having been kindly meant.

May 27.

Today the selectmen approved my petition for the place
on the night watch. Mary accepts my new occupation
without complaint, despite the disruption to our lives that
will result from the night hours, and despite my reduced
station in life.

It is obvious that between the 16th and the 27th of May
something induced me to accept an employment which I had
previously considered demeaning. It might be assumed that it
was a simple question of material need, of debt, of accepting one
humiliation to free myself from another, reluctantly accepting
an adverse fate, but this was not the way it was.

Rather, it was my pride asserting itself in earnest. I discovered that I had no need to worm respect from a community that dared not stand in judgment of me. I would walk their streets at night with an appearance of humbleness such as has never been seen on this Island!

November 30.

"Horrible Mutiny!!!" So begins the *Inquirer*'s account of a most dire tale of brutal officers, an insubordinate crew, mutiny, and murder on board the Nantucket whaleship *Globe*. The chief perpetrator was—to the surprise of no one who knew him—a wild young man, with a snarled and dreamy mind—Samuel Comstock. A boatsteerer on board the *Globe,* he persuaded a number of the crew to mutiny with the object of freeing themselves from the harsh discipline of the vessel and becoming kings of a Pacific island. In the dark of midnight, Comstock, accompanied by several others, descended into the cabin and hacked to death the captain and his three officers. He and his mutineers, keeping others in terror, then set a course for the Marshall Islands to claim a kingdom there. Ashore, Comstock and all but two of those with him were stoned and speared to death by natives. Five others, having eluded the mutineers, sailed the *Globe* to Valparaiso. One of the survivors, a Joseph Thomas, has been arraigned in Nantucket as an accessory to mutiny and murder. He will stand trial in the Federal Court in Boston, where it is to be hoped that mainland jurisprudence will shed light on this murky matter, so that justice will be done and the public consoled.

Dec. 4.

Jephthah Clasby reported today that while fishing offshore he saw a sea serpent. Quahoging with Pease.

Jan. 20, 1825.

Nancy Coffin came to our house at 7 P.M. She told us that Ann was very sick and wanted to see me. I went with her and on the way asked how ill my cousin was. "Dying," said she.

In the last of the dusk we stepped up on the porch and entered the dark house. I followed Nancy up the stairs and down the hall toward the back bedroom door, which stood open.

My young cousin lay in bed motionless, her face white and skeletal. Slowly she turned her head toward me and smiled gently.

"Hello, cousin," she said. "I'm glad you've come."

"I'm sorry to find you ill."

She started to answer but was taken by a fit of coughing that racked her frail body. When she could speak she said to her mother, "Have you told him?"

Nancy did not reply.

"Please. You promised."

Nancy then said, "I forgive you, George." But there was no forgiveness in her voice.

Ann, pained and desperate, half rising on one arm, said, "Forgive him in your heart, Mother. You can."

Nancy looked at me, then closed her eyes, and when she opened them again I felt that she was seeing me as I had been to her long ago.

"I had no reason to blame you," she said. "So I have no reason to forgive you. I wish you peace."

Ann lay back in repose. After a silence she said, "God will forgive us all our sins. God bless you, George." She reached out, and I took her hand. "Say a prayer for me."

"I will," I said. And I did.

For the first time in my life, from depths of myself unknown to me, I prayed for the salvation of another human being.

Jan. 21.

Ann, last child of Hezekiah and Nancy Coffin, died of consumption today.

4

May 1, 1826.

Last night an encounter with Caleb Mitchell. We met on Main as I was trying the door of Miss Macy's shop to verify that that trusting lady had locked it. I said, "Good evening, sir. Fine evening." He looked at me in astonishment. My old antagonist, who had always quailed before me, was completely at a loss. He stammered, "Good evening—Pollard." I said, "Captain Pollard, sir." The other looked at me in dismay. "Captain Pollard." I smiled and touched my hat.

An interesting entry. We are shown the nightwatchman exulting in confounding his "old antagonist" with his false servility, then bringing him up short with a bullying demand to be addressed by his old rank. The tone betrays the diarist's strenuous evasion of true feeling.

Oct. 30, 1826.

Today John Francis, Jr., sighted a sea serpent off Rose and Crown Shoal. For the first time Henry Coffin attended the Unitarian service. May he too find what he is seeking. The *Inquirer* reports that the Congreve Rocket was used successfully against nine whales in less than one hour. The future is upon us.

Feb. 1, 1827.

Nancy Coffin Wyer has returned from Providence for the purpose of selling her house, furniture, and belongings and of showing off her new husband, a short heavy man, a decade her senior, who, it is said, complains of the smell of whale oil here. They will make their nest in Providence. My aunt appears determined to be content in the company of Mr. Wyer, defiant toward the town, delighted to be leaving. For the sake of form she paid a farewell visit at Polpis. None at Centre Street. She made it plain that she did not wish to see me, and I kept out of her way. May she find happiness and peace at last.

March 3.

Mrs. Wyer departed this P.M. on the New Bedford steamer, and I shall surely never see her again in this life.

Dear God, if only that prophecy had proved true!

July 6, 1828.

This morning in the predawn hours Zenas Coffin died. Late this afternoon the funeral Meeting took place and at dusk the burial at the Quaker cemetery. So passes an excellent man. If there is whaling in the hereafter, he will make the most of it.

I remember that day well. During my rounds I found all the windows alight in Zenas's large plain house on Pine Street. Through the panes I saw women laying him out. Even then my thoughts were less upon the death of this "excellent man" than upon its immediate bearing on myself. For it happened that Mary was a friend of Zenas's widow, Abial, and her circle, and this meant that she would ordinarily have ridden to the cemetery with those friends in one of the leading carriages. But what of me? Was the nightwatchman with his lurid past to share a carriage with Quaker lords and ladies? I had no wish to put the question to a test. Later that morning, to make matters easier for Mary, I said that I would not go to the burial, and she said that we were both going and that was that. And so it was. At four, when the South Tower bell tolled for Zenas, she and I joined the crowd outside the Pine Street house, where carriages awaited the Friends inside. Through the open door and the windows we could see them, standing mute for ten minutes as the bell went on tolling, then exchanging handclasps, after which the unpainted pine casket was borne outside by men of the family, sons Charles and Henry foremost, and raised onto a plain gray cart. Then Abial came out and her sons were helping her into the leading carriage when she caught sight of Mary, then me, hesitated, spoke to Charles. That gentleman came toward us, raised his hat, and said, "Mrs. Pollard, my mother would be pleased if you would accompany her to the cemetery. We have one place." Without hesitation Mary replied, "Please thank her, Charles, but I will walk with my husband."

And walk we did, with the crowd in the dust of thirty-seven carriages that followed the rude hearse to Zenas's unmarked grave.

April 6, 1832.

In these thriving times a nightwatchman is not without importance. There are acres of oil casks at the wharves, cash in the banks, fine merchandise in the shops, and mansions are being built on Main Street that would astonish the old Quakers. There is much to watch over.

I remember those days, the Golden Age of Nantucket's whale fishery. Charles and Henry Coffin were building their twin brick houses across the street from each other. And soon Joseph Starbuck did them one better, putting up three bricks in a row, up the street, for his three sons. and Joseph's son-in-law William Hadwin would build, just down from them across the street, his two great houses with columned porticoes. All this from whales and well-thrown irons.

Aug. 12.

Saw Chase last night at the new shipworks. Lost in reflection on his good fortune. The first whaleship ever built on Nantucket is being built for him. The *Charles Carroll* will be launched in two or three months; 395 tons. I did not interrupt his thoughts.

The moon was out that night. Chase, standing on the Brant Point beach gazing up at his nearly completed vessel, had not heard me approach. Remembering how he had bemoaned his ill fortune when I had been given the *Two Brothers,* I could not help smiling. Chase had by then become one of our most successful whaling masters. After the death of his first wife, Peggy, he had married the pretty widow of our once shipmate Matthew, Nancy Slade Joy. He had four children. He owned a house on Orange Street. He played cribbage and gammed with other captains at the brick Pacific Club at the foot of Main, where I had never chosen to venture. Between his cruises we would sometimes meet in town. A ritual developed. We would

ask after each other's families, then about the other survivors
from the *Essex*'s boats. Surprisingly perhaps, all three, including Ramsdell, eventually returned to whaling, married, settled
off-Island, and were on their ways to successful careers in the
fishery, when Chase and I began to lose track of them, then
interest in them. In those early years, Chase, remembering
Chappel, would take his leave of me with a "See you in Liverpool," but that custom wore thin, and as time passed our en-
counters were more and more perfunctory, finally uneasy. As
memories of his recent cruises crowded out those of the *Essex,*
I became a living reminder of what he dearly wanted to forget.
I came to know pretty well how his thoughts ran when we met.
No longer in the least interested in guessing what made me tick,
he would say to himself, "How the poor fellow has come down
in the world. I must not let him know that I see it." Only then,
that night, as I turned away from him without letting him know
I was there, did it strike me that I must appear to Owen Chase
as not so long ago Silas Bench had appeared to me.

5

After the Chase entry the diary breaks off. From the record it
appears that for fifteen years—between 1832 and the present—
nothing happened in my life worth noting. Outwardly this is so.
I walked my rounds at night. Bluefished with Pease. Gammed
on the benches at Old North Wharf—never, of course, speaking
of the *Essex.* Once when a Vineyard man persisted in question-
ing me on that subject, I got up and walked away without a
word. This action was reported and made an excellent impres-

sion. In these years I cultivated a deferential, humble manner, suitable to a member of the night watch. I lived a quiet, sober, unobtrusive life. I watched over the town by night, kept out of the way by day. Little by little I let happen what Worth had warned against; I let myself become what the Island saw me as: a man with a fouled past, stripped of consequence, a town character. At first the change was only an outward one. Gradually it worked inward, until I knew myself only as the humble nightwatchman.

I remember the morning in the spring of 1834 when the news reached town that George Worth's body had been found rolling in the surf below his house in Sconset. It was thought that he walked into the sea. I came back from the wharves to the house, feeling low, so low, in fact, that I said a foolish thing. I told Mary what had happened, then, not thinking, added, "My only real friend in this world is dead."

At that she twisted her mouth to one side, as she does when she's vexed, and said, "I'm sorry to hear it. I'll fix some tea."

I sat at the kitchen table while she brewed tea, neither of us saying a word, then she put the cups on the table, sat across from me, studied me a while, then said, "Good a time as any for a talk, Captain Pollard."

"What about?"

"You."

I waited.

"Should be easier now," she said.

"What?"

"Hiding from yourself. Hiding what happened to you. Hiding your thoughts about it. Now that your only real friend in the world is dead."

Only then did I see what was bothering her. I said, "Didn't

mean to include you, Mary. You're more than a friend."

She sniffed. "Am I now?"

"You're my wife, and you've stood by me more than I ever could have expected. It's just that Worth—he knew what I went through, and not just at sea. He knew what it means to a man to be beached."

"Ever occur to you that a woman's born beached?"

"Always figured that was their choosing."

"Just try being a woman and choosing something else!"

"There are wives of whaleship masters who ship with their husbands."

"Not the same. Not that I'm complaining. But a wife's for more than standing by you. A wife's to love, George Pollard."

"I do love you, Mary."

She thought this over, then said, "You're doing your best."

"I thought I pleased you."

"Didn't mean that. You 'please' me just fine. What I meant was, you're doing your best for a man who won't let himself near what he feels."

When I didn't answer, she went on, saying what she must have been holding back for a long time. "My friends say, 'What strength your George has to come through what he has so easy in his mind,' and I say, 'Ain't it so?' but I know better. You haven't come through it. Instead you've shut yourself off from the memory of it, from this Island, from me. You blame yourself for what couldn't be helped. You fight it alone—that's what's wrong!" Near tears, she said, "George Worth was the loneliest-seeming man I ever met!"

"He was a whaleman, like me. Whalemen aren't famous for feelings."

"Not for sharing them. That's for sure."

"Who was it said, 'Sooner you forget about it, sooner everyone else will'?"

She smiled a little and said, "A wife's for making mistakes."

"I do love you."

"You just better. We're beached together, George Pollard, and don't you go forgetting it."

6

During the late 1830s my family's life on the Polpis farm grew harder, finally desperate. My father's back was worse than ever, and finding that he could no longer make a living on his own, he came to depend on neighbors who worked the farm for shares. People deal with adversity in different ways. My mother burrowed in the Word. In the Book of Revelation she found signs that Nantucket was facing its day of Judgment, when the sea would give up its dead and the Quaker cemetery would give up its dead and all who were not written in the book of life would be cast into the lake of fire. For our sins. For killing whales. For my sins. She predicted that a great conflagration would consume the Island. Nobody believed her.

My father had a different vision. In his eightieth year, crippled, with no capital but what little the farm would bring, he got the idea of moving to Ohio and starting over. Why Ohio I don't know. The idea was crazy any way you looked at it. No one was more rooted on this Island than he. It was home, church, everything to him. He couldn't move without pain. The notion of "starting over" at his age in such circumstances seemed like a sure sign of dementia. I took to visiting more often, in the hope of getting to know him better before he failed or died.

One afternoon Susan had seen me coming and came out on

the road to meet me. She was a middle-aged woman now, and I had come to realize that in her way she knew everything important there was to know about her world except that it was very small.

She said, "George, Father says we're going to Ohio soon. Will you come with us?"

I took her hand and we walked toward the house. "I have to look after Mary," I told her.

"Bring her too. We'll all be together."

"Mary wouldn't go. She loves the Island too much."

"Keep a secret?"

"Yes."

"We'll never leave either. Don't tell Father. It would kill him to know."

Later, alone with my father, I asked him how Tamar took to the idea of leaving Nantucket. He only said, "A change'll do her a world of good."

"You're really planning on going?"

"Soon as I'm fit."

"How does Mother feel about it?"

He smiled. "Can you keep a secret?"

"Yes."

"She thinks it'll never happen. Susan too. They both humor me. Just like you're doing."

On that and other visits we did get a little better acquainted. He died the same year, in November. My mother survived him by six days. Susan came to live with us for a time, then with Betsy and Tom at Hudson, where she is now.

Since my father's death I have come to understand what lay behind his Ohio project, at least to my own satisfaction. There must have come a time after the soil and his bones and joints all gave out on him when he knew that he could no longer endure the pall of calamity which my mother cast over that house without growing to hate her. He needed a vision of hope if he was to go on caring for her, a faith that all would be well in Ohio if he was not to abandon her to the dark of her mind, an affirmation that there was a reason for their needing each other. The Ohio dream was no mere clinging to his peace of mind through a delusion; it was an act of love.

The strange thing was that my mother's forebodings all came true.

7

Tamar had often said that Nancy would come to a bad end. In fact, once she said that she would be clothed in Hell Fire, and to that I swear. Except for that one time, what she said were ordinary things for an older sister to say about a flightier, prettier, younger one, whom she disapproved of and had probably envied at one time. I don't know whether or not my mother somehow knew about Nancy and me, but if she did it would help explain the bad blood between the sisters. But whether Tamar did or did not know, looking back, remembering what she said and how she said it, especially her saying that Nancy would be clothed in Hell Fire, I cannot help believing that she somehow foresaw that dreadful July night in 1846.

Not two weeks before, Nancy Bunker Coffin Wyer had returned to Nantucket, alone, in fragile health and, it was soon apparent, unsound mind, arriving unannounced on the New Bedford steamer and, with no house of her own now, had taken an attic room in Mrs. Robertson's boardinghouse on Federal Street.

Why she had come back without her husband or the son she'd had by him was a mystery at first, but not for long. The morning after Nancy's arrival, Clara Robertson spread the word that Mrs. Wyer had gone on a crying jag and told her that a month before, her son had for reasons unknown taken his father's pistol and ended his thirteen-year-old life with one shot in the brain and that, not long afterward, Mr. Wyer had left her a note saying that he was going to the Far West and not to look for him. The reason, according to Mrs. Robertson, was not hard to find. That Temperance lady had happened to observe no fewer than seven Dr. Damon's Elixir bottles among Mrs. Wyer's things, three empty, and she let everyone know that only Christian decency had prevented her from throwing her out in the street.

I never did see Nancy then, except one night on my rounds as a stout, unsteady shadow on the wall of a dormer window.

On those early summer nights while my aunt was destroying her brain and body with an alcohol-and-opium-laced patent medicine, another Nantucket woman was sweeping the skies with a powerful telescope, installed in her father's observatory on top of the Pacific Bank.

Since this formidable young woman figures prominently in the July calamity, and peripherally in the nightwatchman's life at that time, I will introduce Maria Mitchell here.

When she had been a child (not pretty but bright as could be) growing up on Vestal Street, where her father had had his first observatory, I used to imagine from the way she would look at me that I filled her with horror. In those days some Nantucket parents used me as a bugaboo to frighten their children into obedience. "Mind, or Captain Pollard will get you," they'd say. I should have known that her parents, William and Lydia Mitchell, being enlightened people, would never have resorted to such threats, and that behind the girl's wide-eyed gaze when we'd pass on the sandy lanes was not revulsion but a curiosity that was both scientific and compassionate; for many don't realize that for all her braininess and crusty ways Maria has a broad streak of kindness in her. It took me a while, but I have even come to understand that her vexed look whenever our paths cross is directed not so much at me as at the problem I present to her. She can never quite explain me out of her mind any way she tries. I think she judges the problem of Captain Pollard's existence to be something like a problem in astronomy, requiring intricate trigonometry rather than plain reckoning. When I stand before her desk at the Atheneum with my monthly ration of books and she looks up at me with her questing eyes that seem to have nothing to do with her set-in-her-ways face, I am sure of this.

A child at the time of the *Essex* disaster, she would have heard from her father how George Pollard had come raging back from the Pacific, pouring out his terrible story to anyone who would listen, to Zimri Coffin of the *Dauphin,* who rescued him, to George Worth of the *Two Brothers,* who brought him home. William Mitchell might even have told his daughter how the young captain then seemed possessed by the need to make known exactly what had happened in the boats, so that the Island could gauge with what proportion of judgment and compassion to receive the survivors, as if this were a matter that Nantucket was prepared to resolve for itself. He might have told her how his effort soon ended in failure, how an interdiction against any mention of the *Essex* was imposed, and how he was given a new command, that same *Two Brothers,* as if nothing had happened, the owners as eager as he to believe that he was not in any way blighted and that lightning never strikes twice in the same place.

Maria Mitchell would have known at least something of all this, as she settled into womanhood, a bride of Science, lover of Milton and Shakespeare, stargazer. Lately, since her discovery of the comet, I see her almost every day. Dressed in plain gray with a white shawl and white cambric cap, she strides spinster-proud past our house on her evening constitutional from the bank to the Cliff and back. Still no beauty—she has the face of an old sea-dog—she has something about her that tells you at once she is someone special. Not that fame has changed her. It would take more than a medal from the King of Denmark and the acclaim of the Western world's scientists to turn Maria's head. She goes on about her business just as she has done for years, checking out books by day, tracking the movement of stellar bodies by night, finding companionship in Orion and the Aurora Borealis; in Vega, Deneb, and Altair; in mighty Antares; just as she had been doing the night of the Great Fire.

8

It started in Will Geary's hat shop on the south side of lower Main, about eleven o'clock at night. I had come up toward Main to Geary's store, where I found young Tom Hussey and Zeph Congdon peering in the windows at a flickering red glow. As I approached I saw that the whole back of the shop was in flames. I then told Hussey, "Tom, you run up Main hollering as loud as you can, and fetch Caleb Mitchell." And to Congdon I said, "Zeph, you run over Federal doing the same and get Ben Bartlett. Quick as you can!" Both looked at me wondering who I was to be giving orders until I yelled at them, "Get moving!" They ran off, shouting the alarm. Soon, people came running out of their houses, some with leather fire buckets, converging on the shop. Sam Macy said, "Come on, boys, let's bust in that door." I shouted, "Not yet. That'd fan the flames. Start a bucket chain from the cistern first, and hope to God Caleb and Ben get those hand pumpers here *now!*" Everyone stared at me, until Charles Coffin, who had just come up, said, "Captain Pollard's right. Form a chain." And they did.

It took the two fire brigades almost five minutes to collect their brigades and bring up the hand pumpers, but I figured that even at that they'd arrived just in time to contain the fire to Geary's shop. What happened next, however, would be hard for a mainlander to believe if he didn't know about that special madness that passes for pride on this Island.

Ben Bartlett ordered his men to run a hose across the cobbles to the cistern on the other side. At this, Caleb said, "Hold on, Ben. This one's ours." (I swear he said that. I heard him myself.)

At that, Bartlett replied, "No, it ain't, Mitchell. Last one didn't count."

"Did so," said Mitchell.

Hearing this exchange, Charles Coffin, now joined by his brother Henry, proceeded to protest, but in a gentlemanly way that had no effect on the rivals, whose determined faces, confronting each other, now shone brightly in the light of the flames.

I then shouted in a quarterdeck voice that none present had ever heard from me, "God damn it, the two of you get those pumpers working, and quick!"

They looked at me, hesitated, then inside the shop there was a crash, a crackling roar, and flames appeared at the second-story windows. A shout arose. Caleb and Ben then ordered their men to run out their hoses, the pumps were worked furiously, the door broken in, streams of water directed inside, while the head of the bucket chain heaved splashes on the fire.

Then the roof roared into flame swirling high into the night. Nearby roofs caught, and soon the whole south side of Main Street was burning. Everywhere people were carrying silver, china, pictures, everything they could carry out of shops and their houses. Freed horses galloped wild-eyed in the streets. Soon the flames leaped Main to the north side, worked west toward the brick bank and the wooden Methodist Church, east toward the oil-soaked wharves.

I ran down Centre, found Mary heaving a bucket of water on the front of our house, starting in for another. When she saw me she asked, "Will it get to us?"

"Whole town may go. Best get up to Mill Hill."

She glanced up at the roaring sky behind me, just as a tremendous explosion, then another shook the ground under our feet.

I shouted, "They're blowing up buildings. Last chance to stop it. I'll lend a hand. Get up to Mill Hill. You'll be safe there."

She looked at me an instant, then said, "You do what you have to, George. I'm wetting down this house." And she went in for another bucket of water.

Down Centre I found a crowd around the steps of the Methodist Church. Beyond lay the blasted ruins of two houses on either side of Orange Street. Maria Mitchell, a cloak over her nightdress, stood on the church portico between two columns. A cart stood in front of the church, a wet tarpaulin over its load. Lieutenant Davis and his men from the Coast Survey ship *Gallatin* were squared off facing a very determined woman.

Davis shouted, "Please, Miss Mitchell, we got to blow up the church to save the west end of town. Come down."

"I told you, Lieutenant, this church goes, I go with it."

I came up and called out, "Got to be done, Miss Mitchell."

She glared at me, then said, "Know what a cyclone is, Captain Pollard?"

"I ought to."

"Then look behind you."

I turned. By then the whole center of town bounded by Main, Centre, Broad, and the harbor was a single firestorm, creating its own winds in the still night, swirling—inward.

"That fire's not crossing this street," she said. "So, Lieutenant, you set your men to wetting down roofs and cart that black powder off somewhere it won't hurt anybody."

I saw that what she said made sense, and the lieutenant did too but was not about to take orders from a woman.

I said to him, "Miss Mitchell's right, Davis."

Twice stung now, he demanded, "Who in hell are *you* to be handing out orders, Pollard?"

I just looked at him. I said nothing. Whatever he saw in my eyes answered his question. I could see that he was calculating how to back down with the least damage. Just then we heard a detonation from the direction of the wharves, then another, then a ripple of thunderous explosions becoming a single great blast that shook the whole town.

The oil casks. The Island's wealth. And with it our means of production, the refineries, storehouses, ropewalks, sail lofts, everything was going up in flames.

Maria Mitchell was coming down the steps, and Lieutenant Davis had ordered the powder cart hauled up Liberty Street and out of danger, when I noticed a woman in a white nightdress seeming to emerge from the flames at Pearl Street, walking toward us in a daze. Her gray hair was tied up in paper curlers. She was carrying a birdcage.

Clara Robertson.

Her eyes were staring, unseeing. She was smiling faintly. The bird in the cage lay dead.

Suddenly I was seized with fear.

Nancy!

I ran to Mrs. Robertson. "Where is Mrs. Wyer?" I asked.

She smiled at me with ladylike sweetness.

"Is she in her room?"

"Oh, dear no," said the other softly. "She can't be."

"Why?"

She looked at me in surprise. "Why, Captain, because her room is burning."

I remember running down Pearl toward Federal. The buildings on both sides were on fire, the winds raised by the blaze driving the flames from roof to roof. When I reached Federal I at first couldn't see the boardinghouse through the flame and smoke. Then I did. It was a tower of fire. Then the flames parted and for an instant I saw Nancy in the dormer window, curtains, nightdress, hair, burning.

I was told that I had staggered out of the inferno with my clothes on fire, then fallen unconscious. Maria Mitchell threw her cloak over me. Lieutenant Davis rolled me in it, putting out the flames. I don't remember any of that.

9

As Maria Mitchell had predicted, the fire had stopped at Centre Street. The Methodist Church still stood, as did all the other structures on the west side, including our house. On Broad, the three-story mansion built by Jared Coffin only a year before was untouched, as were the buildings down that side of the street (including Nancy Coffin's former house) down to the harbor. But out our front windows what had been the center of town, acres of houses, shops, commercial buildings, all the industries on which the fishery depended, along with the entire waterfront with its countinghouses and offices, containing the logs, oil books, shipping papers, the records of two centuries of whaling, lay in blackened ruins.

I did not speak for four days. I had swallowed a gulletful of flame. I lay in our bedroom as Mary tended me, soothing my burns with compresses and calling me every kind of fool for almost getting myself killed. As the pain of the burns eased and my memory returned I found myself in a state of black anguish worse than any I'd ever known before. My old nightmares returned, more terrible than ever. I was leading the boy to the stone on the mountaintop. I could not look at him. Then we were in the boat, Ramsdell raising his pistol to the boy's head, firing. I butchered the warm, limp body, severing the head violently so as not to look into the eyes, letting it fall into the water. Then we shared the blood, the liver, the limbs. I was awakened by my own howl, trapped in my seared throat. I feared that I had gone beyond the point of no return to my reason.

Mary was sitting by my bed. I called her name, then burst into racking sobs. She said, "You've been holding back much too long, George Pollard. Stubborn. Just plain stubborn." And she let me weep myself out.

I slowly recovered. The burns healed. The black depression passed. I know for a certainty that without Mary I could not have come through that crisis with my sanity.

A week or so after the fire we were sitting in the parlor one evening. By then, we were finding it natural and easy to share thoughts that we would have kept to ourselves before. Of course, there were dangers to this, and one was the subject of Nancy Coffin.

That night after a silence between us, I said, "I could have saved Nancy. If I'd once thought of her there, out of her head and helpless."

Mary replied coldly, "Even in death."

"Do you hate her so much?"

"I hate what she did to you."

"She had reason enough to curse me."

"Of course she did. If you were guilty, she could be innocent. She could poison herself in peace."

"You're too hard. She lost everyone close to her."

"Not everyone."

"I should have saved her."

"George Pollard, will you ever stop blaming yourself for what couldn't be helped? My Lord, those Bunker women! Tamar made you think you weren't meant to walk proud on this Island. Nancy tried to prove it to you."

"Nancy always said I should marry you."

"Did she?" demanded Mary. "Night after night?"

When I didn't reply, she said, "Day of our wedding she took me aside and said, 'Now he's yours, dear Mary.' But her look was saying plain as day, 'He'll never be yours. He'll always be mine.' And she was right, even in death."

"She was wrong," I said.

She studied me a moment, sniffed. "Was she?"

"I love *you,* Mary Pollard."

She looked happy and vexed at the same time. "Took you long enough to say it like you meant it."

"Thought you could figure it out for yourself."

She wiped the tears that were starting with the back of her hand. "Oh, George Pollard, you thought you had to conquer the world all by yourself before you could let somebody matter to you. What a fool I married!"

. . .

So in a way, if Nancy had kept us apart all those years, it was Nancy who helped bring us together.

10

Within a year the town was mostly rebuilt, bigger and better than ever. Of the new buildings the one we were proudest of was the Atheneum, a grand white edifice in the best Greek style, containing a library and a museum on the main floor, a capacious lecture hall upstairs. When it was finished, the Atheneum trustees, led by Charles and Henry Coffin, decided that for its official opening nothing but the best would do, so they invited the most famous lecturer on the mainland, and to everyone's surprise he accepted. The Sage of Concord, Waldo Emerson.

And so the stage was set for that celebration, and, as it would turn out, for the first and only public appearance of Captain Pollard of the night watch.

Mr. Emerson arrived on a fine morning in early May, when the lilac was out. He was given a full-scale distinguished-visitor welcome, always a strenuous experience. No sooner had he been escorted to his room at Mrs. Parker's boardinghouse than he was jounced over sand ruts between Sconset and Madaket, viewing the moors and ponds. He was tea-ed at fine parlors on Main Street. He was taken on board the Coffin brothers' whaleship *Constitution*. He was presented to William Folger, who showed him the astronomical clock he had invented that not only tells time but displays the movement of heavenly bodies. He was shown the town from the South Tower, from the Second Congregational Church, from the Pacific Club looking up Main to the Bank and from the Bank looking down Main to the Pacific Club—and Mr. Emerson came through it all with flying colors. He expressed interest in everything, in the Island's history and the whaling trade, always ready for more, an ideal guest, in fact—until the second night, when (as I would learn later from Henry Coffin's man Will) Mr. Emerson suddenly announced out of the blue that he had heard that Captain Pollard of the *Essex* still lived on the Island and he asked if that was true. As Will would tell it to me, everyone fell silent then, until Henry Coffin allowed that it was true, but in a voice that should have made it plain that the subject was not a welcome one. Mr. Emerson, however, was not to be put off when his curiosity was aroused, so he asked squarely whether it would be possible to meet me. At that there was more silence, after which Henry Coffin said that it surely might be, perhaps tomorrow, or the next day, or at some other time, and brother Charles put in that Captain Pollard wasn't always the easiest man in the world to find. And that should have ended the matter right there, but it didn't.

Emerson's first lecture was at seven the following evening. Of course, no one had done anything about arranging a meeting with me. Knowing nothing about his interest in having one, I decided to attend the lecture.

Mary and I found places at the rear and to one side of the large crowd. On the stage, in an arc of chairs, sat Maria Mitchell, James Starbuck, Walter Folger, the speaker of the evening, the Coffin brothers, and William Mitchell. Everyone present was admiring the spacious new hall, which smelled of new wood and paint, and sizing up the celebrated visitor. With his large, serious blue eyes and lofty brow, his presence bespoke a spiritual nobility, which immediately put off the rougher sort of men present, a good many of whom were munching on nuts, or apples, or chewing tobacco in a way that seemed to defy the off-Islander to tell them something they didn't know already.

William Mitchell introduced the speaker. He went on for some time, and after a while even Mr. Emerson's attention drifted and he gazed around the audience, then leaned and whispered something to Henry Coffin, who searched the rows until he found me and whispered back, and suddenly there was the most celebrated philosopher in America studying me with intense curiosity.

When Mitchell wound up, Mr. Emerson arose to polite applause, mostly from the women present, and began to speak.

I had never heard anything like it. No one had. We had all heard fancy speakers before—preachers, phrenologists, anti-slavery and Temperance people, travelers to the Nile and China —but nothing like this. Emerson's clear, strong voice filled that new-smelling auditorium with such torrents of ideas that all you could be sure of was the faith they flowed from, for there could be no mistaking the faith in that voice. Listening to him I felt as if I were again in the open boat, in a storm, rising on one wave to peer for an instant across the thrashing sea, before sinking again into the trough. I would catch hold of a phrase, cling to it, only to lose hold when the next wave of words broke my grasp. His main thrust seemed to be that we are all part of a Divine Entirety, in which we navigate by Reason and Faith, advancing against Chaos and the Dark. He believed in the worth of the individual man. His heroes were those who are obedient only to the impulses of their unique selves, those who live without fear of the opinion and censure of others, in harmony with the Universal Mind. Nothing less.

At first I resisted that voice, that blue gaze, which often fell on me. Like most of that Island audience, I resisted being tossed about in that squall of high-sounding notions, until, having stopped trying to follow his meaning, I found that thoughts of my own were being kindled by sparks from his. When he declared, *Heroism is the avowal of a quality in one's self that is negligent of life and of a will that is proof against all that might oppose it,* I thought of the red-sailed whaleship that as a child I had seen clearing the harbor, bound for the Pacific, when my life was outward bound. *The Hero,* he went on, *does not submit to what is called Fate. Fate,* he said, *is a name for facts not yet proved under the fire of thought. Fate is unpenetrated causes.* The voice went on, but I held fast to that idea, for if it was true, then I was no Jonah, no pawn of Fate if Fate was only the dark in my own mind, where I had not dared to enter. It struck me that since my return after the wreck of the *Two Brothers* I had permitted that quality in me that had first attracted me to the Pacific, against my mother's warnings, almost to perish. I had come to accept my banishment from the quarterdeck, the interdiction, the night watch, my quarantine from Island life, as being my due, the price I must pay for my crime, my survival. Little by little I had let my inner being die. Now, in the spell of that voice, I felt that youthful spirit awakening. *Trust thyself,* the voice said. *Self-trust is the essence of heroism. What you must do is all that need concern you, not what people think. Who so would be a man must be a nonconformist. Congratulate yourself if you have done something strange and extravagant, and broken the monotony of a decorous age.* I felt panic and joy at once. I discovered in myself the terrible and marvelous idea that I alone was master of my life, and that I need feel no guilt or shame before those who know nothing of it. The voice rose, resonant, clear. *Let a man know his worth and not skulk up and down like an interloper in the world which exists for him. Every jet of chaos which threatens to exterminate him is convertible into wholesome force. Let him live, not expiate.*

I bring you one doctrine—the infinitude and power of the private man.

It was over. There was applause, then a great scraping of chairs. From the quantity of tobacco juice, apple cores, and nut shells that littered the new floor, it was plain enough that the Sage of Concord had lost most of my fellow Islanders from the start. Behind us, I heard a young man comment, "Sure talks like a coof, don't he?" So much for the Universal Mind. Up on the stage Emerson was looking my way and again speaking intently to Henry Coffin. I couldn't see what happened next, but then Henry Coffin's lanky son Charles Frederick was pressing through the crowded aisle, toward me. He came up and addressed me, loud enough for everyone around to hear, "Captain Pollard, Mr. Emerson requests the pleasure of making your acquaintance."

At that, everyone around fell silent, watching me. Some of those leaving turned back, sensing that the evening's entertainment was not over. My old fears stirred. I sought some pretext to slip away. Mary sensed what was going on in my mind and, taking my arm, whispered, "George Pollard, you're going up on that stage and meet Mr. Emerson and I'm going with you." And that settled the matter.

We followed Charles Frederick down the aisle and up toward the podium, where the speaker of the evening awaited me. Henry Coffin introduced us.

"Dr. Emerson, this is Captain Pollard of our night watch. And Mrs. Pollard."

The philosopher bowed to Mary. "Honored, madame." Then, turning to me, he said, "And former master of the *Essex,* I believe?"

Well, there it was, the forbidden subject, out in the open. I knew that everyone was wondering whether I would turn tail and walk away, as I had done with the Vineyarder. I looked from one familiar face to another. Miss Macy, Tim Jenkins, Will

Pease, Caleb Mitchell, Jason Starbuck, Mrs. Robertson, old Gideon Folger, the Reverend Mooers and his wife, widows, young people, old ex-captains and mates, and near me on the stage, Zenas's sons, William Mitchell, and Maria, all waiting to see what I would do. I glanced at Mary. She looked back at me, confident and proud. I said to myself, It's time to stop hiding, Pollard. Time to square things away.

"The same, sir," I said.

Mr. Emerson, for all his philosophical gifts, had no idea of what was happening between me and that Nantucket audience then.

"Some years ago," he said, "I read an account of the tragedy and was struck with admiration for your amazing feat of seamanship and courage."

"I am gratified, sir. Not everyone has understood our story in that light."

"Surely no one would pass judgment on what was obviously justified by necessity?"

I looked out over the silent crowd. I let their silence answer for me.

"Surely, Captain," he said, growing uncomfortable, "in the boats you must have felt the presence of Almighty God?"

"I felt that we were alone."

"Guided only by your knowledge of the Pacific?"

"And by our fear of what was unknown to us."

At that, Mr. Emerson appeared distressed. I added, "In the last extremity we were guided by something else."

"And what was that?"

"A custom of the sea."

Now Mr. Emerson looked lost. You could have heard a pin drop in that auditorium. Then, carefully, he said, "The drawing of lots?"

"Yes."

"A custom known to you?"

"From the sea itself."

"You were driven almost to madness by hunger and thirst, and even then you did not become—as beasts. You found the way to act as men."

I looked out at the audience then, and spoke to them. "We acted as men."

"Surely no one can condemn you for that."

"None perhaps but ourselves."

"But it was done fairly."

"It was done."

"Chase stated that you offered to take the boy's place."

"Chase was not present."

"Then—"

"I offered to take his place. I said the words. Had he accepted, I would have taken his place."

"Surely no one would have done more."

"I made the offer, but even as I did, even as I pleaded with him, I knew that he would not accept it." Unafraid now, I looked again at that Nantucket audience. "There *are* things more important than life, sir. Owen Coffin knew that then. I know it now."

A strange thing was happening. Mr. Emerson was undergoing a transformation before our eyes. Only minutes before, he had stood on that stage as the bearer of Truth, Enlightenment, Reason. Now, to me and to that still audience, it was becoming clear that there were things of this world, well known to us, about which the Sage of Concord was ignorant. He didn't know anything about matters that did not fit easily into his Divine Entirety. He didn't know anything about darkness. He didn't know anything about Cape Horn. Especially, he didn't know anything about Islanders. He couldn't make out anything from their silence, or mine. He couldn't know about the understanding—you could almost call it a joke—that was passing between them and me then.

He said, "Surely every fair-minded person must understand what happened?"

Silence.

"Surely no one condemns you?"

Silence.

Then, to the audience, an edge of desperation in his voice, he called out, "Who would dare stand in judgment of you?"

Silence.

Then, one by one at first, then in bunches, those Nantucketers stood up and, still not speaking, made for the door. All you could hear was the shuffling of their shoes on the new floor.

11

It was about eight o'clock when Mary and I left the Atheneum and started up India. I was feeling considerable satisfaction, and she knew it. As we turned down Centre I saw, in the clear twilight, birds sweeping and diving over the chimneys of our house, a new moon behind.

"Nice night," I said.

"So 'tis."

My attention on the house, I said, "Got to get that weathervane up."

"I'll believe that when I see it."

"First thing in the morning. House isn't a proper house without a weathervane."

We walked a few steps, then she said, "I was wondering when you were going to start living in that house."

"Where do you think I've been living?"

"In your head. With all the sins of the world."

I looked at her then, in the dusk, suddenly feeling that I was really seeing her for the first time.

We reached the stoop and she started up the steps. I followed, saying, "First thing in the morning."

We went inside.

"Welcome home, Captain Pollard," said my Mary.

EPILOGUE

So ends the captain's journal. Virtually nothing is known of his life after 1847 except that he continued to reside on the Island, probably as a member of the night watch, until his death on January 7, 1870, at the age of seventy-eight, having lived long enough to witness the death throes of Nantucket as a whaling port. His wife, Mary, survived him by twelve years. The site of his grave is unknown. No portrait of him exists. His obituary in the *Inquirer and Mirror* mentions the loss of the *Essex,* the ordeal in the boats (with no reference to cannibalism or the execution), and the loss of the *Two Brothers,* concluding:

"He was still a young man when he retired from the sea and closed the strange, eventful part of his life. For more than forty years he has resided permanently among us; and now leaves the record of a good and worthy man as his legacy to us who remain."

Only one incident in the captain's later life is recorded. In July of 1852, Herman Melville visited Nantucket for the first and only time and met Pollard. The year before, the thirty-three-year-old writer had published *Moby-Dick,* having based the climactic scene in which the *Pequod* is struck by the white whale on Owen Chase's account of the sinking of the *Essex.* Nothing is known of what passed between Melville and Captain Pollard that summer of 1852, but the meeting left a strong and lasting impression on the former. In old age, his eyesight failing, he scrawled in green crayon on a margin of his copy of Chase's

Narrative:

". . . I—sometime about 1850–3—saw Capt. Pollard on the island of Nantucket and exchanged some words with him. To the islanders he was a nobody—to me the most impressive man, tho' wholly unassuming even humble—that I ever encountered."

A NOTE ABOUT THE AUTHOR

Henry Carlisle is a writer who has been, among other things, an editor of trade books and the president of the American Center of PEN. He is author of several novels, including *Voyage to the First of December*, which won the Putnam Award for fiction in 1972, and *The Land Where the Sun Dies*. Carlisle lives in San Francisco with his wife, Olga.

A NOTE ON THE TYPE

The text of this book was set in a type face called Times Roman, designed by Stanley Morison (1889–1967) for *The Times* (London) and first introduced by that newspaper in 1932.

Among typographers and designers of the twentieth century, Stanley Morison was a strong forming influence—as a typographical advisor to The Monotype Corporation, as a director of two distinguished English publishing houses, and as a writer of sensibility, erudition, and keen practical sense.

Composed, printed and bound
by The Haddon Craftsmen, Inc.,
Scranton, Pennsylvania.

Designed by Amy Berniker.